Praise for *Tamar of the Terebinths*

"This is a haunting story, full of poetry, wisdom, drama and deep-seated intrigue. Looking forward to the next book in the series."
—Stavros Halvatzis, PhD
Scarab, Scarab II: Reawakening, The Level

"Sikorski and Silversher have created an embellished backdrop for one of the most mysterious stories in Judaism, a backdrop ... framed by history, seeped in realism and enchanted by the depth of character development the authors have created. *Tamar of the Terebinths* will fascinate the reader, and Tamar's voice telling her own story accentuates a possibility of truth."—Patricia Ann Carratello
Author and award-winning educator

"As I read the story, I could not stop from comparing the characters to modern day women living in the Middle East. Even though Tamar had to suppress a lot of her feelings and spirit, she found a way to survive. Witnessing her growing pains was a pleasure ... it is the story of survival and the strong spirit of women of all time."
—Charline Evers, retired educator

"Tamar of the Terebinths is biblical historical fiction at its finest. This story resurrects and brings to life the voices that are all too easily swept aside or even silenced in history: the women. Tamar gives me hope and courage. The words in the book are literally alive ... bringing to light what is so often covered in darkness and oppression."
—Katrina Bietz

"I was surprised and disappointed when this book ended. I was enjoying it so much I couldn't put it down. So looking forward to Book Two of the Trilogy. I hope it comes out soon. Kudos to the authors. I highly recommend this book."
—Dorothea (Dottie) Goldfarb

TAMAR
of the
TEREBINTHS

Book One
Judah and Tamar Trilogy

Also by Joy Sikorski

Singing Through Life With Your Mouth Closed

TAMAR
of the
TEREBINTHS

Book One
Judah and Tamar Trilogy

JOY SIKORSKI and MICHAEL SILVERSHER

Whisper Voices Publications
Idyllwild, California

This book is a work of fiction. Although based on stories from the Bible, the characters, events and story lines are created from the combined imaginations of the two authors.

Tamar of the Terebinths
Book One of the Judah and Tamar Trilogy

Cover art by Rona Liu

ISBN-13: 978-0-9913325-1-9 (pbk.)
ISBN-13: 978-0-9913325-0-2 (eBook)

Library of Congress Control Number: 2014943536

Whisper Voices Publications
Idyllwild, CA
books@whispervoices.com

Printed in The United States of America
First published in the United States by
Whisper Voices Publications

To the women and girls
who wait for their voices to be heard

Authors' Note

If you like to discover unusual words when you read, we trust that you will enjoy our use of transliterated words from several different languages, including, but not limited to, Hebrew, Arabic, Persian, Akkadian, Phoenician and Armenian. Additionally, we created a few new terms by combining bits and pieces of words, or sounds from different languages, or by utilizing sounds from no language in particular simply because we liked the way the new term might hint at a feeling to describe a thing.

For instance, one of the words we created is "noorshma." You will find the meaning to this word and others in the Glossary at the end of the book.

We also use transliterated Hebrew names for characters occurring in Genesis, such as Yehuda for Judah, Ya'akov for Jacob, etc. All of these words, and many others you may not be familiar with, can be found in the Glossary, although in most cases, you will probably understand them from the context of the story.

Other than that, we wish you a sense of discovery as you delve into a new way of looking at the Genesis 38 account of Judah and Tamar.

Gratefully,

Joy Sikorski and Michael Silversher

Prologue

"I have placed life and death before you, blessing and curse, and you shall choose life so that you will live, you and your offspring."

—Devarim 30:19

Land of Kn'n, circa 1,665 BCE

"Please let me hold the child. Let me see the child's eyes."

"No, Trinjah, you're too weak."

"Is it alive? Is it well?"

"The child is well enough. Save your strength."

"It doesn't matter now, Anush, I must hold it before I—."

"Careful, Trinjah, careful. Let me help you."

"Yes, please help me."

"There now, here's the child, but only for a moment so that you can see its eyes."

"Yes, its eyes. Is it a boy or a gir—"

"Trinjah! Stay with us. Can you see me?"

"Yes, Anush, I can see you, but why are you so far away? Please tell Yergat..."

"Of course, Trinjah, there's plenty of time for that, but now you must rest."

"Rest."

"Breathe deeply, Trinjah. Think of the cave."

"Cave."

"That's better, a little smile now. Lean on me and keep breathing."

"So tired."

"Shoosh-shoosh, Trinjah-jahn, shoosh-shoosh."

* * *

"Did she suffer long, Anush?"

"There was much blood and much pain, Yergat, but she bore it well, blessed the little one's eyes in Ditzah's name and went quickly, mercifully."

"And the child? Is it dead too?"

"No, may the gods be praised. The child is well."

"I am not sure about the praise of the gods. They could have done better to save Trinjah from the vengeance of Lilith."

"We mustn't blame the gods, Yergat. We carry enough sorrow from the loss of Trinjah. You don't want to bring their curses and more sorrow down on us, do you?"

"No. Not down on us. Down on the chi—"

"Shh! Yergat. Don't say it."

"No, Anush, for the sake of Trinjah, I won't say it. But I feel it in my heart. Better that the child had been taken than Trinjah."

"Yergat, you're the only remaining son of my dead sister, Kohar, and the heavens alone know the full weight of the sorrows she bore before she died. What I saw of it was beyond anything you can imagine, beyond death itself.

"If she were here now, she would tell you to war against the bitterness that bites at your soul. She would tell you to seek the mercy of El, the mercy of Asherah and the mercy of Ba'al rather than allow Tiamat to drag you through the doors of Chaos and cast you into the jaws of Mot.

"Even though she's not here, I speak in her name for the sake of your life, for the sake of your child, and for sake of the memory of Trinjah, your cherished and gentle wife."

"You fight unfairly, Anush, but I will let you win... for the moment. Have you anything else you wish to say to me?"

"Two things only, Yergat. Trinjah told me to tell you that she loved you, and that she wanted you to name the child Tamar."

The Ghost, the Cat, the Bird and the Cave

"Abuse, if you slight it, will gradually die away; but if you show
yourself irritated, you will be thought to have deserved it."

—Tacitus

I SQUEEZE MY EYES SHUT and tense my toes before I peek to see
if the ghost is still there. In the murky moonlight that oozes
through the tiny window above my bed, I see it swaying in the
entryway across my sleeping room and feel its fiery eyes peer
at me. My heart thumps loudly inside my ears. Will I die this
time?

Earlier in the night, I remember crying out into the darkness
before the ghost appeared. Maybe the sound of my voice gave
it the signal to draw near. Maybe it thinks I have summoned it.
Maybe it will pounce and swallow me whole.

Without warning, it smashes a clay bottle against the mud
brick wall nearest it, and liquid explodes into the room. A
nasty odor fills my nose, but I do not flinch.

The ghost curses and staggers, teetering toward me.

I stay silent, close my eyes and will my eyelids into dead
things that know not how to blink or twitch then relax my
toes and breathe more quietly, more slowly.

When the ghost leans over me, I can feel the leer of its
hatred, feel its foul breath surround me like a swarm of
mosquitoes, feel the stench of its oily body odor that reeks of
sweat, urine, rotted sheep hides and lebonah gag me. Usually,
I love the smoky smell of lebonah and the way it calms me

before I sleep, but right now, the way it mixes with the fetor of the ghost makes me want to give up my lentils.

I steady my stomach and lie as still as a cat watching a mouse, except my cat eyes are still closed.

"Tamar," the ghost slurs, "are you awake?"

It must be a pretty stupid ghost to ask such a question.

"I have something to say to you, you little sharmuta," it snarls.

I am only six and do not know the meaning of that word, but it sounds like a nasty thing, so I stay in my dead-eyelids-relaxed-toes cat mode.

Suddenly, the ghost shouts into my face, "You know you killed her!" Putrid spittle spatters onto my eyes and cheeks.

Still I do not flinch. Instead, I will the sound and speed of my breathing to imitate deep slumber and pretend that I am in a dream world beyond spit and nasty words.

I am not sure if I fool the ghost or not, though, because it throws back my nice warm sheepskin blankets, grabs my shoulders and screams, "You can't fool me. I know you're awake."

It shakes me hard then stumbles over its slurry words while rambling on about nonsense. I pretend that the shaking and slurring are part of a game that's made for a very limp cat, which is what I have now become.

Its fingers dig into my flesh and I want to yowl, but I ignore the pain, for now I am a very dead cat that cannot respond, not even to the ache in my head from the ghost's joggling of it.

With one last jolt, the ghost releases its grip and shoves me down. I melt into a heap on my blankets as it turns away. I still do not move, though, because I am not sure what magic powers a ghost might have, like maybe eyes on its elbows, or ears that can turn inside out to know if my breathing speeds up or not.

Stumbling sounds now move away from me, so I peek with my barely squinting cat eyes to see if I am safe.

6

I am.

At least I think I am as I watch the ghost stagger back through the doorway and lurch off to the left.

Still, I listen and wait, my cat ears alert for the nasty thing's return.

Finally, I hear loud snoring coming from the direction of Yergat's room. Off my bed I leap and land ever so softly on my cat feet, then creep through the doorway and off to the right, quickly padding into Anush's room.

Crawling into her bed, I cover myself with her blankets and cry my quiet cat tears.

* * *

"What's this, a little katu in my bed?" Anush's warm smile mixes with the early morning sunshine that trickles into her room. She gently pulls me to rest against her big bosom. "What is going on under this swirling cloud of blushing onyx today?" she asks as she strokes my long curly hair.

"Why do you call my hair that?" I ask her as I nestle in closer.

"Because it looks like the red Calanit flowers on our hillside have kissed its blackness from the inside out." She kisses the top of my head. "And it's so curly and thick and seems to have such a strong mind of its own that it moves like an uncatchable cloud whirling around in the sky." She gives me a gentle hug.

"Oh," I say as though I understand what she means, even though I don't. But I like the sound of her words, so I snuggle in closer.

I love it when Anush holds me and surrounds me in her softness. It makes me feel like I am floating on top of a pile of fresh sheep's wool.

"Why are you here *this* morning, Tamoosh-jahn?"

Anush often call me Tamoosh-jahn, my pet name, and rarely Tamar, my real name, unless she is angry with me. I like my pet name because it means that she loves me. When she holds me close, like she does now, and wraps me in her squishy arms near her squishy breasts, I always imagine that she is my Imma, my mother, and I am her darling, her Yakiri.

"The ghost," I whisper. "It came to my bed and shouted at me again last night." Tears form in my eyes.

"Shoosh, shoosh, my little Katu. Don't let that old ghost fool you. It's only an unhappy soul who means you no harm."

"But this time he told me that I killed my Imma."

I feel the heave of Anush's breasts as she sighs.

"Ah, Yavrik, my little one, he should never have said that." She stares at the ceiling like she sees right through it. "His words ache my heart," she says.

Pressing my right ear deeper into her breast so that I can hear the ache in her heart, I hear nothing but her normal heart.

She shifts her weight now and holds me by my skinny shoulders as though she can will away the aching words by gently touching me with her work-worn hands.

"We haven't been to the cave in a long time, have we, Katu? Would you like to go there today?" She smiles down at me and kisses me on the top of my head.

I throw back the covers and jump from the bed. "Oh yes, Anush-jahn, yes!"

"Not so fast now. We have to make our beds tight, wash ourselves up, eat and do our chores."

"Do we have to?" I pout. "Now?"

"You know my rules, Tamoosh-jahn."

I crinkle my nose and frown at her.

In spite of the great bulk of her body, she bursts out of bed and chases me around her room, lumbering and laughing, grabbing at me as I race away and out of her reach. By the time I run through her doorway and into the hall, I am flying so fast that I do not see the ghost before I plow into him.

He pushes me back and bellows, "What do think you're doing, you brat? This is not a house for your stupid antics. Stop your nonsense and get to your chores."

The fire in his voice burns my ears.

"Anush," he barks, "come here this instant!"

I watch my dear noorshma walk out of her room without even so much as a smidgen of fear on her face.

"What is it this time, Yergat?" Her voice remains calm as she peers at him like his outburst is none of her concern. "What's your trouble today, nephew?" She turns and winks at me.

"Don't you go and teach that child your wicked ways. She's bad enough as it is."

"Hogoc." Anush rolls her eyes. "Yergat, Yergat, Yergat. When will you learn? A six-year old isn't ba—"

"*Don't* tell me what a six-year old is or isn't. If I say she's bad, she's bad and that's that."

He turns to go, but there I am, right in front of him, standing taller than before and imitating the fearless way Anush looks at him. He glowers at me with sunken eyes as black as a cave that allows no light to penetrate it. His unkempt and oily hair, which matches the black of his eyes, falls around his face like a shredded curtain whose sole job is to keep his skin from seeing the sun.

I feel my own eyes widen, but I hold my ground.

"Abba." The sound of my voice in my ears is like a stream of sweet cool water in summertime. "Do you want me to go away? Forever?"

I usually do not call him Abba, but today I feel like maybe he will answer me more gently if I use the word that other children use with their fathers, the word that speaks of love and kindness.

For a brief moment, I see a sliver of sadness pierce his eyes, but then his face only darkens all the more as he shouts at me to keep my dirty little mouth shut. Next, he turns and stomps out of the hallway and into the courtyard that leads to his business room near the kitchen.

Anush sighs, shakes her head and wags her finger at me. "You're a clever little Katu, Tamoosh-jahn."

I look at her as though she has given me a puzzle to solve. "You shamed him and now his nose has fallen."

I peer at the floor. "I do not see his nose on the ground, Anush-jahn, not even in the cracks between the stones. Did he leave it somewhere else?" Dashing around the room I search for his nose. Her eyes crinkle with merriment as she watches me.

Then I remember the other word she used and rush back to her. "What does shame mean, Anush-jahn? And where did his nose fall?"

"Hah. His nose fell," she says as she stops and sticks her nose high in the air and flips her right index finger under it as though she is sending it to the ceiling, "because he thinks he's too high to admit when he's wrong." She looks down at me again. "Shame means that your question told the truth about his poor behavior, and that made a light shine into his dark places to make him think. That's what shame is, and believe me, my clever Katu, he can use lots more of that kind of shame. Someday he will..."

I do not listen to her as she rambles on about things I do not understand nor want to understand. What I *do* understand is simple: when she goes on and on like this, I can do something else without it upsetting her.

To speed things up a bit so that we can get to the cave as fast as possible, I dash to her bed, straighten her covers and plump her pillow then run out of her room to do the same thing with my bed.

As she follows me, her laughter tickles the sunshine that streams through our house.

Despite the ghost, I know it is a good day.

Up in the stone-strewn hills near our home in Adullam there is a cave where I go to play as often as I can. I am not old enough to go there by myself, so I must always wait until Anush is able to go with me. Usually, she works so hard to take care of the ghost and me, there are never enough times when she is able to pull away from the chores. Never enough times by my rules anyway.

But, today… Oh, the air! Oh, the colors!

I skip over rocks on the dusty pathway that leads to the cave and dance past clusters of blue flowers on either side of me. The flowers look like tiny bells ringing out songs of joy, and their notes find me as I sing in my happiest and highest little voice. Then I zoom upward and lift my arms to fly into the clouds and float there in contentment.

I do not think about the ghost at all.

"Tamoosh-jahn."

I hear Anush like she is an ant and I am an eagle, but I do not answer her. Instead, I imagine myself soaring over the Great Sea I hear so much about but never get to see with my real eyes and feel the cool breezes kiss my cheeks. Only my bird eyes can see that place, only my bird eyes can know what is there and what I long for.

"Tamoooosh-jaaahn."

Anush speaks my name more loudly now. She always gets louder when I fly. Maybe this happens because she has forgotten how to fly. The last time we came to the cave and I asked her to soar into the clouds with me, she told me she didn't remember how to fly.

"Tamoooosh-jaaahn," she calls again.

I still do not answer her, for now I sail far above the clouds; a feeling captures me in its memory and I wonder where I am. When I open my bird eyes, however, I am still standing on the dusty pathway near the flowers, and watching Anush huff and puff toward me, her face all wet.

Drawing out each syllable, she again says, "Taaa-*moooosh*-jaaahn*," and wags her finger at me when she reaches me.

I blink, grin and run circles around her. She coughs at the dust I stir up.

"That's enough, Katu. You'll turn me into a hogh of Araratyan!"

She tries to hide her smile but I see the twinkle in her eyes.

11

She loves to come up here too. I know it.

Slowing down and stopping directly in front of her, I grin and hug her as though I can stuff her into my heart if I just squeeze hard enough. She reeks of garlic and za'atar, but I don't mind at all.

"Ah, now, Katu, here we are again at last."

Saying nothing more, she wraps her arms around me and we stand together in happy silence. I think this is what my Imma might feel like if she were here instead of Anush.

When I am happy like I am now, my skin gets a kind of itch on it. No, that's not right. The itch is *inside* my skin and feels like it wants me to burrow myself into it. No, that's not right either. Burrow *through* it to the other side of things, to the bottom of it all, wherever that is. The only way I know how to scratch this itch is with my "rubbies," as I call them, and right now I feel the itch!

Like a cat cleaning it whiskers, round and round I rub my face into Anush's clothing.

* * *

The first time I felt my skin itch me this way—I call it my joy itch—all I could do was nuzzle my head (especially the space above my nose between my eyes) in quick movements against Anush's soft woolen halug. Her legs on the other side of the fabric became my "rubby-posts" until she burst out laughing and asked me what in the world I was doing.

"I have the rubbies!" I cried out as I pressed my nose, cheeks, lips, jaw, eyes and forehead deeper into her halug. "I cannot stop until the rubbies tell me to stop."

There is so much joy in rubbing out the rubbies that I think everyone must get them like I do, especially my sweet Anush.

"You feel the rubbies too, don't you Anush-jahn?" I twinkle as I look up at her then rub out my rubbies again.

"Yes, child, I feel *your* rubbies," she says, laughing as she gently takes me by the shoulders to stop me, "but never have

I ever once felt the rubbies like you do." Her voice becomes more serious as she continues. "Although I do remember something that might be like them."

Eager to know there might be a different kind of rubbies than my own, I ask, "What is it, Anush-jahn?"

She hesitates for a moment before answering. "I used to listen to the strong heartbeat of my beloved Ishkahn, and it often felt like I could get inside his heart if I just pressed enough of my love into his chest."

With these last words, Anush's face sags as though her words bleed out all her happiness. Her mouth droops too. Whenever she mentions her dead husband she gets quiet and sad, although I don't know why.

* * *

"Run on ahead now." Anush scoots me on my way.

Happy to play again, I dart along the path as fast as I can to get to the terebinth tree that grows next to the entrance of the cave, and plop down on a large rock by it. This rock is my favorite place to watch and listen to the birds, the wind in the trees, and the clouds in the sky. I always sit here before I go into the cave. I imagine the cave as my real home where no trouble can find me, where the ghost does not get drunk and yell at me, where Anush does not pester me with chores, or this and that.

The cave is where my Imma lives, I am sure of it. She is beautiful, kind and wise. I am sure of that too. Most of all, she loves me and lets me talk forever and ever without once yelling at me to keep quiet like the ghost does.

"Boop-boop-boop... boop-boo." A dukifat hides in the terebinth and sings to me. I sing back to her, "Boop-boop-boop... boop-boo." She chatters and changes the tune. "Boop-boop-boop... boo." I echo her then ask her to come out of hiding so that we can play. She chitters then repeats the first and second tunes. I twitter and answer her the same way, but end my singing by asking her to *please, please* come out of hiding. She ignores me and sings again.

I do not want to sing again. I want to see her and talk with her. I raise my voice and spread apart the branches near where she is hiding. "Come out, Doookifat!"

I see a flash of cinnamon-amber color—the hattah scarf she wears. It covers her head, neck and half her chest. The backside of her head looks like the long dark beak in front of her except that it shoots out behind her. It is thicker and has four black spots on it. The last spot looks so much like her beak that I am not sure if she is coming or going.

"Silly Dukifat. You do not know your front from your back. That is okay. Never mind. Come play with me." I pull the branches further apart.

She hops toward me, then spreads wide her white and black striped wings, swooshes over me and shows me her white belly. As she flutters into the azure sky like a large butterfly and trills that I should meet her up there, I clap my hands in delight. I prepare to join her, but suddenly she disappears behind the hill where I cannot see or hear her.

"Hogoc, I'm finally here." Anush drips with sweat, garlic and za'atar as she lowers herself onto my rock.

"Why did you do that?" I accuse.

"Do what, child?"

"Scare away my friend."

"What friend?" Anush looks around.

"Dukifat!"

"Dukifat?" Anush chortles. "A bird?"

"Why are you laughing at me?"

"Oh child, I'm not laughing *at* you. It's just that your ideas amuse me, that's all."

She looks away.

I jump off the rock and stand before her then stamp my foot. Dust flies.

"Yes you are, you *are* making fun of me." I cough through the dust. "I was going to fly with her but you scared her away because you do not know how to fly anymore and don't want me to either. You are… you—" I stamp my foot again. "I am going to tell my Imma on you!"

I scowl and run into the cave before she can grab me. Coughing, she calls after me, but I ignore the cough and her voice, then wedge myself between two rocks deep inside the big cave, away from any light that might let her see me. I peek through a crack between the rocks to see if she follows, but she does not. I wait long enough to be sure, and when I still do not see her or hear her call my name, I crawl back out of the rocks then walk further into the cave until I find my secret spot, the spot where my Imma lives.

Anush knows where it is but rarely comes inside the cave this far anymore. Besides, she is probably too big to get to it now anyway, so I think I am safe.

My spot is a place so deep inside the darkest part of the cave that it makes me feel like I am on the inside of a dream. The secret to this magical place is a small crack in the highest part of the cave that allows in light belonging only to my Imma. Her light points to me, and no one else. *Only* me. It has powers too, powers that let me talk to her.

"Imma, I am here. Can you hear me?"

From high up in the cave I hear a rustling sound.

"Yes? Good. I hear you too."

The rustling continues.

"Oh Imma, I am so angry right now. Anush chased away my friend and then made fun of me. She makes me do chores, and tells me that the ghost does not mean to hurt me, even though it hates me. No one listens to me but you. I wish Anush would turn into a toad and the ghost would disappear into the clouds forever!"

I breathe rapidly and blow air loudly through my nose.

The rustling stops.

"No, Imma, do not be angry with me. Please, just tell me what to do."

She answers me with silence.

15

"Imma?"

The light fades and nearly disappears.

Tears brim over my eyes and roll down my cheeks. I brush them away with my hands and touch my halug to wipe them off, but suddenly the light comes back and makes my tears twinkle and shine on my hands. I remember a feeling from long ago and search for something that seems to be right behind my eyes.

The light shifts away again.

I feel naughty for having been so mean to Anush and worry that she will go away, just like my Imma went away the day I was born. Maybe the ghost is right about me after all. Maybe I *am* the one who killed my Imma.

Tears gush now as I turn and rush out of the cave.

Anush sits quietly on the rock. She has not moved at all. A pinkish-orange glow from the sun that is ready to go to sleep shines on her face. She watches me as I run to her.

"I am so sorry, Anush-jahn."

She opens her arms to me, and I sob into her squishiness. My words race so fast that I can barely breathe.

"I did not mean what I said... please do not leave me... it was my meanness that killed my Imma, wasn't it? The ghost is right. I know it now."

She holds me fast but says nothing. I bury my head between her breasts and hear her steady heartbeat. I feel her hands stroking my hair.

We sit like this until a sound stops my tears.

"Boop-boop-boop... boop-boo, boop-boop-boop... boo."

I un-nuzzle myself from her bosom and look up. My Dukifat sits on the branch of the terebinth. A deep sigh shudders through me and I yawn.

"My friend did not disappear after all, did she, Anush-jahn?"

"No, she is still here. She came back after you ran into the cave. I have been watching her and listening to her song. She is beautiful, isn't she, Katu?"

"Oh yes, Anush-jahn. I am so glad you think so."

Anush touches my nose lightly.

"She is beautiful, like you are."

"What do you mean? I don't have a cinnamon-amber hattah like she does." I speak the next words so low that I hope she will not hear me. "And I cannot really fly, at least not the way she does."

Anush goes on as if she does not hear my confession about flying. Another sigh shudders through me.

"Ah yes, Katu," Anush hugs me closer to her heart as she speaks, "it is true that you do not have a hattah with her colors, but you have something else, something that makes all her colors pale by comparison."

"Do you mean my eyes?" I ask without looking at her. "Right now they feel like they must be the color of worn-out dirt."

"Ha-ha. No, Tamoosh-jahn, not your eyes, although they certainly are beautiful. In fact, they are as rich looking as the finest Tyrian purple made from the finest shells found in the Great Sea. If I mixed that color with the darkest and most fertile soils of our Elah Valley... *that* would be the color of your eyes."

"You mean my hair then?" I ask eagerly.

"Tch-tch, no, not even your hair, although it adorns your head like a swirling cloud of blushing onyx, as I have always said."

I am not exactly sure what all her words mean, but hearing her say them makes me feel better.

"No, my little one, my Yavrik, I meant that the bird is beautiful like you are because she flies away when something startles her, but always returns to where she belongs."

"I don't understand. Why is that beautiful?" I yawn again.

"Beauty is something that happens inside you when you know where you fit into the world around you," Anush answers as though she is far away from the rock, the terebinth tree and me.

"Dukifat belongs here?"

"Yes. Didn't you see her nest?"

"She has a nest?"

I sit up straight and eagerly look around, but the branches of the terebinth block my view.

"Yes, it's behind those branches. When you pulled them apart, she flew away to protect it. That is what Imma-birds do. When something or someone gets too close to their nests, they fly from them, flutter around, and squawk to distract and draw away whatever it is that threatens their eggs or their babies."

I settle back into Anush's bosom and think about this for a few moments. Anush continues to stroke my hair.

"If that is what Imma-birds do, is that what my Imma did too?" I ask shyly. "Fly away because something wanted to harm me?"

Anush stops and reaches down to gently tilt my chin toward her. Her eyes are the color of a terebinth tree trunk, and the strength in the way she looks at me reminds me of one too. Her wrinkly lips curve into a partial smile; she kisses the top of my head again. This time, though, she keeps her lips there and speaks ever so gently through my hair.

"No, Katu, your Imma did not *choose* to go away. There was nothing that could harm you the day you first breathed in the air of this world. No, she wanted to stay and hold you, take care of you, and tell you that you were her Yakiri, her darling."

Anush pauses, as though weighing whether or not to go on.

I say nothing, for she has spoken the one word I long to hear: Yakiri. I am my Imma's darling.

"I was there, Yavrik. She spoke her last words to me, and…"

Through my hair, I hear nothing but the sound of Anush breathing.

I shake loose and tilt her chin down to see my eyes. "And what, Anush-jahn? What did she say?"

She laughs, "Oh Tamoosh-jahn, you are all that Trinjah

told me you would be before she... before—"

"Before she flew away?"

"Yes." Anush's eyes cloud over. "Before she flew away."

"But what did she tell you about me?"

"Ahhh, that." Anush sighs deeply and takes a long breath, then lets it out slowly. "She told me you would see life beyond the way others see it, that you would love to hear stories and..."

She pauses to look at the terebinth tree.

"And what, Anush-jahn, what did she say?"

"Oh, it was nothing important."

I pull at her halug. "What, what?"

"Only that you would..."

I hop off the rock and dance around like I need to pass water. Dust flies.

"That's not fair, Anush-jahn." I cough and laugh. "Tell me, tell me."

"All right." She sighs as though it is a big effort for her to continue. "If you insist." Her words seem to come out as slowly as a moon changes from a full ball to a sliver of light.

"Only that you would drive... me... crazy!"

"Oh Anush-jahn." I laugh and twirl around her. "She didn't say that, did she?"

"No, Katu." Her voice softens to a mere whisper. "She didn't have time to say much before she flew away. But she did have time to see your face and bless your eyes in the name of Ditzah, her Imma, your Grand-Imma."

I stop in front of her, silent.

She cups my chin gently in her hand again and lifts it lightly to look deeply into my eyes.

"Your Imma made me promise to tell you about her life. She wanted you to know about her family too, her Imma's family, and her Imma Imma's family, and all the way back as far as she knew. All the way down through the generations of Immas in her family back to—"

Returning her hands to her lap, she looks away.

19

JOY SIKORSKI ~ MICHAEL SILVERSHER

"Now you are driving *me* crazy, Anush-jahn, with all your secrets, stops, and starts. Back to where?"

She doesn't say anything else, and her silence, coupled with the gentle cooing of the birds at the end of the day, makes everything seem like a dream somehow, like a mist has filled the air, like we are in a sacred place.

I crawl back onto the rock and rest against her again as I look down at the Elah Valley below us and at our city of Adullam with its outer walls of stone, which now seem golden in the last light of day.

"Are all those Immas my family too, Anush-jahn?"

"Yes, Katu, but that's enough for now. Would you like me to tell you more about Ditzah on the way home?"

I clap my hands and jump from the rock. "Oh yes, yes!"

Anush laughs, stands up and takes my hand as we head back in the direction of the setting sun toward Adullam.

Angry Anat and the End of the Ghost

"For every minute you remain angry, you give up
sixty seconds of peace of mind."
—Ralph Waldo Emerson

As Anush and I walk hand in hand down the pathway toward
Adullam, the sinking sun, hovering low in the direction of the
Great Sea, turns the ground into the color of roasted carrots
and makes the bushes look like they burn with fire. Birds
perch in branches and call out their final songs of day before
they will tuck their heads under their wings and sleep.

Anush's hand feels like the rough tops of the sheepskin
slippers I wear at night after I take my bath, but it is large and
strong, and comforts me much more than the slippers would
if I were wearing them over my fingers right now.

"A long time ago," Anush begins the story of my Grand
Imma, "long before you were born, long before your Imma
was born or I was born, Ditzah, your Imma's Imma, who was
from the family of—"

"Do you think birds dream?" I look up at her.

"Hogoc." She sighs and rolls her eyes. "Don't you want to
hear the story?"

"Yes, of course I do, but I also want to know if birds
dream."

"Hogoc." She rolls her eyes again then glances at one of
the birds. "How should I know?"

She looks down at me and sees my face fall.

"Oh never mind," she responds. "If it's that important

to you, then perhaps they do." She shrugs her shoulders. "Perhaps they don't."

"Anush-jahn." I protest. "That is not yes, and that is not no. We dream, so they must dream too," I answer with a slight pout in my voice.

"Not necessarily." She ignores my tone. "We are different than the birds."

"Anyone knows that, Anush-jahn. But does anyone know if they dream or not?"

Taking a deep and drawn-out breath, she replies, "I don't suppose so."

"Well, *I* think they do."

She smiles and squeezes my hand, but says nothing.

Bleating sounds drift to us from the lush green fields outside the walls of our city. Newly sheared sheep slowly munch their last meals before they too will sleep for the night. I look in their direction and see our neighbor, the big man called Yehuda, as he herds them together. His dog, K'lev (the one I love so much), darts and barks here and there at the back of the flock to keep the stragglers together.

"Are you sure we cannot have a dog, Anush-jahn?"

Since the day I first met K'lev, I have longed for a dog of my own. We got acquainted many moon cycles ago on the morning after the ghost came to my room at night for the first time. Anush felt it would be good for me to get my mind off of the ghost, so we had visited our neighbors, Yehuda and Illit and their three sons.

Every other time we had been in their home, K'lev was not around. This time he was standing in the courtyard like a panting statue, and when he saw me he dashed over and licked my face like I was his long-lost puppy. I fell in love with him as quick as the winking of a star.

Anush frowns slightly. "You know my answer, Katu. Your father will not allow a dog in our house, so there can be no more discussion about dogs."

"But Anush-jahn," I say in a whining tone, "why does the ghost always spoil everything?"

24

Stopping, Anush wraps her fingers over my shoulders and turns me to face her. She bends down, and in the dimming light her face looks like a big pomegranate with brown holes where her eyes, nose and mouth should be.

"Tamar, if I'm to tell you the story of Ditzah, then you must promise me you will never call your father a ghost again. He's my dead sister's son, which you already know. What you *don't* know is that he carries sorrows you cannot understand. No matter how mean he acts or how wrong it is, he's still your father, and without him you wouldn't be alive."

Her words smack my stomach, and I try to wriggle free, but she does not let me.

"Do you want to hear the story of your Grand Imma or not?"

She sounds like she actually might not tell me about my Grand Imma if I do not bend to her bargain, but at this point I am not so sure I care enough about the story of Ditzah to quit calling my father a ghost. I stop wriggling, but clench my jaw so tightly my lips feel like two sticks tied together.

I turn my head to look at K'lev again as he runs to the left then to the right. Hearing Yehuda's strong voice call out his name, I watch as K'lev dashes to Yehuda's side and Yehuda crouches down to take K'lev's head in his hands and scratch his ears and under his chin. I inwardly groan, for it's easy to see the love that Yehuda has for his dog and the love his dog has for him. I want to feel that kind of love too, and cannot understand why the ghost is so mean that he has to keep it from me.

Yehuda looks up then, sees us and shouts out a greeting. Anush lets go of my shoulders and waves. I stay as still as a stick in honey. Yehuda waves back at Anush then turns to attend to the sheep again. K'lev bounds off toward three of the animals that have drifted away from the flock, and I want to go racing through the fields alongside of him.

When Anush looks at me and sees that my jaw is still clenched, she shakes her head and starts walking toward home without me. As her heavy body sways to and fro along the pathway, her large backside looks like a wet halug hung out to dry and flap in the wind. I wait for her to look back, but she does not. The sun is gone, and the darkness suddenly feels like a real ghost might jump out from behind the rocks, so I scurry to catch up with her.

I hate the idea of not being able to call Yergat a ghost anymore, but I try not to let her hear it in my voice when I finally answer her.

"I *do* want to hear the story, Anush-jahn."

"All right then, Tamar, this means you are giving me your word... your promise not to call your father a ghost anymore."

Without looking at me, she pauses and waits for me to reply. When I say nothing, she tries again, but this time a sterner tone in her voice demands an answer. "Yes or no?"

"Yes." I scrunch my face into a raisin and hesitate before saying, "I promise."

Suddenly, a rumbling sound races across the field from the direction of the cave, and the ground trembles beneath us. Then, like lightning in wintertime, a loud *boom!* cracks the air and shakes the ground the way the ghost shakes me at night. Anush grabs me and holds me close.

"What is it?" I cry out as I wrap my arms around her and bury my face in the folds of her halug.

Anush plants her feet more firmly and strengthens her hold on me. "Don't worry, Katu, it is only angry Anat. She's just shaking El from his bed..."

I've heard of this violent goddess before, and everyone knows who El is—the father of all the gods—so I peek out to watch Anat's anger as she causes the ground to rise and fall like waves of barley in a fierce wind.

"... So that she can demand a palace for her brother Ba'al."

Crying out as Anush and I struggle to stay upright, I cling to my noorshma. She continues to tell me the story of Anat, El and Ba'al, and her strong voice soothes and wraps me in a cloud of safety. I know in that moment that Anush will do anything to protect me for as long as she lives.

Finally, the rolling and rumbling of angry Anat slows down to a few jumbling shakes. Anush and I hurry along the pathway and I see the ghost (or should I say my father now?) hurry toward us. He looks worried.

"Are you both all right?" He's out of breath by the time he reaches us.

"Yes, we're safe. And you? The house?" Anush's voice rushes like the wind.

"I am fine. I did not know where you were, but Yehuda came running through the city, saw me and shouted that he had seen you both out here on the path. I came as quickly as I could."

He looks at me. For the first time in my life I see sparks in his eyes the size of the most far-away stars in the night skies. Those tiny flickers make me feel like he might actually care about me. My breath draws in suddenly, as though it has been trapped since the day I was born. Then, as suddenly as angry Anat unleashed her fury, darkness snuffs out the light and he turns away to finish speaking with Anush as if I don't exist.

"There is some serious damage to your room," he answers then pivots his head in my direction without looking at me and snarls, "hers too."

The way he says "hers" makes me sound like sheep dung, but I pay no attention to him because I now know what's hidden behind his eyes and his nasty words.

"We will need to bring in workmen as soon as the shake-afters sto—"

Another jolt of Anat's anger convulses the ground beneath us. I cling tightly to Anush, but Anat does not seem as angry as before, and the trembling earth quickly quiets itself again.

"Don't worry, Katu, the shake-afters will settle down in two or three days." Anush's voice is calm. She never seems to get much rattled by anything.

"And the roof, Yergat?" she asks. "Is the roof still standing?"

I know that if the roof has fallen down, the laundry Anush and I hung out to dry before we went to the cave will have to be washed all over again. Or, maybe if it is buried under the rubble we will never have to wash it again. That thought makes me smile, but no one notices.

"The roof is fine, but many of our cups and jars were broken." My father's voice sounds hazy and far away now. "One of the gods too."

"Which god, Yergat? Which one broke?"

He cannot look at Anush directly, and when he answers I can barely hear his voice.

"The one I bought to give to Trinjah so that we could celebrate the birth of..."

As his voice trails off, and in spite of the darkening of dusk, I see a tear form in his eye. Anush puts her hand on his shoulder and suddenly I am not so sorry I cannot call him "the ghost" anymore.

The Royal Game of Ur

"It is rare that one can see in a little boy the promise of a man, but one can almost always see in a little girl the threat of a woman."

—Alexander Dumas

YOU CAN'T DO THAT!" Er shouts at me.

"Oh yes I can," I shout back. "I'm the one who knows how to play this game the best, and you can't tell me what I can and cannot do."

"Nuh-uh. Can too. You're just a stupid girl, and I can tell you to do whatever I please."

Before I can blink my eyes, he grabs his side of the board, flips it on end and sends all the player pieces flying, then he twists his face into such an angry red knot that it seems like he might choke away all his breath. He looks so ridiculous I want to laugh, but since his fists are so close to my face, and because I like my nose too much to risk breaking it on those fists, I press my lips together, and do not let out even so much as a peep.

Shelah, Er's youngest brother, laughs then claps his hands and runs after the pieces. Shulgi, Aqhat and Bushra's son, imitates everything Shelah does, so he dashes away too, then they both scramble to see who can get the most markers. They are both four years old and act like inseparable twins, except they don't look anything alike and don't have the same parents. Onan, who is Shelah's older brother, and the same age as me, sits near the courtyard pond, ignores us, and stares at nothing.

This is not unusual, for he hardly ever talks or plays games. He tends to look at just about everything around him as though it were a story going on inside his head that will never be told to anyone. Shulgi's two older sisters, Hazibah and Mirah, are off in a corner of the courtyard by themselves, huddled together on a stone bench, paying no attention to any of us as they whisper secrets from their pesky private little world. That's nothing new, though. They always snub me because they are older than I am, and think that all I want to do is play with the boys, which isn't necessarily always true.

I make a face at Er. "Now look what you did. That's not the way to play the game, you goat."

Er stands up and glares at me. "Who're you calling a goat?"

I stand too, plant myself and glare back at him. "You. You are a goat."

"Am not. You're a goat!"

He kicks the board out of the way and charges at me yelling, "Goat-girl, goat-girl, goat-girl."

I stop him from bashing into me by holding out my arm like a terebinth branch that will neither bend nor break, then place the palm of my right hand firmly on his forehead.

Flailing his arms about like a bird that can't fly, he continues to shout, "Goat-girl, goat-girl" then turns his head to the right and tries to shake me off. Even though I am six and he is seven-and-a-half, I am stronger and bigger than he is (and smarter too), so he can't get away. When he steps backward, I step forward. When he moves to his right, I move to my left like I am his mirror image shadow.

Out of the corner of my eye I see Anush hurry over to us from where she has been sitting and chatting with Numa.

"That's enough Tamar."

"He started it." I do not pull away my arm.

"I saw what happened, Tamar. Now let go of him."

I continue to glare at him and do not let go.

"Tamar! This instant!"

I frown and stick my tongue out at Er, keep the pressure

on his forehead as strong as possible, wait until he pushes the hardest he can push at me, then let go at just the right moment. He stumbles forward, falls into the courtyard pond and lands with a splash right next to Atagartis' stone fishtail flipper. Atagartis does not even blink. She continues to lie sideways on her rock with her right hip curved upward and her big stone breasts curved outward.

"Eeek," Er squeals as a fish brushes up against him.

He leaps out of the water and runs to Illit, his Imma, who stands near the doorway that leads into her home. Er hides in the folds of her halug, and she scowls at me. Shelah runs after Er and stands behind him. Shulgi runs after both of them then hides behind Bushra, his Imma, who stands next to Illit. Bushra's two daughters, Hazibah and Mirah, don't seem to notice any of this. They are such old snooty-pots.

I take in the entire scene with a swoop of my eyes and mutter under my breath, "Babies, stupid babies, all of them."

Anush grabs my shoulders hard and propels me to the bench where Numa, Illit's servant and Anush's friend, sits on the other side of the courtyard. The bench is as far away from the pond and Illit's screechy eyes as I can get, and I am glad of it.

"What do you think you're doing, Tamar?" Anush accuses.

It is not a question I have to answer. I know this because whenever she calls me Tamar and adds a question to it with that certain tone of voice, a lecture follows that will not allow me to speak.

"Sit down," she commands.

I sit but do not look at her, or Numa, who sits on the other side of me.

"You know better than to behave like a wild auroch. We're guests here and you're acting like you own the place."

I stare at Atagartis and the fishpond. Onan still sits near them and traces his fingers through the water, oblivious to us all.

Atagartis is an extravagance belonging to Hirah, one of the

wealthiest tamkarum in our city. She is his favorite goddess, and it amuses him that she has a flipper rather than feet. It amuses me too, but I dare not smile while Anush scolds me. Instead, I swing my feet back and forth, pretending to have a flipper too.

Hirah keeps the pond filled with rare fish grown from rare fish eggs he buys in Ebla when he goes on his merchant trips. I found this out the first night Anush and I came to stay with him in his big house after angry Anat shook the earth. Hirah shares the pond and this courtyard—the biggest and best in all of Adullum—with Shua's family, but none of the people there like Atagartis or the fish as much as Hirah does.

"Tamar, Are you listening to me?"

"Yes, Anush-jahn," I say without meaning it, "I am listening to you."

She is too angry to call me on my lie, but I know she knows that I am not really listening, so I stop swinging my feet yet continue to look at Atagartis.

Anush drones on. "No one knows how long it will take the workmen to fix the walls that were damaged in our home after Anat's earth-shakes, so we may need to stay here longer than you think. It's important to your father and me that we don't wear out our welcome. Very important, Tamar."

I turn to face her. "What do you mean about wearing out our welcome? How can we do that? Do you mean the wool kilim we sat on when Hirah welcomed us the first night at the dinner? Is that what will wear out if we sit on it too much?"

My thoughts are on the food from that night, so I am not actually *trying* to make her laugh, but when I see her cheeks crimp up then down then up again as she holds back a smile, I feel better on the inside.

"No, Tamoosh-jahn, not the kilim."

"What then?" I beam up at her because she used my pet name, and that means she is nearly done scolding me.

"Ah-ah, no you don't." Her cheeks drop again and she frowns at me. "This is serious, Tamar."

Now my cheeks drop. I scrunch my closed lips over to the right side of my face and stare at Numa for support. She gives me none. I look back at the fishpond and the goddess.

* * *

That first night after Anat's anger shook the earth, Anush and I came to stay at Hirah's home until the repairs on our home were finished. He's such a nice man, and what I like about him is that he laughs a lot and that a twinkle crinkles his eyes when he does. He loves to eat—maybe more than he should—and had served us his favorite food: masgouf. I had never eaten it before and neither had Anush. We knew it was the kind of food people with lots of silver and gold and jewel-stones eat, but we had both looked at it suspiciously. That had only made Hirah laugh, but everything that night seemed to make Hirah laugh. He told us it was very rare and tasty and made from the fish in his pond.

To be honest, I had not been at all excited about eating a slimy old fish from his pond, but when I finally agreed to try it I was amazed by how smoky and succulent it tasted. I looked at him and said, "I never want to eat anything else in my life!" Of course, he had laughed at that too. Anush did not care much for the fish, but she is more polite than I am, so she had smiled and said nothing.

After Hirah belched loudly to signal that the meal was finished, the three of us stood up. I walked over to Hirah to thank him for the wonderful dinner, but when I looked up at him I could see nothing but his meaty belly, which jiggled with his booming laughter. He bent down, picked me up, swung me around, and told me I was the prettiest little thing he had ever seen.

I like Hirah. If he had a wife and children (he doesn't), I imagine they would be just as nice as he is.

* * *

"Tamar!" Anush rasps as Numa jabs me with her elbow.

I gasp and come back to attention.

"Hogoc! You're not listening." Anush seems even more irritated than before. "You need to learn that you can't treat other children the way you did just now, especially Illit's children. And in front of Bushra, no less."

Anush pushes her breath out with a loud "hehh," then leans forward and looks in Illit's direction. Next, and to my utter vexation, she smiles and waves at her. Numa waves too. I want to grab both their hands and say that Illit is an ugly old goat, that her three sons are even uglier, but that Bushra and her brood are the ugliest of all. Instead, I remain silent and stare harder at the goddess. I want to make sure it is clear to Illit that I prefer the stone statue to her, and that I don't give one barley grain for Bushra and what she thinks either.

"Now we are going to go over there, and you are going to apologize to Er." Anush is adamant.

I nearly come off the bench. "What?"

Anush places her right hand firmly on my left thigh and Numa uses her left hand to hold my right one. I try to wriggle free, but they are not about to let me go.

"You keep your head forward, and don't you dare speak loudly enough for them to hear you."

Anush keeps the silly pasted smile on her face, and nods to Illit. Numa nods too.

"No fair. Why do I have to apologize?" I whisper sideways to both of them because I want to be able to walk again. "It was stupid Er who kicked over the board. He should apologize to *me*."

Anush answers out of her Illit-smile lips without turning her head. "You don't understand a thing yet. There are ways in this world you're just going to have to learn to accept. You'll either do that the hard way or the easy way, and which way it's going to be is entirely up to you."

I do not like the idea of the hard way. It sounds too much like Anush is going to turn my head into stone, like the head of Atagartis. And maybe she might even turn my feet into a stone flipper. I imagine myself in a courtyard as a stone goddess with a flipper and slimy old fish swimming around me. I do not like the idea at all, so drop my shoulders, take a deep breath and force myself to relax.

"That's better," Anush says as she continues to smile at Illit. "Now you are going to get up off this bench and walk with me past Onan, past the pond and the game board then all the way over to Illit, where you are going to tell Er that you are sorry you made him fall into the water."

When I stiffen again Anush and Numa instantly tighten their pressure on my legs.

"Ouch, do you both have to squeeze so hard?"

"Only as hard as you harden against apologizing," Anush replies. "So which will it be? Easy or hard?"

I am getting powerfully bored by now, and really just want to go back and play again with the board game. And since Bushra's daughters always treat me like I'm a leper, and since the only other children for me to play with are Illit's dumb ol' boys and Bushra's silly Shulgi, I give in.

Anush and Numa release their tight hold on my legs then Anush stands up, straightens her dark green halug and takes my hand. Numa remains on the bench. I stand up and silently walk with my noorshma across the courtyard, past the overturned game board, past Onan and the goddess and her flipper. I stare at Illit the entire way and do not lose eye contact because I have secret powers she doesn't know about, and there is no chance at all I am going to bend to her. I will bend to Anush, but not to her, not to that woman who is going to let her stupid son get away with his stupid temper tantrum and blame me for every stupid thing that happened.

I stare at Illit with my secret powers and make her fly through the air and into her house where she turns into a statue that looks like Atagartis, but with the body of a goat and four flippers. I see her father—Shua, King of Adullam—and Yehuda, her husband, argue about what to do with her.

Yehuda wins the argument, and Illit flies through the air again only to land in the pond of the real Atagartis. With a loud swooshing sound, Illit disappears when a giant fish gobbles her up.

Anush's honeyed voice breaks my spell. "Hello, Illit."

To my dismay, Illit still stands in front of me without flippers and looking nothing at all like a goat. Anush sounds so sickly sweet I want pull back and give up my lentils right then and there, but she clutches my hand so tightly I cannot move it. She nods to Bushra then turns back to Illit.

"Tamar has something she would like to say to Er."

Anush looks at me, her dark eyes belying the smile still pasted on her lips. I don't budge. Her eyes get darker as she nudges her head slightly in the direction of Er, who, still clinging to Illit's halug, smirks at me.

Anush squeezes my hand even tighter. "Don't you, Tamar?"

I look straight at Er and speak as fast as I can, "I should not have made you fall into the pond." I look away.

He says nothing and keeps hanging onto Illit.

To my surprise, Illit unwraps his hands from her halug and says, "Er, what do you have to say to Tamar?"

He frowns as she nudges him slightly toward me.

I look at him and wait.

"I… uh…" He spurts out the next words. "I should not have shouted at you and called you a stupid goat-girl." He sinks back into the folds of Illit's fabric.

Shelah steps out from behind Er, smiles at me, and opens one of his chubby little hands to reveal a black game piece. Shulgi comes out from behind Bushra and shows me a white one. I smile at them both. Then, almost at the same time, they grin at me and open their other fists. Each one holds a single pyramid die.

Er watches all of this then suddenly lets go of Illit's halug and asks me if I want to play again. I scrunch my lips to the left side of my face and say nothing.

"You can be white this time so that you can go first," he

says nicely, as though that will take away the sting of having had to apologize to him.

I look up at Anush. She smiles and lets go of my hand, then Er, Shelah, Shulgi and I run back to the game board where it juts from its landing place among the clover. Er picks it up and sets it straight again. As we sit down Shelah and Shulgi dance around us. Onan takes his hand out of the pond to look at us.

I gaze back at Anush, Illit and Bushra. They all smile and follow us with their eyes. Numa observes everyone from the bench across the courtyard where she still sits. Hazibah and Mirah continue to ignore us all. I scrunch my lips tightly and breathe loudly through my nose. I wish they would let me play with them so I wouldn't have to play with these goaty ol' boys all the time.

"Now you shake all four of your pyramid dice," I say to Er, as though I am his teacher, "then tumble them onto the board."

He shakes the dice and tumbles them. Two land with their white tips up and two do not.

"That means you can go ahead two steps on the board."

"I know, I know." He sounds like he doesn't want a teacher, especially not one who is a girl to whom he has been forced to apologize.

He moves his black board piece forward two steps and lands on one of the rosettes.

"You're lucky, Er. Now you get to throw again."

Er smiles smugly, as though he knows how to play this game better than I do. He throws his dice again, and this time only one lands with its white tip up.

"So what does that mean? Remember?"

"Of course I do," he answers haughtily.

"Korseedoo." Shelah loves to echo his older brother, but still has trouble speaking words clearly.

"Korseedoo," Shulgi chimes in like a twin.

"It means I get to move this forward one step." Er sits up

taller, lifts his eyebrows, tilts his head back and looks down his nose as though I am far, far beneath him. He moves his piece. "Your turn now," he says while looking through me as though there is a pill bug on the other side of me that is more interesting than I am.

I shake my four pyramid dice onto the highly polished olive wood board. They clatter onto several of the twenty carved squares. This board is not like our board at home. It has little bits of shiny white, pink and yellowish shells embedded into each of the squares, and the rosettes are made with tiny pieces of amber that twinkle in the sunshine. I think it is the most beautiful thing I have ever seen, and I wish our board at home were half as nice.

"Where did you get this board?" I ask Er.

"Oh, my Abba brought it back from one of the trips he takes with Hirah. He always brings something nice back when he goes away. Does your Abba go away and bring nice things back to you?" His voice has an edge to it that makes it clear he knows perfectly well my father does not bring back such nice things for me.

I want to punch him. Instead, I look away. I am still not happy that I can't call my father the ghost anymore, and the way Er refers to Yergat as my Abba vexes me.

"He goes away sometimes," I casually croon, "and he brings pretty things back too," I speak the lie without hesitating, "but nothing quite as nice as this." My smile zooms straight into his eyes; he blinks as though the moon stands before him.

I pick up one of my white pieces and ask him if he knows what it is made from. He does not, but I do. Turning it over, I point to the prettiest piece of green stone I have ever seen.

"This part is made from a famous kind of stone that grows underground." I am smug in my superior knowledge, but do not tell him why I know what I know.

His eyes open wider, as though the moon before him has grown as full as a giant pumpkin. "I've never heard of stones that grow on trees underground. Do you think my Abba went below the ground and picked this one out?"

"Oh, probably." I shrug and look away.

I act like I am not the least interested in the stone anymore, even though I happen to know that it is very valuable. I had once seen a smaller and less polished one in our home and had asked Anush about it. She had told me that the stones are found only beneath the ground in the Timna Valley, and nowhere else in the world. That is why they are so valuable.

I turn the playing piece over and point to its top. "And that, oh, high and mighty Er, is pure pearl, the most valuable thing ever."

"Oooo." He stares at the pearl layered on top of the green stone as though he has never seen it before.

I too stare at it in awe. This Royal Game of Ur contains seven of these valuable pieces, and I wish my family had only one such piece. I reach over to pick up a black playing piece where it sits on the ground next to Er.

Eying me suspiciously, he juts out his arm to stop me. "What're you doing?"

"Nothing, silly." I turn away from him and cross my arms over my belly, look at Atagartis and pretend to be fascinated by her flipper. "It just so happens that I know something about the black pieces too, not that you would be interested or anything." I yawn, and do not look at him as he ponders my words.

Still suspicious, he huffs a bit, but finally gives in. "Okay. You can hold it. But only for a little while, and only if you tell me what you know."

I smile sweetly and turn back to him. He extends his open palm to me, and I take the piece. The top is layered with a black stone, but the bottom is green, just like the pearled pieces are.

"See here?" I motion for him to come closer. "Watch what happens when I turn it in the light just so." Slowly turning it until I see what I want to show him, I ask, "Now what do you see?"

He peers at the stone suspiciously. Then his face lights up

and he claps his hands in delight. "I see red lines… red lines deep down inside the black of the stone!"

Shelah claps his hands and attempts to match the words of his older brother. "Ded dines, ded dines." Shulgi does the same. I smile at them both and then turn back to Er.

"Yes, that's right. Pretty, aren't they? And did you know that this stone comes from very far away?" I whisper in my most mysterious voice. "Far above the Salt Sea, all the way to where the mountains blow smoke!"

The two younger boys open their eyes wide, as if the moon stands before them now too.

Er frowns when he looks at me. "Mountains can't blow smoke, Tamar. Only men blow smoke." He purses his lips, snorts through his nose, and brings his chin down sharply and then back up as though he has had the final word.

"So you say, but I know better."

I turn away to study Atagartis' flipper again. He exhales with the sound of defeat. Shelah and Shulgi wait to see what will happen next.

"If you do not believe me," I say testily, "you can ask my noorshma. She is very smart about these things."

He looks over at Anush and Illit, who chat like old friends, even though they are not old friends. In fact, they are not friends at all. Anush says that Illit is too high in the sky for anyone else but herself. So why does Anush smile at Illit and pretend? And why does she do the same thing with Bushra when, according to her, Bushra is even worse than Illit?

The three women watch us with their eagle eyes.

Er pinches his lips shut, tightens his jaw, and glares at me before he gives in. "All right. I believe you. Now can we play again?"

"Almost," I reply. "I did not tell you about the rosettes yet."

"I don't care anymore. Do you want to play or not?" He asks gruffly, as though he is going to make a ruling similar to what Shua—his Grand Abba, who is the King of Adullam—

might make.

"Pay, pay," Shelah and Shulgi cry out.

Onan says nothing.

"Silly Shelah. Silly Shulgi. I don't have to *pay* anything to play with Er."

Er looks like he will not hold back his ruling much longer.

Bored now, I act as though I am making a huge sacrifice. All in one motion, I blow air from my nostrils and make a "humph" sound, then force my shoulders down, pinch my lips, scrunch my right cheek, turn my head slightly to the right and roll my eyes up into their top right corners, as though I am trying to look at the insides of my eyebrows, then drop my jaw, and push my voice downward like a bird driven and beaten by the winds. "O-kaaay," I say without enthusiasm. "We can play again, but it is still my turn."

He rolls his eyes.

I smile sweetly then move my green stone pearl piece forward two places. In the rosette that it lands on, bits of amber sparkle in the late morning sun. Looking at Er smugly, I shake my four onyx pyramid dice again. All the pearl tips turn right side up. Now I know I will win today.

Turning to wave triumphantly at Anush, my confidence falters when Illit pierces me with her screechy eyes.

It's time to turn her into a goat again.

The Shuk

"The quality of decision is like the well-timed swoop of a falcon that enables it to strike and destroy its victim." —Sun Tzu

Six years later

OH, ANUSH-JAHN, they're so beautiful." I admire my two new bracelets as they jingle and sparkle in the bright morning sunshine. I want to hop up and down, but hopping doesn't seem dignified enough for someone with a sprouting chest and five hairs on her Hill of Asherah. Instead, I rest my braceleted hand on my hip—which has begun to make a curve where none existed before. "Where did you get them? I've never seen any like them."

Anush smiles, "I have a few secrets hidden in my sleeves, Katu." She shakes her index finger at me in mock warning as I stare at her sleeves. "And secrets they will stay. The only secret you need to concern yourself with today is the one that reveals you are old enough to go to the shuk and shop without me until your heart is full." She grins at me like a sly soothsayer who knows how her customer will respond to a prediction before she even makes one.

"What?" I gape at her, then hop up and down, twirl round and hug her, all my dignity disappearing in an instant. "Do you mean it, Anush-jahn? Do I *really* get to go by myself and look at whatever I want, anywhere at all?" I jiggle my bracelets over my head then dance about her, swishing her halug with my fingers as though searching for more hidden secrets. I feel like a small child again.

"Hogoc, Tamoosh-jahn," Anush tries to pretend that I am getting too carried away, but I see her smile widen until her chipped and yellowed right front tooth seems to grin as well.

I continue to dance and swish her halug and jiggle my bracelets until I cannot help but sing.

"She rises early in the morning
She wipes the dew from the grasses
She carries the cloud on her shoulder…"

I finish one snippet then begin another from songs she has sung to me ever since I first knew the sound of her voice.

"A golden bird sings at the top of the tree
And what do you think his little eyes see?
A forest, a mountain, the sun and the sea
And you in the flowers looking for me
Dai-da-dai… dai-dai-dai-dai-dai-dai-dai-dai hey!"

I start another song, and she laughs and claps her hands as she sings along with me.

Curling her fingers into mine, I lead her in a dance that takes us out of her small square room. We chortle as we sway down the narrow hallway where I bumped into the ghost six years ago; we roar with delight as we wend our way into the courtyard that separates our sleeping rooms from Yergat's business room and the kitchen and storage areas.

In the courtyard we dance a wild mecholah around the perimeter of our garden, which is filled with edible and medicinal herbs: black ka'mun, mint, marjoram, oregano, thyme, hyssop, dill, crocus and rose. The soil around our plants looks like a mixture of crushed almonds and cinnamon bark that blushes with unexpected joy. Round and round we go, laughing, singing, swaying and stretching our faces to the azure sky above, inviting shafts of sunlight to join us.

We nearly stumble now and again over the uneven ground beneath us, so through her laughter Anush tells me to slow down; but our wobbling only adds to our fun, and I cannot help but speed up until she drops my hands, bends over, laughs and pants with a hand over her heart. I continue to clap and sing in front of her until she catches her breath, then we both giggle our way through the front doorway and onto the main street of Adullam that leads to the shuk.

Everywhere, birds on the rooftops of the homes in our little city sing the renewed songs of a flower-blooming spring. Leaves freshly awakened from their budding tremble from a slight breeze weaving its way through the terebinths outside our city walls. Hungry lambs bleat for their Immas' milk, and a waft of roasted peppers and barley makes my tongue eager to reach the shuk.

I dash off to the right and run ahead on the stone-paved street then call out over my shoulder, "Hurry, Anush-jahn, hurry. We're going to miss it."

She laughs and calls back, "It'll be there all day, Katu, until the sun itself tells it to stop, so wait for me before you go into it."

Of course she is right, for the shuk is alive with colors, foods, smells and voices every day of the week until sundown. Every day except one, that is, but today is not that day. That day will come tomorrow. Today is my day. All mine.

I am twelve years old today, and even the sky above me does not seem too far away to touch with my fingers. I jingle my bracelets again and race ahead past all the stone houses on my right and left until I reach the central well.

The fragrance of roasted peppers and barley is stronger here and mingles with spices that tell my nose about far away places. I want to charge on but know that Anush will want to tell me the rules for my big adventure before I can enter the shuk, so I stop and look back at her. She waves and smiles.

I wave back, and then, as though waving at myself, I motion with my fingers for her to catch up with me. "Come

JOY SIKORSKI ~ MICHAEL SILVERSHER

on, Anush-jahn. Hurry."

During one of the many times she and I sat on the rock near my cave, we saw a bear in the bushes below us. It barely seemed to move, but when it did, its movements looked like an enormous batch of lechem being slowly kneaded from side to side. As Anush makes her way toward me in this moment, her movements remind me of that bear.

To quell my impatience I gaze beyond her to look at our house on the left, and then across the street from it to Aqhat and Bushra's house. Whenever I look at their house I think about the way Bushra treats me like a servant because Aqhat is much wealthier than my father. But Aqhat is not at all like Bushra, for he is nice to me. Anush once told me that he loves to help widows and orphans, and that Bushra doesn't like it because she thinks it takes too much gold and silver away from her snooty old daughters.

As I think about this and look at the rooftop of their home, I can still feel the sting of Hazibah and Mirah's haughtiness toward me when we ate lunch up there together last week. As if it wasn't bad enough that their mother treats me like a servant, they acted like I wasn't even *worthy* enough to be their servant! Although the gods know I tried my best, nothing I said pleased Hazibah and Mirah, everything I did to have fun irritated them, and they criticized the way I sat, the way I ate my food, and even the way I smiled. No matter what I do to make them like me so that we can be friends, those two ugh-uglies hate me worse than ever, and gossip behind my back all the time.

The only one in that household who treats me kindly (other than Aghat) is Shulgi, and since I am not allowed to play with any of the other girls in Adullam, the girls who are lower in stature than I am (whatever that means), Shulgi is my only real friend now. I almost wish he were here with me today so that we could explore the shuk together. But that is okay. Never mind. No one would let just the two of us go by ourselves anyway. Besides, if he were here with me now, I'd have to make sure he was happy with what I chose for us to do. No, being alone and doing what I please, rather than trying to please someone else, will be much more fun today.

I look back to Anush and see her bend down to grab something at the bottom of her halug. "Anush, why are you stopping?" I call out, but she doesn't even look up, so I sink back into my thoughts about our neighbors.

Past our home and Aqhat's home sits the well we share with his family, Shua's family and Hirah. Actually, we also share it with Yehuda and Illit and their sons because they live with Shua. Usually, a woman goes to live in the home of her husband's family when she gets married, but because Shua is the King of Adullam and his wife is dead and Illit is his only child, he wants to keep her under his roof. Besides, Yehuda doesn't have his own home, only an ohel outside the walls of the city that makes it seem like he is ready to pack up and move at any moment.

I asked Anush about this once, for I thought it strange that the King of Adullam would let his only child marry a man who owns only an ohel rather than a house. She told me that it had something to do with Hirah—who is Shua's business partner—having told Shua that Yehuda was one of the smartest and most successful tamkarum in the sheep business that he had ever seen, and that because Yehuda treated his workers with great respect and taught them the best ways to produce the highest quality sheep in the region, he turned out the best wool, meat and hides… on and on she went, and I got so powerfully bored that I didn't ask any more questions. "Oh," I had said when she finished, "*that* explains everything," even though it didn't.

Behind the shared well, Shua and Hirah's houses stand side-by-side, separated only by the courtyard where I have played with Er, Onan, Shelah and Shulgi all my life.

Today, the only person I want to play with is Shulgi. Onan is the same as he has always been, and hardly ever says a word to anyone; Shelah can't seem to make up his mind about anything and still tries to imitate Er; and although Shulgi continues to imitate Shelah enough that it sometimes vexes me, he is still the nicest of them all.

Er will only occasionally play the Royal Game of Ur with me now because I still win most of the time, and that irritates him more than ever. He is almost fourteen and thinks he is a man, and so should be able to beat me at anything. Besides, he likes one of the older girls in the city and doesn't want to be bothered with a girl like me who doesn't have the breasts of a goddess yet.

"I'm here, Katu. Where are you?" Anush's voice shakes loose my thoughts.

I grin and jiggle my bracelets. "Oh Anush-jahn, you know you can see me. I am right here."

The wrinkles around her deep-set brown eyes crinkle as she laughs. "Let's go then, *old* girl."

I shout to the sky, "Old? Me? Yes, old enough to go through the shuk on my own!"

Even though I want to run, I walk hand-in-hand with her past the central well, past the rows of smaller and more tightly packed homes to our left, and even more of them to our right. We get caught up in the swell of people heading toward the city gate, the temple and... the shuk!

Suddenly, Anush calls out, "Numa, Numa," over the noise of the crowd.

I tug at my noorshma's halug. "Please, Anush-jahn, not now."

"Shoosh," she retorts, not unkindly.

"Hogoc," I say, slumping my shoulders and parroting the way she always shakes her head when she uses the word that signals she is mildly frustrated or vexed. Then I look up at her and frown slightly.

She laughs at my imitation but continues to steer me through the crowd toward Numa, who is easy to find because she towers above everyone around her, including us.

I cannot stay unhappy when Numa greets us with her usual

twinkling smile and says, "You are both shining today."

"That's because it's Tamar's twelfth year celebration." The pride in Anush's voice is unmistakable.

"My, my, that's good news." Numa bends down and kisses me on the top of my head; I smell faint traces of lavender and lebonah.

I like Numa. She is Illit and Yehuda's servant and Anush's closest friend. Whenever I see her, any gloomy thoughts I might have fly away like smoke on a breeze.

I grin and jiggle my bracelets before her. "See what Anush gave me?"

She claps her hands and says, "Aren't they quite stunning?" She looks up at Anush with the knowing silence of the moon in her eyes.

Anush mirrors back to her that same knowing glance then nods her head as though answering an unspoken question.

I do not know what they know that causes these moon eye exchanges between them, but they have passed secrets back and forth to one another in this manner for as long as I can remember. I gave up trying to figure things out long ago, for they made it clear they would share their secrets with no one, not even me.

"Yes, and not only that, Numa, Anush-jahn told me that I am now old enough to go through the shuk all by myself." I grin and grow at least a zeret taller, thrust out my chest and beam.

"Oh, you are, are you?" Numa teases. "Then I think you might want to have this with you to show how beautiful you are now that you are twelve." She pulls a gift from behind her back.

"Oooh, Numa, it's so beautiful… and purple too. Thank you." I wrap a hattah of purest silk around and over my head and kiss her hand. "It makes me feel all grown up."

She laughs and says, "You're welcome, Tamar. And since purple is a color fit for royalty, may you feel like a queen today as you roam through the shuk all by yourself."

Anush's eyebrows furl slightly as her eyes ask Numa a silent question.

Numa shrugs, smiles and winks. "Er, Onan and Shelah."

"Illit, you mean." Anush winks back.

Numa quips, "Certainly not Yehuda."

They both laugh.

"What do you mean?" I ask loudly.

They look at me as though I have been somewhere else during the entire time of their exchange.

"Never mind, Katu." Anush hugs me. "It's just silly old woman talk, but look over there now," she cries out and points ahead.

We have arrived at the entrance to the shuk!

Anush issues a somber warning. "You can go anywhere in there you like, Katu, but stay inside the city and do not go outside the gates."

"Yes, Anush-jahn," I reply, "anywhere but outside the city gates."

She looks at me solemnly. "And you must be back home before the sun sets."

"Yes, I will. I promise." Eager to enter the shuk, I hop on one foot.

She holds up a kisum. "Here's something for when you get hungry."

I stop hopping. I have seen this leather pouch many times, and the fact that she is going to give it to me surprises me.

"I have taught you how to use what's inside, so be sure to bring back any clay tokens the stall keepers give you when you buy something. And use one of the silver slivers to bring me back half a shekel's worth of salt. We are nearly out at home."

She hands me the kisum. I open it and take out the bulla. My eyes grow big, for I have never used one on my own before. The only times I have used a bulla at all were with Anush beside me, showing me how to keep a close eye on the stall keepers when they weigh items on their bone scales.

"Truly, Anush-jahn? You think I can do this by myself?" I

ask in a whisper.

She smiles. "Yes, Katu. After all, you are a *big* girl now. Why, you're almost a woman!" She winks at Numa.

I ignore her teasing and turn the bulla around in my hand. On its top and sides are imprinted shapes that represent my family, or at least Yergat's part of the family, that is. The horns of an auroch holding up a half-moon show my father's preference for the gods Moloch and Yarikh. Inside the curve of the half-moon, two crossed knives show his status as a tamkarum of meat and tanned animal skins. Everyone in the city of Adullam knows the symbols of Yergat, so it is a great privilege for me to be trusted with this bulla.

I take off its lid to see what Anush has put inside. Bits of silver glinting in the sunshine mix with tiny clay shapes—pyramids, balls, boxes and nails—that show the value of something sold or purchased. Each hand-molded piece is carved with Yergat's symbols in miniature.

"Anush-jahn, are you sure?"

"Not only am I sure," she replies, "but Yergat himself is the one who insisted that I give you the bulla today."

My eyes widen and my stomach ties itself into knots.

"I... I..."

"Don't worry, Tamar. You'll do just fine." Numa pats my hand.

I smile but am not sure she is right.

"Tuck it inside your halug and be sure you do not leave it anywhere," Anush exhorts.

My voice trembles slightly. "Of course, Anush-Jahn."

"Now go fill yourself with the delights of the shuk."

I do not have to be told again.

I dash away; the day explodes into colors and sounds. Bright banners, fabrics, kilims and halugs hang from every stall: a rainbow I can walk through. From every direction voices cry out with the intensity of brisk bargaining, buying and selling. Fires from cooking pits fill the air with crackling noises and the fragrances of sizzling meat. The smells of lamb, chicken and—*oooh*—cinnamon and cloves capture my nose. Not until now do I realize how hungry I am. Where to go first?

The street shrinks in size as I feel the press of people and stalls on both sides and in front of me. I slip on stones, smooth from years of treading feet, but catch myself before I fall. I am sure-footed and refuse to be embarrassed on this day, this magical day. I want to hop up and down just to hear my bracelets jingle. I shake my wrist instead.

"Girl, look! See this?" Men's voices rise as they shove hattahs and trinkets in my face. A heavy man points at my wrist. "The bracelets I have here are better than that trash you have there. Here, try this on. It will make you feel beautiful!"

"No, thank you." I pull away.

As I weave my way toward a food stall I hear his voice trail behind me. "Come back here. Come back you stupid hen!"

One hawker shouts and lifts a stick of succulent roasted meat near enough to my nose that I want to instantly bite into it. "Smoky lamb... and spices to make you dream." He entices. Other smells and voices pull me away.

Deep brown carob pods, each one looking like it has been dried around a large round stone, hang together in shiny semi-circles as though they are gossips that cannot bear to be apart. Someone bumps into the flaxen-tied bunch of them and they clatter-chatter to make sure the others will not miss any part of their tasty stories.

Pots of steaming lentils boil here and there. My stomach shouts for me to stop and eat.

"Pistachios," cries out an old man, his desert-sand eyes barely open, "dipped in wild sage honey from Ur." He breaks a nut piece in half and curls my hand over it. "Eat." He smiles. "Enjoy. Then come back for more!" He grins and I see that he is missing three teeth. I smile, thank him then plop the nut into my mouth and savor the sweetness as long as I can before chewing it.

A barefooted woman sits on the dirt by a tabun and bakes lechem. Her husband, with his long beard and yellowed eyes, stokes the fire with sheep dung chips that their small son hands to him. Smoke from the tabun drifts through the shuk and mingles with smoke from the meat pits. It is almost sickly sweet, but makes me even hungrier.

"Chicken," a high female voice sings out, "soaked in salt from the Great Sea." Louder now, she trills, "Dipped in olive oil, rolled in almonds and ka'mun." She barely takes a breath before she continues. "Simmered with cardamom and barley fresh from the fields." She sounds like the leader of a celebration dance.

I dance a few steps toward her and she smiles warmly at me. With a stick she holds up a piece of chicken. "Would you like a piece, my sweet one?"

I nod my head up and down. "How much please?" I pull out the kisum Anush entrusted to me.

"Today," she whispers and pauses as though considering what to say next, "to you and to no one else, I will give this tasty dish for only one small silver piece." "Her white teeth flash in a ray of sunlight that has managed to make its way into the heart of the shuk.

Remembering how Anush barters, I raise my eyebrows, shrug my shoulders, pinch my right cheek and eye and tilt my head to the right all at the same time. "Eh," I say.

She scoops up some of the cardamom barley with a clay cup and brings it closer to me. "Smell its juiciness," she insists.

Indifferently, I sniff. My stomach dances its own dance that is definitely not a celebration dance. I can barely hold back. Still I make to walk away.

"An extra portion," she cajoles before I get too far. "One for you and one for your beautiful Imma." She looks at my purple hattah. "Same price for both of you."

I turn and look at her carefully. Does she know me? Does she know I have no Imma? I hesitate. She waits. I see the red, black and honeycombed colors of her skirt and decide that she must be one of the daughters of the roaming Elamites. Anush tells me their stories so that I will understand why some people come and go in their ohelim, their moveable dwelling places that keep them from being tied down in one place, like we are.

"Do you come from Hayk?" I ask and step toward her.

She eyes me curiously, forgets about the food. "You know Hayk?"

"I haven't been there, but my noorshma tells me tales from there."

She looks at me quizzically. "Your noorshma? I do not know this word."

"She takes care of me. My Imma died when I was born." I watch to see if she will think badly of me because of this.

"Hogokak," she sighs with a sad look in her eyes.

Relieved, I smile. "That sounds like my Anush, but she says it like this," I say "hogoc" the way I know how to say it.

She laughs, "Yes, they both sound similar. Is your Anush from Hayk?"

"No, but she told me her family came from there long ago."

"Ha!" She grins and brings the chicken back to my nose. "We are all family then, and you can afford this piece of chicken!"

"Hogoc," I say then roll my eyes and take the bulla out of the kisum and open it. "For the sake of family," I proclaim proudly as I hand her the smallest sliver of a silver piece from the bulla. She takes it and hands me a large grape leaf filled with chicken and cardamom barley.

"A few raisins for you too." She tosses them on top of the chicken.

I smile. "Thank you."

She pats my head and turns to sing again, "Chicken, soaked in salt…"

I find a place to sit away from all the dirty feet, wipe my hands on my halug, and eagerly devour the delicious food with my fingers. After I am finished, I suddenly remember that I am supposed to get a clay token from the chicken woman to show Anush, but when I go back to claim it she is gone. I search with my eyes everywhere through the smoke and people, but cannot find her. I shrug and turn back into the flow of the crowd. So much for family.

Color everywhere: the reds, yellows and oranges of peppers; the greens, golds and browns of fresh vegetables, grains, figs, dates, raisins and nuts; too many flowers, roots, leafy spices and herbs to name; textures that shift colors in the light into more colors; and fabrics vibrating with brilliance enough to dizzy even a twelve-year-old girl.

Then there is the crowning color of them all: purple. Like Numa said, it means royalty. Anush once told me this is because it is rare and costly and can only be made from a certain shell found near the Great Sea. I touch my hattah. To think I have this glorious color on my head today! I whisper to myself, "Thank you, Numa," then reach my arms wide enough to wrap up all the colors in the shuk and take them home with me to brush away the darkness of Yergat's ongoing moodiness.

Even though I have not called him the ghost since Anush made me promise when I was six years old, he still acts like a ghost more than ever before. And yet, Anush said that he wanted me to have the kisum today. Still, I do not trust him.

I lower my arms and sigh.

In front of me and to my left, a hollow-cheeked man with skin the color of thin mud, and eyes the hue of spring water stands on a well-worn kilim of interwoven woolen threads of red, yellow, brown and blue. Surrounding him and suspended above him swing kinnors, flutes and drums. The instruments hang from flaxen ropes tied to sticks that are bound tightly to the roof of the stall.

"May I hold one, Adon?" I use the formal term of politeness. "Might I pluck its strings?"

In the doorway behind him stands a cumbersome looking woman with a baby propped on her hip. A boy about two years old clutches her halug and picks his nose. She eyes me suspiciously.

The skinny man looks at her, shrugs and moves his hands up and apart. "Eh, why not?"

The woman sniffs and says nothing. The baby jiggles around on her hip, and the boy wipes snot on her halug. She continues to stare at me.

"I will be very careful," I say in an earnest and honest voice.

He smiles and looks back at the women. She squints her eyes.

"Sit here," he says and points to a spot on the kilim.

I sit. He sits.

"This is a very special kinnor," he tells me with a mysterious voice. "It was made in a place far above us and near the Great Sea." His voice lulls me like a lullaby. "Have you ever been to the Great Sea?" he asks.

I lie and shake my head yes because I think maybe he will not let me touch the golden streaked wood of the instrument if I have not been there.

"Ah, good," he says. "Now, set the bottom of the kinnor on the ground between your legs and tilt it like this." He demonstrates.

"You see how I put the top of the kinnor against my left shoulder?" He looks at me intently.

I watch and nod.

He smiles at me like I am a jewel. It makes me feel shy but I smile back. He is a nice man.

"Watch my hands," he says then begins to play. His left hand plucks the thicker sheep gut strings at the bottom of the kinnor while his right hand lightly dances over the top strings. The melody he plays pulls at a memory in me that feels like—

Abruptly, he stops. His face has a stricken look to it; I wonder if I have done something to offend him. But he ignores me as he stands up and strides to the woman, hands her the kinnor then rapidly grabs as many instruments as he can from where they hang. As he pulls them down, the strings that held them dangle like lifeless arms. One of the kinnors will not come loose, so he leaves it there. With children in tow, his wife slides from view.

"Go quick," he urges and tilts his head toward the stalls at the end of the street. With his arms full of instruments he disappears through the doorway, slams the door shut.

I turn to look.

A scuffle of some sort.

People shout. Baskets of food spill into the street. Fabrics fly. The shouting gets louder. I turn to run back the way I had come. Blurs of color race by and knock me off the kilim then down to my knees. My bracelets clang as they strike the ground.

Someone steps on my hand.

"Ow!" I roll over as people kick and scream; I crawl forward then try to stand.

A deep voice roars, "Stay where you are!"

I gasp as a foot pushes me down.

A big hairy hand grabs at my bracelets.

"No!" I bite the hand. The pressure on my back lets up enough for me to roll aside.

A large nasty-looking man bellows and swings an axe at me. His blade strikes the lone kinnor still hanging above me and tangles in its strings; the shattered wood swings and pierces his eye. He yowls, then quickly wipes at the blood with one hand while pulling at the axe to dislodge it from the kinnor with the other. The flimsy roof of the stall comes down in outbursts of dried mud and branches.

I cover my head and curl into a ball. Pain strikes my hands.

The man growls, flings dirt and branches aside as I scramble for a way out.

The axe whizzes near my ear. I jerk sideways. The axe strikes the ground a knuckle's length from my nose.

The man's movements and voice detach from me as though I am under water and he in the sky. An acrid smell bites at me. I cannot see anything around me as my entire twelve years dance before my eyes.

A crashing noise thrusts him away.

A familiar voice yells. Yehuda. He pulls me behind him

before plunging forward, knife in hand.

Blood spurts. The attacker drops his axe, pulls at the knife in his flesh. Yehuda lunges. They lock and roll across stones, slam into baskets of tomatoes and eggs. The knife glints above them; I cannot tell who holds it.

Spit, blood and sweat smack my face. I wipe it off, see the axe and crawl through the rubble to reach it. The foul man throws off Yehuda, lunges at the axe. I grab for it. He blocks my wrist, grips me hard. I wiggle around to kick him. He raises his other fist. Yehuda punches him.

Knife in the air. Yehuda rams it into the man's back. The man jerks, lets go of my wrist. I pull the axe away. He bellows and comes at me. Yehuda roars, stabs. The man drops. Yehuda jumps over him, snatches the axe, strikes him full force on the head with the blunt end. The man crumbles near my feet. No movement. Yehuda drops the axe.

My head rings. I stare, transfixed by the twitching of the body as blood from its nose, ears and mouth seeps and joins into a single pool on the stones.

Yehuda crouches beside me, breathing hard. "Come, Tamar, there is more fighting behind us."

He picks me up, pants and limps down the street and out of the shuk. The shouting dies away as we pass others rushing to their homes.

I look at Yehuda's face. "You are bleeding." I frown.

He looks down at me. "But not you," he answers with a smile.

It is then that I become aware of his strong arms around me, the smell of his sweat and blood, the pounding of his heart near my right ear. I smile back at him and look as far into his eyes as I can see. My body trembles all over, and suddenly I am very cold. He holds me closer, and says with a voice that rumbles low like distant thunder, "It is over, Tamar, and you are safe."

I know in that moment that I will never again feel unsafe when he is near.

Fever Dreams

"Healing is a matter of time, but it is sometimes also
a matter of opportunity."   —Hippocrates

SHAPES PULSE TOWARD ME... away, then back and forth again
like waves of barley in the brewing of a late winter's storm.
An endless succession of smells and colors push my head
from side to side. Food dances, faces leer, and instruments
play while voices hover and fade like erratic flocks of starlings
plunging and surging upward as one, then splitting apart and
tumbling in and out of the wind only to unite and split, unite
and split in ways that defy all predictable patterns.

"No, Yehuda, no!"

More shapes and voices. Something cool on my brow. I
drift deeper into smoke. Carob pods appear out of nowhere,
whisper and clack my head as though I am one of them.

"Ow. No, no, no!"

A single voice. A cradle of arms. Water down my throat.
Water dripping from me. Something soft on my skin.

A giant bracelet jangles loudly. A purple hattah floats by.
I reach for it. It wraps around my hand. "Tight, too tight." I
tear it off.

I force my eyes open, but I am under water; a dark cloud
towers over me. I kick to swim away, but dried clods of mud
roar down on me, and I cannot breathe. Red bubbles float up
into darkness.

Someone sings "Hogoka, hogoc, hogoka," and I run after
a round clay ball. It rolls down a dirt street until it flies into

the flames of a smoking tabun and disappears into ash on the wind.

Jumbled snippets of songs filter through the smoke: "I rise early in his forest eyes; I eat on the top of the tree..."

A sparkling knife made of jewels and an axe made of dung dance together. I clap the rhythms and breathe hard.

"Yehuda?"

How long I thrash about in this world where dream and reality merge, I cannot tell. Light comes and goes, comes and stays. Goes again.

Finally, I am quiet.

Finally, I sleep.

Finally, I do not dream phantom dreams.

* * *

Early in the morning Anush sits near me. I know it is my noorshma because I can smell the familiar smells of her body: garlic, cinnamon, sweet basil and sweat.

"Tamoosh-jahn," she coos softly, "Tamoosh-jahn, wake up now." She fans my face with something. "Tamooooosh-jaaaahn," she almost sings this endearment, drawing it out as though the entire sky might like to hear it.

I groan.

She sings it again. "Tamooooosh-jaaaahn. Time to come back to us and eat. You have to eat something, Katu. I have nice lentil cakes with warm date syrup and fresh ewe's milk. Come now, sit up and lean on your old Anush-jahn." She shifts her weight.

My eyes flutter open and there she is, smiling down on me with a plate of food in her hand.

"There you are, my sweet Katu. There you are."

Feebly, I look up at her and see a tear in her eye.

She quickly wipes it away.

"Now eat. You must eat."

She sets the plate on the other side of the bed and helps to prop me up against her.

I lean into her as she encircles me with her right arm. I have not felt her nearness this close for a long time; her large breasts feel like the comfort of heaven's clouds against my head and neck. She sets the dish on my lap and tucks a pillow behind me so that I can also use the wall for support.

"Hogoc," she says through heavy sighs. "I thought I'd never get any rest with all your thrashing about and calling out."

"How long did I do that?"

"Here now, take some of these nice lentil cakes. I ground the flour for them this morning." She kisses my head and makes sure I take a bite before she answers, "Two nights and one day."

"That long?"

"Yes, that long and then some, for Yehuda brought you home long before sundown."

At the sound of his name, I perk up.

"Is Yehuda all right?"

"Yes, he is healing well." She ignores the eager tone in my voice.

Dreamily, I say, "I'm so glad he was there to rescue me and carry me home."

"Isn't that date syrup nice and warm? Now take another bite."

I oblige her.

"You've have had a tough time of it, Yavrik. But that is all behind you now," she says without looking at me.

I take another bite. "And Yehuda?"

"That's right, eat. Always best to eat whenever there is trouble." She sounds like she is hiding words inside her words, but I am too tired to question her about it.

"May I have the milk now please, Anush-jahn?"

"Yes, of course, Katu. Here you go." She puts a clay mug to my lips. "Tilt your head back now, just like you used to do when you were a little girl."

I tilt my head and drink a few swallows of the milk. It's still warm from the Imma sheep and the taste of it soothes me.

"That's good. Now eat some more."

I yawn.

"Good, that's good too. Yawning helps you eat."

I manage a wan chuckle as I look into her eyes. "You and your eating, Anush-jahn. I think I will grow as big as a terebinth tree the way you feed me."

She strokes my hair and sighs again. "Yes, yes, as big as a terebinth." She looks out the window toward the hills where my cave always waits for me to come and play. It seems like I go there less often than I did when I was younger.

Her eyes briefly cloud over.

"What is it, Anush-jahn? What do you see?"

"Nothing, Katu, nothing." She looks back and smiles at me.

"That was not nothing, Anush-jahn. What are you trying not to tell me?" Whatever she is trying to hide piques my curiosity enough to tease her. "You know you cannot hold secrets."

"Hold secrets... hmm, no, I suppose I can't." Her eyes have such a far-away look to them they do not seem to see what is in the room around us.

"What is it?" I set the plate aside. "Please tell me. I promise I will finish my food, but I'm all aquiver now."

"Hogoc, Tamoosh-jahn. You never give me a moment's rest."

I say nothing and pick up my plate again.

"After you finish, we will talk. But now I need to rescue my arm before it falls off my shoulder. You are not as light as you used to be. It must be all those lentil cakes I feed you."

"Oh Anush-jahn." I start the ritual we have played forever. "Did I ever tell you that I love you?"

"No, never once."

"Not even once?"

"No, not even once."

"Well, I do." I reach up and kiss her cheek, holding my plate to make sure it won't spill over. "Now, will that do?"

"Yes, Katu, that will do nicely."

She kisses me on the tip of my nose, then on both my eyelids and my chin, and finishes with a wet rapidly blown kiss into the crease of my neck that makes a sound like a duck splashing as fast it can to try and fly.

It tickles, and I scrunch my chin to my shoulder while I laugh her away.

She hugs my head then shifts her arm from bracing me so that I lean only on the pillow and the wall.

We are silent together on the bed long enough for me to finish all my food, but not my milk, so she takes the plate and tells me she will come back soon.

While she takes the plate to the kitchen, I look out the window. Did she see someone like that nasty man who—

I try to block the memory of the shuk, but the images are still too raw. The walls and ceiling pull away from me, and I feel myself shrinking and sliding into a dark hole. Sounds slink back too. The last things I hear before the hole closes shut and dark steals over me are Anush's far-away voice and the crash and shatter of the milk cup as it hits the stone floor.

White milk drips onto a kilim. I kick at the milk and it oozes into a red river. A harp plays. I get up to dance, but slip on smashed tomatoes and eggs.

"Chicken and salt, barley and honeyed nuts for an axe. Good price for both of you. Here, let me slice them for you."

"No, my Imma... dead."

The red river slaps me in the face and pushes me under.

"Hurry, hurry."

Running but can't move my legs. Breathing but can't move my lungs. Tangled strings tie my feet together.

"Hurry, Yehuda, hurry."

A hand shakes my shoulder roughly. "Tamar. Stop. You are making too much of all this." The hand shakes me harder.

"Stop your screaming," the voice yells. "Stop it, stop it now!"

I scream. "No, you can't have it!"

The dark shape with the angry voice move away.

A different shape moves in.

"Shoosh, shoosh, little Katu."

"Yehuda, hurry…"

A gentle touch on my cheek.

"Shoosh-shoosh, my sweet one. Shoosh now. You are safe. Shoosh-shoosh."

"Anush-jahn?" My heart races and air returns to my lungs.

"Yes, child, it is your Anush-jahn. You are safe."

"What happened?" I open my eyes and try to sit up.

"No no, stay still. You just went away for a while again. Never mind. You will be all right soon. Close your eyes and rest. Shoosh-shoosh. Rest, just rest. Shoosh-shoosh."

Anush continues to quiet me; I sink back into the pillow. She "shoosh-shooshes" and says "there now, there now" over and over until I am nearly asleep again.

She moves away from my bed. I hear her in the hallway talking with someone. The voice sounds like Yergat's. They must think I am asleep, but I am not. They raise their voices; I lie still.

"Do not be so hard on her, nephew. She has had a terrible shock. It will take time for her to heal."

"Time, I don't care about time. It serves her right. Look at my bulla. Smashed. All the tokens smashed. At least she didn't lose the silver."

"Yergat, how can you say such a thing? You can buy a new bulla and tokens. She was nearly *killed*."

"It would have been better had she died."

I hear a slap.

"You didn't say that. I didn't hear you. She's your daughter, for Moloch's sake. Your daughter, your only child, Yergat."

"No! Not *my* daughter. *Trinjah's* daughter, *Trinjah's* only child. I would still have Trinjah except for *her*."

His hatred hits me like an ax. I neither move nor blink.

"I don't believe you. You are not my sister's son. You are not a man. What is wrong with you? Can't you think of anything besides your sorrows? Don't you think I have sorrows too? And the child?" Anush's voice grows louder. "Do you think Tamar and I live just to break your spirit? Do you?"

I hear different slap, rougher than the first.

"Old fool of a woman. Who do you think you are talking to me like that? You came to me and I took you in. How *dare* you speak to me this way?"

"Yergat, try to—"

"No. I am done trying to please you and that child. She thought I was a lousy Hyksos bandit, for Moloch's sake, a lousy Hyksos. And she called for Yehuda, not me. I am done pretending I should care. I am done with your nagging and controlling ways. This is the end of it. You will be fed and have a roof over your heads. I will do that much for you both. But that is all. I am done, I tell you, done with you both. And since she calls out for Yehuda in her dreams, let her have *him* instead of me!"

I hear his anger follow his loud footsteps into the courtyard, out the door, and onto the street.

Anush cries. I have never heard Anush cry before, and now I am the one who is angry. Angry with myself for imagining Yergat might ever grow to love me. Angry I have held onto hope since the day of Angry Anat's shakings when I saw the slightest bit of light in his eyes. Angry I thought the silly bulla and its silly contents meant he cared for me. Angry I haven't run away before. Angry I can't protect Anush from him. Angry because of his stupid words about Yehuda.

He is right about one thing only. This *is* the end of it. He will soon find out that he is not the only one who is done. *I* am done. I will never look into his eyes or smile at him again.

I fall into a fitful sleep, and this time when I wake up Anush is not there.

"Anush-jahn, where are you?"

I hear nothing.

"Anush-jahn?"

I try to make my voice louder, but it sounds like it is under water. I try to turn to my side, but a force within my belly I cannot name clamps down on my insides, and holds me bound. My thoughts feel pinched from within the center of my head, and the air around me presses down so hot and heavy that every thought is a boulder I must remove before I can reach for the next thought.

Then I hear—no—*feel* a sound reach for me. It sneaks through the hallway and blunders its way toward my room like a storm cloud clumsily possessing a mountain. My belly tightens even more, and I push harder to move the boulders off my thoughts. A foul odor races ahead of the sound coming at me, I want to get away, but I cannot.

Barely able to open my eyes into a motionless squint, I see Yergat snarl into my room. "Zonah." He spits out the word like it is something putrid in his mouth. "You're nothing but a zonah, a liddle biddy zonah with liddle biddy breasts that couldn't sadisfy a man even if he would die withoud'm."

He lurches to my bed and leans over me smelling like the inside of a wine flask that's been soaked in his given-up lentils.

I say nothing and will my eyelids into dead things that know not how to blink or twitch.

He grabs at my blankets. "I know you're awake. You can't fool me with those sheep eyes of yours, you liddle zonah."

Feebly, I try to hold the blankets in place.

"You want to play, do'ya? I'll show you howta play." He bats away my hands and rips off the blankets.

My eyes pop open to glare at him, but I worry that my voice will betray my fear, so I do not speak.

"Lookin' pretty, are we now? Good. I like pretty liddle zonahs." He strokes my hair.

I will my head to pull away from his filthy hands, but I can summon only a barley grain's worth of shudder.

"So thatz how it's gonna be, izit?" He grabs a fistful of my hair and yanks it.

I'm surprised to hear my voice. "What do you want?" I'm even more surprised that it doesn't tremble.

"Whadoo I, whadoo I want?" His eyes look like scum on top of a pool of water that hasn't moved since time began. "Whadoo I, whadoo I want?" His face twitches as he pauses to consider the answer that has become his own question.

He claws at my bedclothes. "Whadoo I, whadoo I? I want a liddle zonah who looks like someone I used ta know named Trinjah."

"No!" I try to grab at his arm, but am too weak to stop him.

He presses his oily face to mine; I struggle to move my head.

He laughs then grabs my chin. "Oh, a hard ta get liddle zonah, are we?"

My eyelids flutter as a sudden urge to sleep weighs me down. It takes all my energy to sputter, "You disgust me."

His brow rucks up until his face darkens into a moonless night.

He thrusts me over and knees me in my back. "I'll show you wha' disguzding is, you liddle brat!" He fumbles with his clothes.

Just when I think my life is over, I hear Anush's voice.

"Yergat! No!"

He gropes for my thigh.

"Get away from her!"

The force of something striking him shudders through my body. As he crumbles to the floor, a crashing sound rips the air. I scream, then hear and see no more.

Lamentations

"If it were possible to cure evils by lamentation, and to raise the dead with tears, then gold would be a less valuable thing than weeping."   —Sophocles

SHUA, THE KING OF ADULLAM IS DEAD, and the people of the entire city mourn. In the courtyard where Atagartis observes the world in silence, I stand and watch Er, Yehuda, Hirah and Yergat as they lift the litter of sheepskin and cedar poles that will bear Shua's body to the temple square.

Er is over fourteen and now wears more of a man's musculature than a boy's. Since Shua was his Grand Abba, he holds the cedar pole at the litter's right front corner, the place of honor. Opposite Er, Yehuda—Shua's son-in-law and Er's father—stands at the left front corner holding a second pole. Hirah stands behind Er on the right, Yergat behind Yehuda on the left, each one supporting the weight of the dead body by the poles' back ends.

I cannot bear the sight of Yergat holding the same pole Yehuda holds. In fact, I cannot bear the sight of Yergat at all anymore.

However, since his muddled mind and selective memory have blanked out the entire incident of his attempt to rape me, Anush tells me that I have to learn to blank out the memory too, and that these things happen in homes everywhere, that men will be men—particularly when they are as drunk as Yergat was that night—and that there is no need to take it too much to heart because we women put up with this kind of thing all the time and know how to slough it off like so much chaff from spikes of barley or emmer during harvest season.

So she says.

But my memory refuses to forget, so I can take no comfort from her words. The way she tells me about "these female details," as she puts it, makes me wonder if she has ever gone through the experience herself.

I lower my eyes, something I frequently do these days. Nine moon cycles have passed since Yergat broke all trust with me, but I can still feel shame as hot on my cheeks as the night I came out of my faint and awoke in Anush's room.

Shua's body lies on the litter under a purple gold-tasseled cloth. The regal covering is blanketed with thyme, tansy, chamomile and lebonah to mask the smell of the body, which is already so strong I want to give up my lentils. It reminds me of Yergat's oily smell that awful night, a smell that seems to cling to the inner parts of all the bones in my body.

I cup my hand and cover my nose and mouth.

Numa, who has done the same thing, whispers over my head to Anush, "Shua fell asleep in his chair soon after the evening meal and never woke up. No one saw him struggle with his last breath when Mot rose from his throne and clutched him away to the never-ending dusts of Irkalla in the darkness of Kur."

Anush whispers through her hand that covers her own nose and mouth, "It's a good sign."

"Why?" I whisper through my fingers. "Why is it a good sign to go to dust and darkness?"

Anush responds even more quietly, "Shh, this is not the time to speak about it."

"Bu—"

Anush puts her hand over my fingers and shakes her head. "Shh."

Across from us and near the statue of Atagartis and her flipper, Illit stands with Onan and Shelah. Illit watches stoically as the litter-bearers stop so that she can place a sprig of rosemary on top of the purple covered mound that is her father's body. Onan and Shelah do the same then the litter-bearers move on. Illit and her sons fall in line behind them.

Yergat passes by me, a faintly veiled sneer on his lips. I want to scream to his face "Liar! Pretender! Foul Drunkard!" and tell everyone else in the courtyard about the filth of who he really is. I want to wake up Shua's dead body so that he, as a king, will judge him the way a king should judge a creature so low as Yergat. Most of all, I want to shake all the women and shriek into their faces that we don't have to simply and silently accept "these female details," and that when we do we share responsibility for the men's continued "foolishness," which is what Anush and the other women of Adullum call the kind of thing that Yergat nearly got away with on his own daughter.

But I am silent.

Like all of them.

As Illit passes by, I look at her profile and the lifeless body of her father on the litter and wonder if Shua ever played out his "folly" with her? I will never know because no one will speak about such details. The men will pretend they don't do these things and the women will pretend it doesn't matter when they do.

Along with Anush and Numa, I fall in line behind the litter and Illit and her sons, and say nothing.

The courtyard gate that leads out to the street and past our shared well is open. A sea of people awaits the king's body. As though on cue, when the litter finishes passing through the gateway, a loud lamentation begins. Accompanying themselves with flutes, kinnors and drums, seven women sing the grieving songs.

"Hear us, oh ancient ones,
And hearken to us, oh Ditanu, king of all our kings.
Remember Shua of Adullam with favor
As you allow his Rapi'uma to join your ranks.

Eat no dust with him,
But allow his feet to walk through
The grain-threshing floors
Until we are all one people again,
Restored and made whole.
Accept now the prayers that we offer
And the flowers we bring."

Illit, her sons, Anush, Numa and I join our voices with theirs. Bushra, Hazibah, Mirah and Shulgi toss flowers as the body passes them.

Looking at Shulgi as we pass by his family, I see a few tears stream down his cheeks. Without intending to, I lean slightly toward him, wanting to move out of my place in the lamentation line so that I can go to his side and comfort him, for I know that his tears are not for Shua, but for his own father, Aqhat, who died of the wasting disease several moon cycles ago. But I pull myself back into formation before anyone notices me. Shulgi notices though, and manages a feeble smile. Then his mother, sisters and he all fall in line behind us to take up the lamentation too.

Even though I don't like Bushra and her daughters, I still feel sad for them, or at least for Shulgi, that is. Since Aqhat died, they all seem to have shrunk in stature somehow, although I do not know why that is. I only hope Shulgi doesn't have the wasting disease too, for he is still nice to me like his father always was. And that is what makes me think that he would continue to be nice to me even if he knew what Yergat had tried to do to me (which he doesn't and never will, if I can help it). As for Bushra, Hazibah and Mirah, I hate to admit it, but I wouldn't mind it a bit if *they* had the wasting disease!

Slowly, we all make our way down the central street past mourners who toss rosemary or marigolds toward the litter then join the procession. The lamentations grow louder as more people finish throwing their floral offerings. As we make our way around the central well even more people toss their sprigs and add themselves to the cortège. By the time we reach the temple square, the purple color of the burial cloth is green, orange, yellow and white. The roar of the crowd's sorrow makes me want to shield my ears, but I do not lift my hands.

Although the square is packed with people, a pathway has been left open so that the body can be taken to the temple. All I see now are flashes of color raining down on the shrouded body and falling to the ground. As the four litter-bearers make their way steadily forward their feet seem to swim through a field of wildflowers. My ears drown in the anguished howls of a city that sounds like the entire world has come to an end.

My world feels like it came to an end nine moon cycles ago; I howl with everyone else, but shed no tears.

Finally, Er, Yehuda, Hirah and Yergat reach the end of the sea of people. No one throws flowers any longer, but their lamentations increase in volume and their sounds make me think of wolf packs joining together to bay at the moon.

Illit and her sons, Numa, Anush and I, Bushra and her children all stand still as the king-bearers ascend the temple steps alone. Priests await them as they take the body inside the temple. Moments later, the four men exit the temple without the litter; the doors close behind them.

Instantly, the heavens roar open with their own tear-laden lamentations, soaking everyone in the square, including me.

Lifting my face to receive the pelting of the rain, I cry openly for the first time in nine moon cycles, but my tears are not for Shua. Nor are they for the memory of Aqhat. They are for me... only for me.

Lechem and Lamb

"Civilization is the lamb's skin in which barbarism masquerades."
—Thomas Bailey Aldrich

"ANUSH-JAHN, WHAT IS GOING ON inside the temple? What are the priests doing to Shua's body?"

Cracking sounds inside my medokah remind me of the snap and pop in Anush's joints when she stands up or sits down. I do not mention this to her as I attack the emmer kernels with the el-ee I hold in my hand.

Anush frowns and shakes her head as she clears a space on our food preparation table, which is made from date palm wood. "Hogoc, Tamoosh-jahn, we're cooking, so keep to your grinding."

I sit on a stool next to the table, and pound the emmer with my stone to make as much noise as possible.

"I know that, Anush-jahn, but I'm curious. I don't understand why we have to wait three days before we bury Shua. It doesn't make sense to me. Why didn't we bury him the first day? His body smelt bad enough when he passed by us on the litter. He must really stink now. How do the priests stand it?"

"Honestly, Katu, do we have to talk about dead bodies right now. I need to get the lamb cooked, and you need to finish grinding the emmer into flour so we can bake the lechem."

I growl and grind away with the stones. Soon I smell the emmer's sweetness as it turns to flour. I wet my finger and dip it into the warm softness of the brownish white powder. I love the taste of freshly ground emmer.

"That's enough with the tasting. Keep to the grinding."

"Oh, all right, I will. But tell me about Shua. I don't care about us cooking while you talk. My stomach will hold my lentils."

Anush lets out a loud sigh. "If you keep grinding while I talk, I'll tell you."

I grind faster. "Yes yes, I will."

"No one really knows exactly what goes on in the temple when they prepare a regal body for burial, but, as far as I can tell there's nothing bad about it. I've only heard stories, mind you, so if you'll be content with stories, I'll tell you what has been said."

"You know I like stories, so yes, go ahead, please."

Anush cuts away pieces of meat off the bone of a lamb shoulder and tosses them into a pot that sits among the coals in the lower part of our cooking tannur, which, with its heavy clay walls, takes up a full corner of the room. Then she shrugs her shoulders and says, "From what I've heard, the priests take out the heart and other parts inside the body, then prepare them with certain salts, herbs and oils I don't know much about. After that they rub down the rest of the body with these same things."

She slices another chunk of meat off the bone, and chops it into smaller pieces before she adds it to the pot.

"Eww, that sounds awful." I grimace as I grind.

"Shua doesn't feel anything." She continues to slice the meat. "At least I don't think he does." She raises the bone to look for more meat. "But then, no one knows for sure."

Content that she has cut off the largest chunks of meat from the bone, she sets down her knife, and begins to scrape off the remaining bits of meat with a flat copper scraper. It is one of Anush's cherished food preparation tools from the region of Hayk. The tools were passed down from Anush's Grand Imma to Anush's Imma, who passed them down to Anush.

"Go on. What happens next?" I dump the emmer flour into a wooden bowl sitting near me on the table then add more kernels to the medokah, and keep grinding.

"Of course, these are only stories, but it is said that the body is wrapped in linens soaked in the black sap from the great cedars that grow in the mountains near Be'eirot. Then a powerful spell is put on it. Except for the priests, no one knows the secret words to the incantation or where the words originally came from. For all time, that knowledge is secretly passed on from priest to priest, from city to city, from age to age.

I say nothing, but the air feels charged with a presence I cannot identify; the hairs on my arms stand straight up.

Anush takes a deep breath before continuing. "After that," she says softly, "the body is taken by procession to the king's burial cave in the hills. In the cave, there is a clay and stone box with carved words and pictures on it to tell of the king's great deeds. The body is put in the box and covered with a lid." She lowers her voice even more. "Beside the box are food, costly clothes, jewels and other gifts for its journey."

I find myself barely whispering, "Its journey? Does Shua's body go somewhere?"

"Not his body. His hogi, his soul."

As though fearful she might wake the dead if she were any louder, she speaks the next words in a voice so hushed I can barely hear her. "His hogi will take the food and clothes, along with the jewels and other gifts, to the Annunaki, who wait before the House of Far Waters and Distant Fire to judge the king." Based on that judgment, Shua will either become a Rapi'uma… or not."

Anush stops scraping the bone.

I shudder and stop grinding. I have heard of the Annunaki, the powerful and merciless group of gods who established the Royal Line of the Dragon Blood Sovereignty, and I do not want to know more.

Old Bones

"Secrets are the things we give to others to keep for us."
—Elbert Hubbard

"I'M GETTING COLD, Anush-jahn."

"Yes, Katu, my bones groan as well. But we must be patient and play our part."

"I tire of playing a part I don't want to play."

"Ssh," without turning her head, she hisses out of the side of her mouth. "Don't let anyone hear you. You have a long life ahead of you and you must learn to play your part. Sometimes what you must do to discover that part is the opposite of what you want to do or think you are capable of doing."

"Seems like a lot of trouble to me," I moan.

"Ssh," she hisses again. "Be clever enough to find the opportunities hidden in your troubles, and you will not only find your part, you will find the strength to play it."

I'm not convinced. "If you say so, Anush-jahn."

She seems to reveal these "jewels of age," as she calls them, more and more these days, and more and more they bounce off my ears instead of landing in my heart. I let out a frustrated sigh, and watch Er, Yehuda, Hirah and Yergat as they wait in front of the temple for the priests to open the doors.

The three days for the preparation of Shua's body is over, and everyone in the city stands in the temple square in the rain that started the day of his death and never stopped. Illit, Onan and Shelah drip with water too, as do Bushra and her family.

I whisper sideways, "Bushra is not looking so good."

"It's true," she grumbles, "but keep your voice down. Even with the rain, here in the square your voice carries further than you think."

I shrug and say nothing.

Finally, the doors open, and the four men disappear inside.

The rest of us wait and shiver. How long can it possibly take to put a body on a litter and cover it so that we can bury it?

As if the priests could hear my question, one of them comes out of the temple, carrying a large pot set on a pillow of purple and gold cloth.

"Are his heart and liver in there?" I ask Anush.

"Ssh, not so loud."

"Okay." I lower my voice. "Is that pot full of his innards?"

"Hogoc, Katu," Anush whispers, "of course it is, but we don't speak about it here."

I roll my eyes. So many rules.

Next comes Shua on the litter. He is a much smaller Shua than he was three days ago.

I make sure my voice is almost inaudible this time. "He seems to have shrunk."

Anush "tsk-tsks" with her tongue, and shakes her head. "You are hopeless, Tamoosh-jahn."

"I hope so, Anush-jahn. I truly hope so."

Illit and her boys, then Anush, Numa and I, Bushra, Hazibah, Mirah, Shulgi and the rest of the people in the square all file in behind the litter the same way we did before. This time there is no lamentation, however. Only silence.

"Can Shua hear us, do you think?"

Anush refuses to answer any more of my questions, so Numa, who stands on the other side of me, answers instead.

"No one knows for sure," she says in a muted voice, "but for myself, I think it's possible."

Now I'm interested because I've never heard anyone say that it might be possible. People have hinted at it, but never said it outright. I turn to her, and whisper soft enough to prevent Anush from hearing me, "Why do you think so, Numa?" She is older than me, but not nearly as old as Anush, and it thrills me that she does not brush me off the way Anush has done.

"I don't know exactly," she says mysteriously, but it's clear to me that she's not trying to sound that way to impress me. Numa isn't like that at all.

Gently, I coax her. "You must have a reason."

"Yes, I do." She looks off to the right in the direction of the Salt Sea and the Ridge Route, neither of which we can see.

I don't hear the sigh that comes out of her, but I see it heave through her body. I worry that if I say anything at all right now she will stop speaking, so I remain silent and act as though I am content to let the subject drop.

Her voice is barely a whisper. "It was a long time ago when I felt it."

As we continue to follow the procession to the cave where Shua will join the bones of his fathers, I wait for her to continue.

"I say 'felt' because I didn't actually see or hear anything."

Without looking directly at her, I can see from the corners of my eyes that her hands fidget with the cloth of her halug. I stay silent, and even the air around me barely moves.

She hesitates, as though she is inside the memory now, inside the feeling she didn't see or hear. "It seemed like it might have been one of my family members. Maybe my Imma, or brother, or Abba. I could not tell for sure."

I take in a huge breath and try not to let her see it.

"Whoever... or *whatever* it was," she says after taking a deep breath of her own, "I wasn't afraid of it. Somehow I knew it came to comfort me, to let me know I wasn't alone."

She stops, but I sense that she is not yet finished, so I still do not speak, which is extremely hard for me to do at this point.

"I don't pretend to understand it, but I also don't pretend it didn't happen either. I've never told anyone about this before,

JOY SIKORSKI ~ MICHAEL SILVERSHER

and I hope you will keep it a secret." She turns her head slightly to look at me, her eyes solemn, her brow somewhat furrowed.

"I will," I whisper. "I promise I will tell no one, not even Anush." I look at her briefly and smile.

The corners of Numa's mouth turn up a little, but not enough for anyone to see other than me. "I believe you, Tamar. Thank you."

"You are welcome, Numa. Perhaps someday I will be able to tell you my secrets too."

"I would like that." She looks at me tenderly before looking away.

We walk side by side in silence while Anush mutters on about the cold.

When we reach the cave where Shua will rest and wait for the Annunaki to judge him, the priest with the pot of Shua's innards walks inside, followed by the litter-bearers of the body, then Illit and her sons. The rest of us have to stand in the rain and wait again.

As the heavens pour down their sorrows on me and my feet begin to get numb, I wonder if the dead get cold like this. I wonder if the man who tried to kill me in the shuk felt the cold after his blood drained out of him?

I never heard anything about what happened to him after Yehuda bore me away. I remember that Yehuda had said there were other raiders that day too. Were they all killed? Were they—along with the one who smashed the harp—all buried in a cave near this one that belongs to the bones of Shua's family? Or were they all burned to ashes in the Fire of the Dead? And if burned to ashes, where did their ashes go? Would their ashes still feel the cold?

And I wonder if any of our people in the shuk got killed that day? I never asked. I was never told. From that day and the next and the days of the following nine moon cycles since, all the way up to this very moment, I have felt like I've been sealed inside bones that will never feel warm again.

Just when I think I will die of the cold, Er, Yehuda, Hirah

and Yergat emerge from the cave. A single oblong-shaped and highly polished lapis-lazuli palm stone lies on top of the otherwise empty litter. Illit, Onan and Shelah walk behind the litter, followed by the now empty-handed priest. That priest joins two other priests. Together the three of them roll a large stone over the cave entrance then pray and pour libations over it to seal the cave from intruders.

When they finish, they take their places in front of the litter. As before, the rest of us fall in behind Illit and her sons. Together, we all silently proceed back to the temple square, where the priests will place the blue palm stone in a secret chamber inside the temple, so that Shua, the former King of Adullam, can commune with them through it from his cave of bones.

It is said that Shua's wisdom will be needed as the priests advise the next King of Adullam, whoever that may be.

Business

"How vain, without the merit, is the name."   —Homer

"Are you sure?"

"Yes, Yergat, absolutely sure. In addition to the scouts that we have set up in the area around Adullam, Hirah and I are getting reports back from other cities in the region. The merchants all say pretty much the same thing."

"Tell me once again what that is, Yehuda, so that I can be sure that I have heard you correctly."

"They tell us that what happened in our shuk last year is happening sporadically in other places as well. The Habiru have begun to join with the Hyksos, who are increasing in their numbers and movements as their rule in northern Egypt begins to falter. Small bands now roam more frequently through Kn'n to steal, slaughter, rape and take over land where they can. Not only that, the Hittites, or Kassites, or possibly Mitannians—no one seems to know who they are for sure—have been coming down from the North and doing the same thing. We are in the middle of a time of a great change, I fear, and it seems clear we must prepare differently than we have this past year."

"So you've come here to tell me that our original plans have changed then?"

"Not so much changed, Yergat, as become more focused and faster in implementing our original plans, especially where the walls are concerned. They need more thickness. And the gate, of course, is the weakest part of our defense, so stronger beams for the gate, yes."

"Are you saying we are slow and careless in our efforts to strengthen our defenses? Is that it?"

"No, not all, Yergat. Why would you think that? You've done your part, as have we all. Have I criticized you in some way, neighbor?"

"Criticized? No. Treated us like you're our leader and we are beneath you? Yes!"

"Not that again, Yergat. I don't understand why you say that. If anything, I feel like I am beholden to the men of this city, and do not deserve to be called leader simply because I am helping to strengthen Adullam."

"Pah. We didn't make you the leader. You set yourself up to rule over us."

It doesn't surprise me that Yergat says something stupid like that. Through a crack in the wall behind baskets of dry lentils and clay cooking pots that sit on a shelf in the food storage room, I glare at him and wish I could turn him into a goat with flippers on his head!

Neither he nor Yehuda know that I can see them from this room, the darkest one in our house. It is situated off of the kitchen and backs up to the room Yergat uses to conduct business, the one in which they are discussing Adullam's walls and gate. That room is off-limits to me, but not this storage room where I am hiding. He and Yehuda are so absorbed in their conversation, and I am so much quieter than a mouse, that they do not even look in the direction of the crack where I crouch. Besides, they think I have gone to the shuk with Anush and the cook, so I am safe to watch and listen as I please.

Yehuda frowns. "It saddens me to hear you say this, Yergat, for nothing could be further from the truth, and you know it."

"I know what I know," Yergat growls.

"Yes," Yehuda says with a certain edge inching into his voice, "I understand that. But we have too many important things to speak about, so let's not take any more time on this subject. We'll sort it out later, you and I, over one of my roasted lambs and a fine cup or two of Aqhat's best wine that I bought from him before he died."

Yehuda looks away for a moment in my direction, and I draw back from the crack through which I peek. I don't think he sees me though, because there is no look of recognition in his eyes, only sadness... from memories of his good friendship with Aghat, perhaps?

Yehuda shakes off whatever it is that he feels and turns back to Yergat. I move back closer to the crack in the wall.

"What do you say?" Yehuda smiles and slaps him on the back.

"Pah." Yergat ignores his friendly gesture. Does Hirah agree with you about the need for speed and thicker walls? And does he also think we should continue to give up perfectly good living space to store even more food and water? Is he still your errand boy or are you now his?"

Yehuda draws in a powerful breath, and I watch his chest swell. His jaw tightens, he squints his eyes, balls his fists, and just when I think (and wish) he'll punch Yergat in the face, he exhales, forces a smile, relaxes his taut muscles, and changes the subject.

"Neighbor, tell me about your dealings with Aqhat's widow and children. Are you still thinking to marry her?"

I squeeze my eyes shut and scrunch up my face. I hate this subject, but ever since Aqhat died, and Yergat revealed his intentions to Anush, who in turn told Numa, who in turn told Illit, which is how Yehuda must have learned about it, I can hardly think about anything else other than Aqhat's ugly widow and her ugly daughters. Oh, they're pretty enough on the outside. It's just that they're so nasty on the inside I can hardly stand to look at them. They're almost as nasty as Yergat, so maybe they all deserve each other. Not Shulgi, though. He's not ugly on the inside, or the outside. He's still my best friend, and we still like each other.

But what about me? What happens to me if Bushra is

actually stupid enough to marry a man like Yergat? From what I know about her, she probably is that dumb, which means my life will get even worse than it already is.

"Don't think you fool me, Yehuda. I know the game you play, but I'll play along with you. So, yes, I believe I will marry her. What do you think about that?" Yergat says defiantly.

"Well, Yergat, it's probably a wise move on your part. After all, it has been over twelve years since Trinjah's dea—"

"Don't mention that name. It only reminds me of my brat, and I have nothing more to do with her. She's trouble and bad luck."

"So I've heard you say before, Yergat. But I have not understood your meaning."

"Understood? How *could* you understand? You have no daughters. You have three strong sons and a beautiful wife. None of your boys caused *your* wife to die, did they? None of them caused *you* to die on the inside. So what could you *possibly* understand?"

I want to scream, "He understands more than you!" Instead, I clench my jaw and can only wish Yehuda would punch him.

"It is true, Yergat, that Illit was fortunate during her birthing times. But I don't see how you can blame Tamar for what happened to Trinjah."

"I told you not to mention that name," Yergat answers hotly. "You are sitting under my roof. Can you not at least respect my wishes?

Yehuda says nothing, and I want to get mad at him for not shouting at Yergat, but I can't. After all, Yehuda is the one who saved my life.

"Besides," Yergat says victoriously as he takes the lead in the conversation, "the house now belongs to Aqhat's son, and there's more space there than there is here, so I can marry off the two daughters then marry Tamar to the son and... well, you get the idea."

I want to break through the wall. I haven't heard this part of the plan before. Me, marry Shulgi? I mean I like him and all that, but *marry* him? Ridiculous! It's bad enough to think Bushra would be in charge of our household, and I would have to put up with the nasty sisters, but marry *Shulgi*? Wait until Anush hears about this!

"Marry Tamar off to the son? You've not mentioned this before, Yergat." Yehuda pulls down on his chin lightly with his thumb and fingers several times.

"No, I haven't, and why should I?" Yergat sneers. "I only just thought of it this moment. You must have inspired me, Yehuda." He laughs.

About ready to race out of my hiding place, I clamp my teeth together to keep myself from yelling, "Come on, Yehuda, fight. Don't let him treat you like this!"

"I don't know about that, Yergat, but I will say you have given *me* something to think about."

I wonder what he means, but am too angry with Yergat to think straight.

"How is that possible, Yehuda? Can it be that this *lowly* tamkarum has inspired such a *lofty* leader as yourself?" Yergat taunts.

I feel my fists tighten.

"Perhaps, Yergat, perhaps." Yehuda stiffens.

Again I feel like yelling, "No. Don't get up now. Don't let him get away with this." Instead, I lean too far into the shelf and almost tip the basket of lentils. I don't think either of them hears me because of the scraping sounds their chairs make on the stone floor.

"It's time for me to go now." Yehuda's voice is as cold as winter snow. "I wish you well in your efforts with the widow, and will be sure to tell Hirah we can all count on you to continue with your help in fortifying the city."

"I never said that," Yergat protests.

Yehuda's deep-set eyes roar with an inner blaze, but his voice is as steady as the rock near my cave. "Of course not, Yergat, but your words today tell me that you will not waver in doing what is best for the success of your business..."

Yehuda stands taller, and the ground beneath him seems to take on a greater firmness. "Even if it is *bad* business for everyone else."

Like a lion that has finished devouring his prey, he turns, glances almost imperceptibly in my direction, and then leaves the room without saying another word.

"Aaaargh!" Yergat explodes, picks up Yehuda's chair and smashes it on the stony place that Yehuda just vacated, then storms out of the room.

Did he know I was watching? I wonder, but I am so exhilarated by the way Yehuda beat Yergat in the match of wits that I can't take time to think about it.

Scrunching my face, balling my fists, then shaking them excitedly, I grin, bend over and whisper in a barely audible but triumphant voice, "Yes!"

Shulgi

"Friendship multiplies the good in life and divides the evil."
—Baltasar Gracian

Hardly a day goes by now that I don't long to escape with Anush, and go live in the cave where I can at least speak to my Imma. Anush and I had to move out of our old house after Yergat married Bushra (I was right that she'd be stupid enough to take him), and now even my dear Anush has very little say about what goes on in the house. Bushra, her daughters, and servants have the upper hand in everything, and I have even less say than Anush.

And Yergat? He's happy he has a bigger house, and has moved up a notch in the eyes of the city elders. Who cares that he now possesses everything that once belonged to Aqhat, even the dead man's lucrative wine and olive oil business? All he had to do was charm Bushra (that nasty ol' fool of a woman), although I can't imagine how he could possibly charm anyone. I can't even imagine him charming a worm.

He acts like all the extra wealth that he didn't even have to work for makes him something special, as though the glitter of it somehow glisters away the darkness of his soul, as though his higher status covers up his cruelty to Anush and me. Such a despicable man.

I cannot help but wonder if a nice man like Aqhat—a man who loved to help widows and orphans—would have allowed himself to become sick unto death with the wasting disease if he had known that someone as despicable as Yergat would dare to take his place.

Pff. Meh!

To make matters worse, Anush and I have lost our privacy, and now have to share a room. It's hard for me to sleep because she snores, and passes loud gas in the night. Too many lentils, I suppose. She mutters too, although I can't understand what she's saying. I only hear snatches of words now and then, but they don't mean anything to me, although they seem to hint at something important to her.

The worst part of this new life is that I have to put up with Bushra. She's ill tempered, nasty-tongued to Anush, rude to her servants, and haughty toward Yergat, not that I mind that last part.

Most of all, she's mean to me. Over and over she points out that her name means "good news" or "good omen," although she is anything but that. I, on the other hand, am "trouble" and "bad luck" according to her.

Hazibah and Mirah (those two haughty birds) take great pleasure in mindlessly parroting Bushra any chance they get, which is most every day. Even the servants in our new household seem infected by the ugliness of Bushra and her daughters, for they too relish sucking up all unkindness in the place, and spitting it out at me.

For my birthday this year—my thirteenth—no one even gave me a present, except Anush, and she barely smiled when she handed me the new halug she had made for me. I almost cried when she gave it to me because she seemed so forlorn and tired looking.

The only one other than Anush to treat me nicely is Shulgi, and I thank all that is sacred in the heavens he is my friend.

Since we are now "sister and brother," we get to do more things together. We play games, go to the shuk together, and sometimes work side-by-side in the fields. However, we are allowed to do these things only under the watchful eyes of Bushra, or her daughters, or Anush, and only in the fields when the threat of bandits is low.

Thankfully, since Yehuda took charge of fortifying our city, things have been pretty quiet on that front. But, as he says, "one never knows when they will strike again, so we must stay vigilant and alert." Some of the men scoff at him for this, but I think Yehuda is the bravest man in Adullam, and that he is right about the danger, so I always keep my eyes open and watch the shadows.

Shulgi doesn't worry much about the threat of bandits. He's too busy warding off the threats of Bushra and his sisters. They think that if we are alone with one another we will do the boy and girl fire-dance, whatever that is. Even though I'm thirteen, and he's eleven, this is all nonsense because Shulgi and I don't have grownup romantic feelings toward one another. We are just friends. Good friends.

Besides, what Shulgi and I like to do most of all is share ideas.

We talk about the purple merchants and the distant places where they go to get their trade items: finely glazed ceramic beads and ivory from Egypt; all sorts of leather goods from Yavan; spices from Magan; copper from Alashiya; lapis lazuli and tin from beyond Paras. Neither of us has ever seen any of these far-away places though. In fact, we have never gone anywhere outside our city except to the fields and caves surrounding Adullam. But we hear stories about the cities in the famous trading regions and like to imagine all sorts of exotic things. For instance, we think that these places might have enormous birds the size and color of the sun that fly down and capture people in their claws. I like to imagine Yergat hooked by one of those birds and disappearing into the clouds somewhere near Alashiya or Yavan.

We also like to talk about the gods and goddesses and how they influence everything that happens, even the way our city gets its king. Adullam has had no king since Shua died, and since the priests have been around the entire time, and they are supposed to be the mouthpieces of the gods, does that

99

mean the god in our temple has forgotten how to do his job?

Shulgi and I ask each other questions like that one all the time, and we laugh at what we call "god nonsense" because the god stories seem so foolish to us. I mean who would believe, for instance, that before the beginning of the world, the goddess Tiamat created chaos? Anyone with half a lentil of a mind can see that men are the ones who create the chaos. Even Shulgi knows that.

The only good thing I can see about the gods is this: every year we get to have a festival in their honor that goes on for twelve days. I love the festival because there's always plenty of food and music and dancing and costumes, and oh, just about everything that makes life worth living.

Gannitha.

It's coming soon and I can hardly wait!

* * *

I peek into the hallway to make sure no one is around. "Let's go, Shulgi, come on."

"I don't think we should. We'll get into trouble." He pulls me back.

"No we won't." I lean forward again. "I can hear Anush snoring, and Bushra and your sisters left for the shuk long ago. If we go now, even the servants won't see us because they're too busy cleaning up in the kitchen. Come on, Shulgi, we can do this."

I lean forward again.

"I don't know Tamar." He shakes his head. "Why do we have to look at that old god anyway?" he complains, as though doing such an exciting thing would be the most boring undertaking in the whole wide world.

"We already talked about all this. You know why."

"Yes, but what's so important about seeing the face of Ba'al today? Who cares if it changes during the festival anyhow?" He digs in his feet.

I blow air hard through my lips. "Oh Shulgi, you're no fun. You're just afraid. Do I have to go by myself then?"

His face turns three shades of red. "I'm not afraid. I want to go too. It's just that…"

"Never mind, Shulgi, don't think about it. Honestly, are you *sure* you don't want to know if it's true or not that some miracle with Ba'al's face will take place during the festival? I know I do. Come on. Let's just go before it's too late. It won't be as much fun without you." I tug at him.

He sighs in exasperation. "Oh, all right, if you really think we won't get caught."

"We won't, trust me." I venture further into the hallway, looking furtively from side to side. "We're safe. Let's go," I whisper.

Together we sneak through the hallway to the courtyard that separates us from the kitchen then quickly make our way out the front door. As I expected, no one sees us.

"We have to run. Let's go." I bolt down the street and Shulgi follows at my heels.

Air, fresh from a gentle rain that drifted through the Elah Valley below us during the night, fills my lungs and I feel more alive than I have in several moon cycles. Shulgi now runs beside me, and I turn to smile at him. He still looks a little worried but I can tell he's mostly happy we're doing this.

As we get closer to the temple square and the entrance to the shuk off to its left, my heart races like a bounding leopard. Memories of the bandit raid flood me for a moment and I feel like someone is right behind us, ready to pounce. I look over my shoulder, but no one is there.

"What's wrong, Tamar? Do you see my Imma?"

I laugh nervously, "No no, it was just a ghost."

"A ghost in the daytime? I've never heard of that."

"Just goes to show what you know. Now watch out. We have to stop here, and see if we can see them."

"See who?" Shulgi grins. "The ghosts?"

That's one of the things I like best about Shulgi. He knows

how to tease me without treating me like I'm stupid or inferior because I'm a girl.

We both laugh.

"There's Bushra," I whisper. I cannot bring myself to use the word "Imma" when I speak about her. Thankfully, Shulgi seems to understand why and is not bothered by it. "Over there at the spice stand on the right side of the street. Do you see her?"

"Yes, I see her... my sisters too," Shulgi whispers as he shirks back into the shadows of the wall nearest us. "Let's go back before we get caught."

"Good idea, Shulgi. Instead of crossing the temple square like I thought we would do, let's go *back* to the well, and down the side street that leads to the alley behind the houses. That way we'll avoid the temple square, and end up at the Gate. Then we'll only have to cross the city's entrance street to get to the window."

He groans but smiles at me.

"See, you're not so bad... for a boy." I grin then turn and run toward the well.

"Ha-ha-ha, just you wait, Tamar of the Untamed Tongue, just you wait. One of these days you'll be someone's wife, and then we'll see what you have to say about boys."

I spin around to face him. "Don't call me that. I hate that name and you know it. What do you know about wives and husbands anyhow? You're only eleven. Besides, I don't plan to get married." I purse my lips and glare at him.

"But you will, won't you? Yergat will make you. In fact, I heard him talking to my Imma about you marrying *me*. So what do you think about that? When we're married, you'll have to do what I tell you because you're the girl." He laughs, smug in his knowledge.

"Oh, never mind. I've heard that old story already. In fact I knew all about Yergat's plans long before he married Bushra. So there." I want to stick out my tongue at him, but I'm too old for that now. "Besides, I'm not going to marry you. I'm not going to marry *anyone*, so that's the end of it. Come on, let's go before it's too late."

We reach the well turn left then left again into the alleyway. The houses here are small and dirty looking. Most of them have no courtyards or second stories. Broken clay pots and animal droppings litter both sides of the alley, and the air smells like the rain never made it here during the night.

Shulgi pinches his nose and makes a face. "Ugh, don't they bury their dung?"

"Yech," I pinch my own nose. "Not only do they not seem to bury it, I don't think that they even pass their water into holes. Let's hurry through here before I give up my lentils."

Shulgi is only too eager to get away from the alley so we arrive at the Gate quickly.

The Gate is open, and lots of people stream in and out of the city via the entranceway, which is known as the Gate Street. On their shoulders, or on the backs of donkeys, they carry baskets or bags full of items to buy or sell. Since the Gannitha festival will begin tomorrow, and since it is barley harvest, and sheep-shearing season after that, our city teems today with exotic colors, foods, fabrics, languages and music from far-away places.

Once I asked Anush about all the people who come and go in and out of our city. She explained to me that because Adullam sits on a hill at the lower end of a valley that can grow many crops, it lies near a road that connects two major trading routes in the region—the Way of the Sea and the Ridge Route. She said that if you stand on certain parts of our city's walls you could see our connecting road and how it follows the path of the rising and setting of the sun.

"But you can't see the Ridge Route," she explained. A dark cloud seemed to cover her face when she told me the Ridge Route follows the mountains that run from the Sea of Kinneret to the Salt Sea. "It starts at Hazor, which is far away from here, and it ends up at Beersheva, which is closer, but not before going through many other cities."

Her voice had seemed sad and soft when she said "many other cities," so I asked her why. She didn't answer. She just looked away, and said nothing else until I asked her to tell me about the Way of the Sea. She had sighed, said that we couldn't see that trading route either, and that it went from Ugarit all the way down the coast of the Great Sea before it ended up in Egypt. Then she had looked away once more.

I still don't know why these trading routes make her so sad, but I never asked her again.

Everyone seems to carry and hide sad secrets, even me, and sometimes it's better not to try and dig them out. Maybe it's the way we learn to pretend we don't care about the memories that created the secrets to begin with.

"Shulgi." I turn my head briefly toward him. "There are so many people here that I don't believe Bushra or your sisters will be able to see us as we cross the Gate Street, but let's peek to see if we can still see them first." I stand as high as I possibly can on the tips of my toes, and cup my hand over my eyes to look for them across the temple square off to the left.

"They're gone. Now's our chance, hurry!" I bolt into the press of noisy and smelly people and animals, and thread my way around them. Shulgi catches up with me; we scurry past the leaders of the city who sit at the Gate and argue about whatever it is they argue about. Thankfully, Yergat is off checking on the workers in his tanning sheds today, and not among them. Neither is Yehuda or Hirah, so we are safe.

Soon, we scramble up the stone steps that lead to the window of the temple. We cup our hands and press our noses to the window so we can see inside. There stands Ba'al!

I whisper, "Do you see him, Shulgi?"

"Yes," he whispers back.

In silence, we stare at Ba'al's face for a few more minutes.

"That's enough. Let's go. We have to be sure to get home before Anush wakes up, or Bushra and your sisters come back."

We scamper down the steps, rush past the leaders of the

city and across Gate Street, then down the stinky alley and onto the main street, where we turn left by the well, then hurtle home. We burst noisily through the front entrance and courtyard, race down the hallway.

Anush hears us and wakes up with a start. "Why are you two panting so hard? What have you been up to?"

"We're hungry," we answer in unison then look at each other and break out laughing.

"Hogoc," she says, and brushes us away with a flick of her wrist.

Shulgi and I run to the kitchen, grab some food, and dash up the stairway that leads to the roof, where we congratulate each other on the success of our secret adventure.

"I think we should make plans to go up on the city walls next time, so we can see the road that follows the rising and setting of the sun," I chatter between mouthfuls of goat cheese and olives.

"Maybe during Gannitha," Shulgi suggests as he chews on a dried date.

I grin.

"Good idea… for a boy."

Gannitha

"The priest is an immense being because he makes the crowd believe astonishing things."   —Charles Baudelaire

"Hurry, Anush, or we'll miss the prayers!" I walk at her right side, and even though I'm too old to behave like a small child anymore, I tug at her halug sleeve.

"Hogoc, Katu, must you be so impatient? Can't you see that my feet no longer follow my head as fast as they once did?"

"I know, I know, Anush-jahn." My words spill out in a breathless procession of song-speech, as though I'm preparing to compose a new verse for the reading of the *Tale of Ba'al*, which is read every year at the Gannitha festival. "It's just that I don't want to miss the opening prayers, for then our festival days can really begin. I'm so excited that I know I will burst with the waiting… and to think that I will get to be the—"

"Yes yes, of course," Anush interrupts. "Naturally you're all aquiver with everything. But me?" She pushes air away with her right hand, as if that will slow me down. "I've heard so many Gannitha prayers and seen so many gods, goddesses, sacred marriages, processions and cups of red mead that I'd just as soon stay home, soak my weary feet and eat nuts and raisins."

I look down at her feet and smile. She seems as strong as a goat, and as stubborn as one too, so I think she is just fine, no matter how much she protests otherwise. I take her hand and squeeze it. Without looking at me, she grunts, smiles and breathes more heavily than usual. The sound of if doesn't sound quite right.

"Are you okay?"

"Fine, fine." She waves me away. "Why shouldn't I be?"

Like I said, stubborn as a goat.

"Well, I'm sure I don't know why, but you sound like you are having trouble breathing."

She waves me away again, but says nothing this time.

On either side of us people swarm toward the temple, where we will all hear and echo the somber prayers chanted by our priest of Ba'al. Back and forth these prayers will go until the noon meal, which we will all share together in the central meeting square near the Gate. After the meal we will continue the prayers until the day is over.

"The only part I don't like, Anush-jahn, is that we have to pray for so long."

"And you're young, Katu. Imagine how my old bones rattle and protest the length of these prayers. You'd think one full day's worth of supplications would be enough to please the gods, but no, tch-tch, I'll have to drag my entire bag of rattles back for the next three days as well."

Her "tch-tch" sounds remind me of water drops spitting from a knife forged in a fire, but I keep my mouth closed, for I am tempted to tease her, and this isn't the right moment. Instead, I blow one quick breath through my nostrils and shake my head.

Anush notices and says, "You don't think it's so hard for an old woman to walk this fast?" She purposefully breathes more heavily to make sure I see how difficult it is for her to keep pace with me.

This time I laugh. "Oh Anush-jahn, you're not that old, and even though you complain more and more these days about your bone rattles, I don't mind." I squeeze her hand again then speak in a softer voice, "I know that you are tired."

The truth is, since Yergat married Bushra, and we moved to Aqhat's old house, I can see all too clearly that the usual glow of her feistiness seems more like a moon coming out of its fullness than going into it.

My dear noorshma squeezes my hand back this time, and we walk in silence the rest of the way to the temple square.

Nothing will spoil the Gannitha festival. I know it.

* * *

Four days of prayers for mercy have brought us to the telling of the *Tale of Ba'al*, and how he gained kingship over all the gods and goddesses.

"I tell thee Prince Ba'al
I declare, O Rider of the Clouds
Now thine enemy wilt thou smite
Now wilt thou cut off thine adversary
Thou wilt take thine eternal kingdom
Thine everlasting dominion..."

Intoning the sacred words of the story, the priest stands at the entrance of the temple and faces the people, who stand packed together in the square listening with rapt attention.

Wedged between Anush and Shulgi, I listen too. Shulgi stands next to Bushra, who stands next to Hazibah and Mirah. Yergat is on the other side of them, and I am glad to be as far away from him as possible.

The entrance to our city faces the direction of the Great Sea. There is a reason for this: during the many years it took to build Adullam, the priests and the kings who lived back then decided it was important to position the temple in such a way as to allow the beams of the setting sun to glow on the faces of the people whenever they stood in the temple square for sacred convocations.

Today the waning sunlight makes us all look like golden statues. Truly, it feels like a holy moment, even to me, the one who doesn't believe in all the god nonsense.

"Homage to Lady Asherah of the Sea
Obeisance to the Progenitress of the Gods
So that she will give a house to Ba'al like the gods'
And a court like Asherah's sons..."

This part of the story fascinates me. Asherah, the Imma of all the gods, builds Ba'al a palace then starts a fire in it that burns for seven days and nights. But instead of destroying the palace, this fantastic fire covers the outside of it with gold, silver and lapis lazuli. I want to see this palace, but whenever I ask about where I might go to see it, no one seems to know where it is.

"One lip to earth and one to heaven,
He stretches his tongue to the stars
Ba'al enters his mouth
Descends into him like an olive cake..."

I grimace; I hate this next part. It's gruesome. But I listen respectfully as the priest intones the words about Ba'al's jealous brother, Mot, and how he kills Ba'al then eats him, and how this fills Asherah and El—the father of all the gods—with so much grief that they maim themselves then cause the water to dry up in the land and the crops to fail.

"Shulgi," I whisper, "don't you just hate this part?"

All he says is, "Shh."

I look around at the golden faces of the people and want to shout, "Do you really believe this part about Mot eating his brother? Would *you* eat your brothers?" Of course they cannot hear my thoughts, or any others for that matter, so no one looks at anyone else and no one says a word; everyone stays focused on the priest.

The priest chants on about how Ba'al's sister, Anath, demands that Mot release Ba'al so Ba'al can come back to life (which he does), and how this makes El and Asherah happy enough to send rain again and restore the land.

> "In a dream, O Kindly El Benign,
> In a vision, Creator of Creatures,
> The heavens fat did rain
> The wadis flow with honey…"

"What happens in those years when there is no rain, and the crops fail?" I silently ask myself. "And why don't El and Asherah fix things during those years?"

I look around the square to see if anyone might know the answer, or at least possibly be asking the same question. All I see are golden statue people staring dully ahead. Am I the only one who sees the obvious?

> "Eat, O Gods, and drink
> Drink the red mead until you are sated…"

The red mead puzzles me. I've never understood what it means, and no one will tell me. When I ask the Anush or Numa, they simply smile the knowing smile of older women and nod their heads.

> "Eat, O Kings, and drink
> Drink the red mead until you are sated…"

What is this red mead, and why do both the kings and the gods drink it?

No one looks like they care about the answer. In fact, I'm beginning to think that there is no answer, and that maybe I'm the only one who is asking the question.

I search the statue faces again. All remain transfixed by the words of the story and the voice of the priest. All, that is, except one of them. It moves.

It's Yehuda.

Like me, he does not look at the priest. Instead, his eyes search the night skies as though looking for an answer there. My heart races to think I'm not alone, to think someone else might be asking the same kinds of questions I ask.

Then, as though he senses that he is not alone either, he brings his head down, turns it slowly, looks at me, smiles and holds his gaze.

I am suddenly warm all over and have to catch my breath as I smile back.

The priest drones on until the gold is gone from the faces of the people, and the skies turn black.

On the way home I look up at the stars. There are so many of them blazing with light that they look like rippling embers in a fire pit.

"Anush-jahn," I whisper in her ear as we walk arm and arm back to our house, "are those lights the gods and goddesses?"

Anush yawns, and looks up for a brief moment then watches her feet so she won't trip. "If you look at the darkness between the stars, Katu, you will see where the real lights are. But the brightest stars take your eyes away from where it's darkest. This is a trick of the gods and goddesses to make you think they themselves are the true lights. If you move your eyes away from looking at the most visible stars—the ones the gods and goddesses use to fool you—and concentrate long enough on the darkness between those bright stars, you will see the lights that fill up what only appears to be darkness. There are many more of these hidden stars than the ones you think are the gods and goddesses."

I look up at the sky again and stare at the darkness between the stars. "It's all black between them, Anush-jahn. I don't see any light there at all."

Anush pats my hand, "You will, Tamoosh-jahn. Someday, you will."

* * *

112

"Shulgi," I whisper to him as he stands beside me, "is he really going to become king today?"

He cups his hand over his mouth, and pretends to cough as he whispers back to me, "Yes, that's what my Imma said."

"I can hardly believe it."

"Me either. I sure wouldn't want to be in his place today."

I nod and watch as the morning sunlight bounces off the jewelry that everyone seems to be wearing today: gold necklaces, silver hairpins and nose rings, copper bracelets, and pale red and blue glass-beaded headscarves. I have on the bracelets that Anush gave me for my twelfth-year celebration, and even Anush has on a necklace of gold, although I am not sure where it came from.

The temple square is full of people again; all eyes are now focused on Yehuda, who stands on the outskirts of the square at the furthest distance from the temple doors. The leading families in the city stand near him, and since Yergat now qualifies as one of the elites because he controls Aqhat's former wine and oil business, our family stands close enough for me to see Yehuda clearly. Dressed in his finest clothes and jewels and holding his seal, cord and staff—the implements that reveal his position and authority—he stands, as always, like a massif with the strength in his body powering out from him in an almost palpable way. Suddenly realizing how handsome he looks towering over everyone around him, I suck in breath and look away before he or anyone else might see me staring at him.

Beside him, a priest lifts a crown into the air and recites an incantation over it. A single red stone in the simple bronze circlet catches the sun, which makes the stone look like a flaming coal. The priest lowers the crown. The crowd holds its breath, not quite sure who is going to become king, but anticipating that it will surely be Yehuda. I hold my breath too. Then the priest surprises us all by placing the crown on Er, who stands next to his father. As we all exhale, sounds of confusion fill the square.

"What? Er, A king?" I look at Shulgi, who shrugs his shoulders. "I thought... we all thought it would be Yehuda. Didn't you too?"

Shulgi shrugs his shoulders again.

"Come on Shulgi, you know that Er is no man and doesn't know the first thing about the business of being king. I doubt that he even has his own bulla yet, so how can he lead Adullam as the most successful tamkarum... as the king?"

He shrugs yet again

Tired of all his shrugging, I frown. "But we heard rumors. Even Bushra told you that it was pretty much a sure thing that Yehuda would become king because he understands business almost as well as Shua did. And Bushra should know these things since she and Illit are such good friends."

Shulgi raises his eyes and eyebrows as if they are the only things he has left to shrug with.

I blow air through my teeth. I don't like it that Yehuda will not be king, and I don't like it that Shulgi has nothing to say about it.

"Oh, sure," I say hastily, "since Er is a few moon cycles older than fourteen now, he *should* be able to represent his family as king, but you know as well as I do that he is not like other boys his age. He's just such a milksop and acts like we are all beneath him." I scrunch up my lips and nose in disgust.

Shulgi smiles and finally speaks. "Well, Tamar, you know how the god nonsense goes. Do you really think those ol' priests know what they're doing anyhow?"

I chuckle. "You're right. It's all god nonsense." I look at him, and even though I am not so sure what the particular god nonsense is that has made Er king, I say off-handedly, "I'm sure glad you and I know the truth about god nonsense. I'm not sure anyone else does though."

"Who cares about anyone else anyhow?" Shulgi grins. "It's enough that you and I know better, isn't it?" His eyes twinkle as he looks at me.

"You're right. It only matters that you and I know how

these things work." I wink at him.

"Uh-huh." He blinks. "But I can't say I like it that Er's now king. He's so full of himself these days."

"I think he's always been that way." I laugh. "When have you ever seen him be nice to anyone? He's such an Imma-boy, Illit's little whiner."

I make faces to imitate how Er's face looks when he runs to Illit and whines about something Yehuda wants him to do. Shulgi and I have seen that happen lots of times when we're in the Atagartis courtyard.

Shulgi snorts, then pretends he is Illit, and lifts his head higher, looks down his nose at me and shakes his finger in my face. Even though Shulgi is two years younger than I am, he is nearly a zeret taller than me now.

We both turn to watch the priest again.

He has finished chanting his incantations over Er and now turns to face the crowd, spreading out his arms. "Hear me now, all you people of Adullam, and welcome your new king, Er, King of Adullam!" His voice booms across the temple square.

The crowd responds with a roar, "Er, King of Adullam."

Shulgi and I shrug at one another, even as we join in with everyone else: "Er, King of Adullam, Er, King of Adullam!" We shake our heads and laugh.

"Just think, Shulgi. I beat the King of Adullam at the Royal Game of Ur just last night. Ha!"

Our families had feasted together with Hirah by torchlight after the recitation of the *Tale of Ba'al* the previous night, and Er had challenged me to a game.

"Tomorrow I'll be king," he had boasted, "so you can't beat me now."

"I think you fool yourself, little Prince," I had taunted. "Just try me. Anyhow, you're not going to be king. Yehuda is!"

We had set up the game board and player pieces; the other boys and my two stepsisters had stood around us as we tore into playing like a kingdom depended on it. They had all laughed and clapped when I won the game. Er had stormed off afterward and wouldn't speak to me for the rest of the evening.

He's still such a baby. That's why shouting "Er, King of Adullam" makes me feel like a liar today.

Now I watch as Yehuda, Illit, Onan and Shelah fall in line behind Er, who follows the priest through the crowd to the temple. Hirah, Yergat, Bushra, Hazibah, Mirah, Shulgi and I follow behind them. Anush stands with Numa on the sidelines, and the two of them nod at me as we pass, then they fall in line behind us. The rest of the people of the city crowd around us, and then we all move together like a herd of sheep toward the temple to chant the ritual words.

"There he is, off on his way to
El of the Sources, of the Floods,
In the midst of the headwaters of the Two Oceans.
He penetrates El's field and enters the pavilion of the King.
At El's feet he bows and falls down,
Prostrates himself, doing homage…"

As we continue chanting, Er enters the temple with only the priest at his side. The doors are left open, so it is easy for me to watch the two of them approach Ba'al at the altar. Er stands sideways; I can see his face. The priest bows before Ba'al and utters another incantation, then shakes his head up and down as though he hears the god say something to him. It must be an order of some kind because suddenly the priest spins around and roars, "I am Ba'al!" Then he rips the crown off Er's head, snatches away his jewelry, seal, cord and staff, then slaps him hard on the face, and pulls hard on his ears!

I suck in air and gasp along with the crowd. Even though I knew this was going to happen—Anush had warned me that this was a long-standing tradition for crowning a new king—it still shocks me. I mean, Er is a baby and all that, but he's still my friend, and I don't like seeing him slapped or having his ears pulled, especially by a priest who pretends to be Ba'al.

But Er doesn't seem to mind, which seems odd to me because he is always so whiny when he scrapes his knee or nicks his knuckle on something.

Er kneels. I hear his every word as he pleads with the priest… the so-called Ba'al.

> "I have not sinned,
> O mighty Ba'al, Lord of the universe,
> And I have not neglected
> Your heavenly power,
> Not even once throughout the past year."

How can Er plead with Ba'al? He can't even beat me at the game of Ur! I want to protest, but instead listen in silence as the priest answers the new so-called king.

> "Don't be afraid of what Ba'al has to say,
> For he hears your prayers,
> He extends your power,
> And increases the greatness of your reign."

Greatness of his reign? Er doesn't even know how to rule his own temper!

Er stands up. The priest returns his jewels, cord, seal and staff, and then slaps him again, harder this time, again and again, until tears spill from Er's eyes.

Once the priest sees the tears, he turns Er to face the people, and proclaims, "Behold, your king who has pleased Ba'al." He then places the crown back on Er's head, and bids us all to join them both in prayers for the earth, for rain, sun, and the new growing season.

I only mouth the words of the prayers this time, for my heart speaks different words after seeing Er treated so violently by of this god nonsense.

* * *

On the way home that afternoon, Anush and Numa walk on either side of me. I ask my noorshma why Yehuda was not crowned king. She hesitates, clears her throat, coughs a bit, fusses with her halug, but says nothing.

I peer at her. "What is it, Anush-jahn?" It's obvious that she wants to avoid answering my question. "What's wrong?"

She looks away, takes a deep breath, but still says nothing. Numa clears her throat too.

The sun is high overhead, the day is hot, my halug clings to my skin with dampness, I'm hungry and tired from the ritual activities of the day, and in no mood to be put off.

Raising my voice too strongly, I ask, "Why did the priest crown Er instead of Yehuda? And please don't tell me that you don't know because you can't fool me on this one. You act like you have the answer, but just don't want to give it to me." I surprise even myself with my brashness. "I don't mean to be rude, Anush-jahn, but what can be so hard about answering such a simple question?"

Anush doesn't even so much as look at me.

"Ouch!" I feel Numa's hand squeeze my shoulder, and I briefly recall the day Er fell into the pond near Atagartis, and how I had to sit between Anush and Numa as they clenched my legs to keep me from jumping off the bench after Anush had insisted that I had to apologize to Er.

Numa now sighs, but does not let up the pressure on my shoulder as she says, "Tamar, Tamar, when are you going to learn that you can't just burst out and demand that everyone jump to your commands when you feel like it?"

I frown, "I'm tired and hungry, and—"

"Oh you are, are you? Pah! Can't you see that Anush is much more tired and hungry than either you or I? You need to think about someone other than yourself right now, Tamar."

It's a rare thing for Numa to voice any impatience at all, and even rarer for her to speak as harshly as she does now, so now I grow suspicious.

"Why are you getting so upset, Numa? It seems to me that

my question is simple enough." I scowl at her.

Anush says nothing during this exchange, but I can hear her inhaling and exhaling with growing exasperation.

Numa's grip on my shoulder tightens. "You little goat. Stop pushing so hard to get your way. If you were my child, I'd make sure that you—"

"All right, all right you two. I've had enough of this nonsense!" Anush puts her hand on Numa's hand and gives her a look that says "forget it, she's not going to understand."

I glare at Numa. She glares at me, but takes her hand off my shoulder.

Anush lowers her voice. "If you two will stop this foolishness, I will answer the question."

I let out a deep sigh. Numa turns her face away, blows air from her nose with a huff, and looks in the direction of the Ridge Route and the Great Sea. She always seems to do this, as though some great secret lies hidden somewhere along the way. Usually, I want to know what it is that she is looking for, but today her gesture irritates me to the point that I can barely hold my tongue. I take a deep breath and let it out with a groan.

"All right, Tamar. That's better." Anush stops for a moment to catch her breath.

Both Numa and I stop too. I feel badly that she and I have had a quarrel, but I think it is her fault, so I'm not about to back down… or look at her.

Anush sees my stubbornness and shakes her head. "The answer is not so simple as you think," she says, "but I will try to make it easy to understand."

I can hear that she is having trouble breathing. "Thank you," I say, feeling a bit ashamed.

Numa turns back to look at her. "Are you sure you feel strong enough to speak about this right now, Anush? You know that it can wait for a better time." She frowns at me as though I am to blame for Anush's rasping breath.

Anush smiles wanly. "No, no, dear friend." She pats Numa's

hand. "I will be fine. It's better to speak of it now rather than later. Waiting won't change anything."

I say nothing, for now I realize that I *am* a goat for putting my dear noorshma through this during the high heat of the day.

Anush turns to me and cups my chin none too gently. "What I have to say is very important for you to know, and I had hoped to wait a little longer to tell you. But since you insist that you must have your answer right now, I will say one thing, and no more, even though there is more to say. Much more. But you must promise me that you will be satisfied with what I tell you, and then not pester me… or Numa, for more. Do I have your word, Tamar?"

Oh-oh. She's using my formal name. Now I know I've pushed too far.

"Yes, Anush-jahn, I promise." I look down as though a pill bug might rescue me.

She pulls my chin back up, and looks me in the eye.

"Yehuda does not have the right blood to be the king. The priests have determined the bloodline that is necessary, and it comes through the mother, not the father. That's all you need to know right now." She looks at me as if to test the value of my promise, then lets go of my chin.

I suck in air, but say nothing.

"Let's go home and get something to eat now," Anush says, and starts walking again.

Numa and I follow her in silence, neither of us looking at one another.

The next morning after sunrise, a large procession of children dressed like gods and goddesses follows Er —dressed as a king—to the Bit Gannitha, the House of Offerings. It's a small stone hut that sits in the middle of the barley fields and holds a replica of Ba'al, who has supposedly been stolen out of his greater palace in the city, and been held captive in the hut.

I am one of the oldest children in the procession and walk

somberly behind Onan, who follows Er, who carries a small god in his left hand that represents El, and a small goddess in his right hand that represents Asherah. Made of mud and straw, they're a dark red color because they've also been smeared with blood. I don't really like this part of the festival, but all the children have to participate, so I hold my head high, look neither to the right or left, and keep walking like the dignified goddess I am supposed to be.

Er carries the two figures to the stone hut, then breaks off their heads and lays the broken parts of the god and goddess on the ground. Next, he turns and faces all the people.

"Behold," he calls out in a loud voice, "El and Asherah have smitten themselves with grief because they cannot find Ba'al."

I join all the people as they chant back, "Smitten, smitten for grief are the parents of all the gods."

Shulgi stands nearby, dressed as a god, hidden from the view of the crowd, but in such a way that I can see him. Suddenly, he stares at me solemnly, quickly gestures with one hand to mimic slicing off his neck, then crosses his eyes at the same time that he bends his neck sideways as though it's going to fall off, and then presses his tongue hard against the bony flesh behind his upper front teeth and blows air hard enough to make his cheeks vibrate with a sound like the passing of loud gas. I know how he makes this sound because I'm the one who taught him how to do it.

Trying to keep my appropriately somber pose, I clamp my lips together and frown. However, my cheeks won't behave themselves, and I'm certain that anyone looking at me can tell I'm ready to burst. I close my eyes for a moment to rescue the grave attitude I am supposed to show, but when I open my eyes, Shulgi's neck still hangs sideways, and now his tongue dangles out of his mouth too.

I feel like I'm going to pee myself!

Er opens the door to the hut with a grand gesture and tells Ba'al that the king has come to rescue him. This strikes me as hilariously funny, and on the heels of Shulgi's antics all I can do is squeeze my legs and buttocks tightly to keep my water in.

Er picks up Ba'al, carries him out of the shed, and everyone cheers. By the time Onan picks up the heads and bodies of El and Asherah, the muscles below my ribs are in spasms from trying to hold in my laughter and my pee. A tiny trickle drips down my leg; this only makes me want to laugh all the more.

I snatch a quick look at Shulgi to let him know that I'm going to get even with him after all this is over. He lifts his eyebrows, turns down his lips then shrugs as though he is perfectly innocent. I show him a little fist and look away before I wet myself completely.

Carrying the broken parts of El and Asherah, Onan now begins to follow Er back to the city. I follow the two brothers, as do the rest of the children who walk behind me, including Shulgi. The crowd follows alongside of us, and soon everyone is back in the temple square, where the people now wave and cheer as we pass by. By then, a few more trickles have escaped down my leg. Now I'm mortified. I take a deep breath; the spasms in my belly stop.

Just before Er enters the temple, he turns to face the people and a hush fills the air. He extends his arms, pivoting slowly from left to right to present Ba'al to the people. Without a single murmur, or cough or shuffling of feet from anyone in the square, Er walks into the temple, and the door closes behind him.

Now comes a frightening moment when no one knows whether or not Er will come out alive. If Ba'al is pleased that Er has brought him back to his sacred palace of the temple, Er will emerge.

The crowd holds its breath, and even though I know Er will come out because whoever is king always comes out sooner or later during this part of the festival, I hold my breath too.

For the next two days, the city feasts and waits for the verdict to be read by the priest. Will Ba'al be pleased or not? Er is not seen anywhere during this time, so no one knows for sure.

Finally, at the end of the eighth day of Gannitha, everyone assembles in the square again. The door opens and Er walks out with a torch in his hand. The priest declares that Ba'al is pleased to be back in his palace. Yet the people do not cheer, for there is yet one more test to go before we can all rejoice.

Er goes back into the palace. Silently, we all go home.

The next day, we do not feast. In fact we do not eat or drink anything at all. Instead, we fast, pray, and wait to see what Ba'al will decide. This is the most somber part of the festival, and if the seriousness of the day does nothing else, it at least keeps Yergat from calling me "bad luck," and Bushra from reminding me that she's a "good omen." Other than that, everything stays pretty much the same in our house.

On the tenth day, we assemble as before. When the last specks of light fade from the sun-shadow post that stands like a sentinel in the center of the square, the temple doors open once more. Out walk the priests, out walk two priestesses, and out walks Er.

The priestesses hold a bowl of water, which they give to Er. He holds it high in the air for all to see. The priests intone a blessing as Er slowly pours the water over the steps of the temple. Now the people cheer, for it means that the last test has been successfully passed, and Ba'al has bestowed on our city another year of blessing and rain.

Now the fun begins as I celebrate with everyone else in the city. I play games, eat more food than what my stomach should ever hold, and dance and sing to the music that chases away shadows from every corner.

I laugh as though I have no more sadness to carry.

Laugh at the moon like a child who has seen no sorrow.

Laugh until that awful moment when I feel something warm, sticky and wet drip down my legs.

This time it is not pee, and there is no Shulgi to blame for it.

Moon Blood

"At menarche a young woman enters her power."
—Native American saying

SEVERAL HOUSES DOWN from where I live I watch dust motes drift lazily about in the air between the spot where I sit and the opening in the crack of the doorpost of the hut. The motes move as though they are part of my breathing, and part of the breathing rhythms of all the women in the hut. At this moment, the stone structure, which is little more than the size of two sleeping rooms in a family house, holds nine women (including me) who nestle within the privacy of its walls.

In various places on the floor, we sit or lie atop piles of dried grasses covered with flaxseed linen and woolen cloths that soak up the pools of Moon Blood coming from between our legs. Bunches of dried lavender, thyme, basil, rosemary, mint and hyssop hang from the ceiling by hemp strings. Our own body fluid odors mingle with the herbs, and the air is sweet and smoky smelling, acrid and pleasant at the same time. We talk and laugh, complain and discuss the problems of men and children, crops and bandits, the weather and the gods, or anything else we choose.

Anush sits beside me, and Illit across from her. Numa is on the other side of me. A few younger women sit in small circles with their Immas or sisters, aunts or noorshmas. Women all, women only, and here I sit, wondering how a little blood flowing from in between the legs makes me a woman.

Was I not playing with Shulgi just one day before Gannitha?

Was I not the one who taught him to make gas-passing sounds with his mouth? Did I not vow to get even with him for making me pee myself on the procession day? I look back now and think about how silly it all seems. Oh, how much can change in the course of three days time.

Three days in the Moon Blood hut, three days of sitting on the grasses, three days of drinking warm herbal infusions and eating lechem and savory lamb and lentil stews, three days of having my feet, shoulders and head rubbed, of oils being gently massaged into my hair and skin. So much gentleness and human kindness in this hut makes me honestly grateful for the bleeding that brought me here, for it keeps me away from anything having to do with Yergat.

Anush had brought me here as soon as she had seen the first red drops on the stones beneath my feet where I stood that tenth night of the Gannitha festival. She had whispered to Numa and asked her to wipe up the blood then had spirited me away from the square and all the people. I remember seeing Numa scowl a bit when Anush had asked her to clean up the mess on the stones, but she must have done it anyway. I don't really know for sure, though, because I never looked back and have not asked about it in the past three days.

When Anush and I had walked to the Moon Blood hut that evening, she spoke to me in a tender and soft-spoken voice so different from her usual "hogocs" and complaints that I had thought she might be someone else, perhaps even my Imma come back to life to welcome me into womanhood.

It had not taken us long to reach this particular hut, the one that is closest to our home (out of the four that are in various places of the city). Fortunately for us, the blood that had spurted down my leg and onto the stones in the temple square that night didn't spurt again until we were safely inside the hut.

I mostly rest here, but often that is hard to do because of the laughter, whispers, groans of pain, storytelling and singing.

Oh, such songs we sing. One of them makes all the women in the hut laugh so hard we sometimes lose our water! But it doesn't matter because we sit on the grass pile that soaks up all our leakage anyway, be it red or yellow.

Ashtoreth, Ashtoreth, why do you bleed us,
Why is the red moon aflame in the sky?
What did we do to deserve such a pleasure as
Red legs and Moon Blood smeared on our thigh?

Ashtoreth, Ashtoreth, why do you need us to
Drink with the moon god Yarikh 'til we die?
Why is the cup that he holds filled with red mead
A power so great it will cause him to fly?

We hoot and whistle and grab our bellies as verse after verse of this silliness breaks the boundaries that so often separate us in the shuk or the temple square. Here in the Moon Blood hut we are sisters, we are friends and equals, we are Moon Blood goddesses with a power so fierce even the most fearsome warrior is afraid of us.

Or so I'm told in story after story that no one gets to hear unless they sit in the Moon Blood hut on a pile of straw and bleed. When I hear the tales about the mystery and power of the Moon Blood, when I hear that it is the sacred source of life that men both fear and desire because it is the only blood that sheds without war or wounding, when I hear how its secrets have passed from woman to woman since the beginning of all wisdom, I begin to understand the silent smiles of the older women, the twinkle in their eyes when any hint of the Moon Blood or the red mead surfaces in conversation.

Snatches of jokes I have heard in the past begin to make sense too: jokes about men, kings and priests, about their intrigues and attempts to staunch the flow of our Moon Blood power, to tame and manipulate it, to use it for their own purposes, or to try and glorify their own names. In these jokes, the men fail… always, especially the kings and priests, the ones who believe they have the most power of all.

At this moment, however, we do not joke or sing. Anush and Illit engage in a serious discussion, part of which involves me, part of which involves Er, and the rest of which involves things I do not wish to hear.

"… So you see, Anush, it is crucial for me to learn the blood lineage of Tamar if we are to set this marriage in motion with the men. Er is the king, and as such can only marry a woman of the Royal Line of the Dragon Blood Sovereignty. You know the rules of the priests, Anush, you know the importance of those rules for the community, and you know how all of this works." Illit's voice of authority lingers on the air.

I wonder what any of this has to do with me. My head suddenly hurts so badly that I feel it will burst and bleed like the place between my legs if I have to hear any more of this conversation. I begin to move my hand toward my temple to rub it. But before I can raise it even a barley's width, Numa sees the movement, quickly places her hand on mine, and presses it back down, none too gently. I stare at her. She doesn't look at me, nor does she say anything as she keeps a steady pressure on my hand so that I can't move it. It irritates me that she thinks she can control me, but the conversation between Illit and Anush is too important for me to do anything about Numa at this particular moment.

Anush doesn't even blink at Illit's words. Neither does she act as though I am even in the hut. I am beginning to feel like she and Numa have rehearsed this moment, and I resent it. Still, sensing that a lot is at stake for me personally because of what I am hearing, I say nothing

"What about Yehuda's blood line?" Anush smiles sweetly, as though she is a queen. She shifts her body ever so slightly in my direction, as if to say, "Pay careful attention to this next part."

Illit does not seem to notice Anush's miniscule movement. My noorshma continues her question. "Is Yehuda of the

Dragon Blood Sovereignty?" Her voice has a slight wrinkle of dryness in it, but not enough to set Illit off.

Again, it seems to me like Anush merely recites words she's long envisioned in her head, as though she has previously anticipated what Illit would say, and then planned her own response ahead of time. I have never seen Anush like this before; it makes me feel restless. Numa keeps her hand solidly over mine… just in case.

"Yehuda?" Illit laughs icily. "Ha! What does it matter? Anush, you sly thing, you know the only bloodline that counts is the woman's. I am of the royal line, and my Imma before me, and hers before her, and so on, all the way back to the time of the Great Rising of Waters at covered the earth. Therefore Er is qualified to carry on the many duties of the king. I know that you and many others in Adullam think that he is too young to bear such great responsibility." She laughs, sits up straighter, holds her head higher, looks down her nose at us then continues. "But, as you all know, he has me to guide him." She laughs again.

So this is why Yehuda will not rule this city, even though he is much more of a leader than Er? Ludicrous! I silently note that she doesn't mention Yehuda's ability to guide Er.

Numa must feel the stirrings of growing anger inside of me, for she presses even harder on my hands. Anush doesn't even so much as blink her eyes or quicken her breathing.

Illit now turns her royal head my way and directs the icy blue of her eyes toward the purple brown of my own. For less than a split blink of time our colors battle one another before she laughs and turns her gaze back to Anush. "That goes for his duties in the temple too." She smiles like an Egyptian cat image I once saw on a box in the shuk.

Instantly, I feel cat claws (from my childhood days) shoot from my fingers until I'd like to scratch out all the blue in her eyes. Numa feels the stir of feline movement in my hands and practically crushes my fingers to stop it.

I want to scratch her too, but I de-claw myself so that I

won't interrupt this conversation. I want to get to the bottom
of the question that was so important to me on the night that
Er was crowned king.

Anush now pets the air with her voice. "Of course, Illit, of
course you are right. Perhaps my old mind does not remember
such important details as these anymore."

Once more the tone in her voice tells me that this is all an
act, and that she knows she is not fooling Illit, and knows that
Illit knows it too, and also knows that neither of them cares
one barley grain for how things stand in their conversation.

I am anxious to know why Anush is doing this because it
still exes me that she never told me about it. Maybe she will
better explain things to me later. From the pain in my hand, I
can tell that Numa certainly won't.

Illit simpers. "Anush, I cannot tell what your mind does or
does not remember, so let us get down to business. What do
you know about Tamar's family? Yergat is your sister's son. Is
he of the royal lineage? Was your sister? Are you?"

Anush says nothing. She simply smiles the same Egyptian
cat smile that was painted on Illit's face a moment ago.

Now I'm getting really worried. Anush? Of the royal
blood? My father? No, I cannot believe this.

"Of course not, Illit," Anush answers. "We are not of the
royal blood, and it would not matter even if we were, for
Yergat is a man, as you, of course, realize. Therefore, even if
his mother was of the Dragon Blood Sovereignty, according
to the rules of the priests it wouldn't count, which you have
so graciously pointed out."

She pauses and observes Illit carefully, as though she can
see back through the ages to the originator of the power of
the Moon Blood itself, all the way back to Tiamat, the Dragon
Queen of the Annunaki!

I shiver. Numa's hand over mine now feels like icy age-old
stone.

Illit's chin and cheeks remain placid as she gathers a slow
breath into her lungs without so much as lifting her shoulders

a barley's width.

I hold my breath without making a sound. Numa seems not to breathe at all, stone that she is.

"And Trinjah? What of her? What of my old friend?" Illit's voice is as soft as the Great Sea mist that sometimes moves over our hillside and down into the Valley of Elah.

Astonished by this question about my Imma, my voice bursts out like an unexpected gust of biting wind on a winter's day. "Friends? You and my Imma were friends?"

Illit now takes her eyes off Anush and studies me. I see a spark of fire within her icy blues, a memory perhaps of my Imma. But I cannot tell for sure because I now realize that I am also looking into the eyes of a Dragon Queen descendent, and am not sure what I see anymore.

I lower my gaze. "My apologies."

I do not see Illit turn back to Anush, but I feel it. The air shifts ever so slightly in the hut, and dust motes flutter around me in disarray, as though they too are shocked by what they have heard.

Illit now waits for Anush to answer, as do I.

* * *

There are moments in time when the history of the world rests on a single word, a minute inflection of the voice one way or the other, the imperceptible quickening of a heartbeat, the crescendos and decrescendos in the sound of blood as it pumps through the body, the flick of a wrist, the tightening of a single finger, or the infinitesimal adjustments in the placement of lips, cheeks or eyebrows.

During these moments it is as if time has neither the power to keep us bound nor hurry us along.

No force exists to cast or break the spell inherent in a choice of words that will change a countless multitude of lives even after the one who speaks the words has vanished into the sands and sepulchers that will eventually silence us all.

In this small Moon Blood hut, far from the greatest places of power in the world, this is one such moment.

* * *

"The tale of Trinjah is a long one, Illit, too long for our short stay in this hut, but I hesitate to tell you, even though it is my duty to do so, that Trinjah is indeed of the royal bloodline. The thread weaves through her Imma, Ditzah, and Ditzah's threads weave back to a regal line all the way to Set, Adama and Havah and…"

Anush pauses, and with the eye of the moon in her gaze she silently probes Illit before saying, "You know these names and what I am saying, is that not so, Illit?"

Illit gauges Anush's words and demeanor to decide whether or not there is truth in what she has said. Anush does not flinch.

I want to shout at both of them because Anush's words, along with Illit's response to them, will seal my fate for all time, and no one has bothered to ask me what I think, what I want, what I fear, or what I believe. Yes, believe about the gods and all their names and stories; about whether I should or should not marry Er, or even whether I should marry at all; about the stars, moon cycles and Moon Blood; about Dizah, Illit, or even Er himself.

Shulgi knows what I think, except for the Moon Blood that is. That is not a subject we are likely to ever discuss. After this is all over, though, should I tell him about what Anush has just said? He'll know that this is all just part of the god nonsense and that my future does not need to rest on the threads of this person or that one just because I now have my own Moon Blood. He'll know that I don't have to marry Er, or him, or anyone else in the whole world if I don't want to. Won't he?

"If the meaning behind what you say is true, Anush, then we can proceed with plans to persuade the men to begin negotiations for the mohar, the nedoonyat, the matan and the date of the nissuin. It will be important that the nissuin occur on the night of a full moon and close to the time of Tamar's Moon Blood flow. You understand why these things are important, yes?"

Anush nods her head and turns to me. I see in her eyes a depth of sadness I have not noticed before, but they also radiate so much love and compassion that I cannot say a word, for I know in ways that cannot be understood that she knows something more than she is telling Illit. Her eyes now seem to speak for my Imma, and she silently indicates that I must give my consent to this marriage arrangement.

Panic runs a race inside of me to see who will control the speed of my heartbeat. I look away and pull my hands from under Numa's heavy hands. She doesn't try to stop me this time. The last thing I want to do is marry Er! He is such a baby, and it's no secret that Illit still controls him more than Yehuda does. If I agree to marry him I'll be under his authority. Not only that, since Illit herself will control the inner workings of the home, and Numa will back her up because she is a servant to the family. I won't have a say in anything. Not anything at all.

Then there is Yehuda...

I slow down my breathing without making a sound, without so much as even moving a muscle, for I don't intend to let on to Illit that I am torn with indecision. After a pause that seems like all the stars in the heavens could fill it, I realize that I cannot run from the choice that has been put before me. I know that the ways of Adullum cannot be changed by me. And even though I do not understand why Anush has set this marriage arrangement in motion, I somehow know that I cannot fight her. I silently suck air deeply then look back at Anush.

I can only answer the plea of her eyes with my own plea for answers. She smiles, and closes her eyes briefly, then opens them to reveal deeper feelings, to show that she understands how hard this is for me, to communicate that she will gather me to her heart later to tell me the secrets that I now realize she has hidden from me all my life. I nod slightly then turn to face Illit.

Hardly believing that I am hearing my own voice, I say with complete composure, "I agree to this proposal. You may proceed with your movements among the men to set your plans in motion."

Illit smiles at me like an Egyptian cat again, and I wonder how I will survive living under her roof. On the other hand, I've survived living under Bushra and Yergat's roof, haven't I?

The Secret Chamber

"A wonderful fact to reflect upon, that every human creature is constituted to be that profound secret and mystery to every other."

—Charles Dickens

INSIDE THE MOON BLOOD HUT, I pass the next four days considering the few moments of conversation between Illit and Anush that will change my life so fully. Is it truly possible that a little flood of blood can wash away everything that came before it, can alter the flow of my thoughts so fully that I no longer feel my life is entirely my own?

During the four days I sometimes I wish I could go back to the days before Gannitha, the days before my Moon Blood could no longer bear to stay confined within what Anush tells me is my secret chamber of life.

Going back is impossible, of course, but memories tempt me to try. Memories of running with Shulgi to see Ba'al through the window, memories of flying like a bird on the clouds of my imagination, memories of playing the Royal Game of Ur with Er, and always winning.

Memories are strange things. Without being something I can hold in my hand, they wield a beguiling power over me. Like a mirage in the noontime heat of summer, they dance before my inner eyes and beckon me to find water where there is no water.

I used to do things without thinking about why I did them. If I wanted to race through the house, I'd do it. If I wanted to twirl around and sing, I'd lift my arms and open my voice to the sky. If I wanted to run into my cave, and speak to my Imma, I never thought about whether or not I should or should not do it. I simply did it.

My choices, and everything around me were so solid and real nothing else seemed to exist or matter at all. Now things once clear to me are fuzzy, and I am not sure what or even *how* to think anymore.

Anush comes to visit me each of the four days. Today, Illit is also here again.

She hands me a gift and says, "This is not the matan from your husband-to-be, of course. That will come later, and Er will present it to you after the negotiations between Yehuda and Yergat are complete."

She looks at me differently than the day of our first conversation in the Moon Blood hut. Now her eyes look softer than before, however, a slight brittle edge in the tone of her voice makes me feel like she is still not sure that I should be the one to marry her son.

I smile politely, and accept her gift, which is wrapped in a beautiful silken cloth, rich in design hues of purple, gold and red. Inside is a tiny goddess figurine the size of half my little finger. The goddess is completely naked except for a headdress that looks like layers of crown circlets stacked on top of one another. Each circlet is slightly smaller than the one upon which it sits, so the shape of the entire headpiece is conical.

"Oh, this is beautiful, Illit! Is it all gold?" I can scarcely take my eyes off the thin strands of gold that form the delicate wings flowing out of the figurine's shoulders.

"Yes, my dear Tamar. It is pure gold, and was given to me by my Imma before she died. It was given to her as a gift from her great aunt, who bought it from a traveling merchant from Midyat. Your Imma knew of it and held it in her hands many times."

Her eyes seem softer as she tells me this. I feel a twinge in my belly—or is it in my secret chamber? I no longer know which is which. The sensation connects Illit's memories to the touch of my Imma's blood in my veins.

My voice trembles. "She held this?"

"Yes." Illit looks away for a brief moment then speaks as though a pleasant memory has touched her voice. "She thought it was the most beautiful thing she had ever seen, and we often spoke about the goddess and her sacred powers. She's Asherah, of course, although some now call her Inanna, who is really Asherah's granddaughter. But then, people tend to confuse these things, don't they, my dear?"

"Yes, I suppose you are right." I don't actually understand the meaning of her question, but it feels safe to answer her in this way, especially since she seems to be treating me almost like an equal, which is something I did not expect.

I turn the goddess over in my hand then gently close my fingers around it, as though holding it near my skin might allow me to feel my Imma's touch in it.

Illit watches my hand as her goddess disappears from sight.

"I must get back to Yehuda now," she sighs as though part of her is gone. "He and I have much to discuss about the terms of the marriage."

"Of course, Illit. Before you go, though, is there a different name I might use when I speak with you, I mean now that you will be almost like an Imma to me and…" I speak shyly, "because you knew my Imma."

She smiles with what I think is a warm smile, but I am never sure what to think when it comes to Illit.

"Yes, of course. You may call me Beleti."

"Beleti." I twirl the sound of the name around in my mouth as though it is honey on my tongue. "It is a beautiful word. What does it mean?"

"In the ancient tongue it means a woman of high and royal birth."

I try to mask my disappointment. "Oh," I say limply.

"It is a good word, and one I do not usually share with others. In fact, Trinjah used to call me by that name."

"Really?" I perk up. "Then I am sure I would like to call you Beleti."

"Yes, I am sure you would. Now I truly must go. Good-bye my dear." She looks at my hand one last time then turns and disappears through the hut's doorway.

Early in the morning on my last day in the Moon Blood hut, Anush comes arrives to get me.

"I'm so glad you are here, Anush-jahn," I say with relief when I see her. "I thought I'd never sit on anything but dried grass for the rest of my life!"

She chuckles. "Let's go, then, Katu. Hurry now, you have to gather the soiled cloths and grasses, and take them out of here."

She hands me a large hemp bag made specifically for this purpose. Quickly, I pick up every unclean thing around me, and toss it into the bag.

"Can we go now? I can hardly wait to see the sky again."

She surveys the space where only moments before the evidence of my womanhood lay under me. Now it seems as though I have never been there, as though everything that happened in the past seven days was a dream.

"Yes, we can go," she says as she waddles out of the hut.

Behind her, I carry the bag. Giddy with being out in the open again, I almost dance. The air so fresh, the sky so vast, the stones beneath my feet so clean! I take the bag by both hands then twirl around so fast and with such force that the weight of the bag pulls at my arms until they feel like stretched out wings. The bag swiftly rises to the level of my shoulders, and feels like it will keep climbing and pull me up with it and into the blue.

The bag swooshes so close to Anush that she must hear the whistle of it because she turns around and hisses, "Stop! What are you doing? Do not display your dead Moon Blood in this manner."

Instantly, I stand still; the bag stops soaring. As I release one of my hands from the bag, it lands behind me, as if no one needs to tell it to hide in shame.

I reach inside the inner pocket of my halug to feel the gold Asherah Illit gave me.

"Then it's true, Anush-jahn? I wasn't just dreaming? I *was* in the hut?" I want to leave the bag of bloodied grasses and rags behind.

"Hogoc, Tamoosh-jahn. Of course it's true. What are you thinking, child?"

"Child? I'm no longer a child. I am a *woman* now!"

I want to twirl again, but the bag of dead Moon Blood holds me back.

"Then start acting like one. We must get these things washed out quickly before we go to the cave."

"The cave?" I can hardly believe it. We haven't been there for so long I almost thought that I must have dreamed too. I want to take her hands and dance the way we always do when I'm happy, but then I remember I am still unclean because of the Moon Blood and cannot touch anyone yet.

"I only have two more," I brag to Anush as I hang my freshly washed cloths out to dry. From where she sits on a palm wood box near the stairs that lead down from the mud and palm branches roof of our house, Anush grunts.

I look to my right and see the Valley of Elah stretching out below me. It seems like everyone in Adullam works in the fields today, harvesting and winnowing barley, scratching and digging with tilling ards to prepare the soil for new seeds, removing dead leaves and deepening furrows around olive and pomegranate trees, staking grape vines and talking, laughing, rejoicing in the warm spring air.

"Ah." I breathe in deeply, tilt my head backwards, and reach my cheeks to the sun.

"Katu, if you have only two more cloths, why don't you

finish so I can take my groaning bones off this insufferable wood!"

I laugh. "Oh Anush-jahn, seven days has not stopped your complaining."

She grunts again then looks off and away from the people working in the fields, past them to the hills and the caves.

"There, I'm finished!" I boast as I look proudly at my first-ever moon cloths dancing on hemp lines in the sun.

"Good." She grunts once more." Then let's go."

I run past her and down two stairs.

"Be sure to take your clean clothes," she calls out before I am out of sight.

"I will," I call back to her before I dash the rest of the way to our room, where I grab a pile of fresh clothing than race back to the bottom of the stairway. Anush huffs and groans as she makes her way down the final three steps; I reach out my free hand to help her.

She flicks her wrist. "I'm not under the earth yet, thank you."

I laugh and let her walk in front of me as we pass through the hallway, through our courtyard then through the front doorway and onto the street.

Anush's tone is hushed and mysterious as we stand just inside the entrance of my cave.

"I want to show you something I've never shown anyone else before."

"What is it?" I whisper.

"You will see. Just follow me."

She walks quickly into the darkest part of the cave and abruptly disappears!

"Where are you, Anush-jahn?" I cry out. "I can't see you."

She calls back to me, "Follow my words."

Her voice echoes against the natural soft-stone walls of the cave. Their creamy and slight yellowish color makes me feel like I'm inside an enormous upside-down bowl of goat's milk and standing where the milk still clings to the sides of the bowl. The dirt beneath my feet is a powdery mixture the color of milk and a tired looking brown.

"I'm coming, Anush-jahn. Please wait for me."

As I recede into the cave, the light from outside dims until I need to feel with my hands to go any further.

"This way, Katu. Follow my voice."

I follow the direction of her voice.

"I still can't see you," I call out.

"Feel for the rock to the left of you that has a sharp edge to it. It's the only one that's sharp enough to stand out from the rest."

I feel for it. "I found a smooth edge. Do I turn here?"

"Since when did sharp mean smooth? Keep going. I know the exact stone where you are standing."

"Hehh." I breathe out and keep feeling my way forward until my hands reach something sharp, sharp enough to cut one of my fingers.

"Ouch!" I suck on the finger.

"Good, you found it. Now turn left and keep coming toward my voice."

I turn left.

"I did what you said, but I still can't see you. Where are you?"

"Patience, Katu, patience. Turn left again when you get to the rock that bumps your head. Be careful not to go forward too fast though."

I move forward before I hear those last words.

"Ouch!"

"Good, you found it, although I told you not to go too fast," she chides. "Turn left now, but keep your head low."

"This is starting to vex me, Anush-jahn. How many more cuts and bumps before I find you?" I keep my head down as far as I can and inch forward carefully.

"No more, I promise. It will be worth it when you get here. Just keep going through that low tunnel area. It will take a few turns before you are here."

As I continue on like a cat searching for a pill bug to bat, a dim light creeps over my toes.

"I can see your feet now. Keep your head down and don't stop. You're almost here." Anush's words sound like they are bouncing around in a space larger than the tunnel.

My back aches but I keep going.

"You better be right about it being worth—"

Suddenly, light explodes around me as I emerge into a shock of color inside a large, high-domed room. Painted figures on the rounded walls show women bathing, resting beside a pool of water, fanning one another, rubbing oil onto each other's skin—all of them naked, all of them beautiful, all of them laughing.

I turn slowly to take it all in then gasp. In the middle of the room a large pool of gently moving water sparkles! Anush stands near it, smiling and serene.

"What is this place?" I ask as though I stand on sacred ground.

"It is your Imma's place," she answers quietly. "She called it her secret chamber, and we came here often—each time she finished the seven days of her Moon Blood, then again when I finished my own seven days, and then," she speaks in a sad hush, "after each of the times she lost her other babies."

"What? Other babies? I never heard about any other babies."

"Yes," Anush says in an even softer voice, "she had other babies, but none of them grew big enough inside of her to live. All of them came out of her with such hardship on her body and mind that she gradually weakened to the point where neither I nor your father thought she would ever cradle a baby inside her again. But she did. *You* were that baby. You were the baby she had longed for through all her many years of marriage. When you were born, I saw her smile again like she had not smiled in years."

Her words rush over me like flocks of starlings suddenly

shivering up and into the winds. The shock of standing in this room, with the vibrant colored figures on the walls and the pool of water near Anush, make me sway slightly.

"Steady, Katu, steady. I have much to tell you."

Forgotten Ones

"Nothing is softer or more flexible than water,
yet nothing can resist it."   —Lao Tzu

AS THOUGH COMING FROM WITHIN THE WALLS of the secret chamber itself, the sound of many voices envelops me. At first I think all the women of the walls speak together on behalf of the stones themselves. Then the soothing melodious rhythm of the sound makes me realize it is a single voice split into a hundred different echoes that swell and die away, swell and die away with each word.

"Your Grand Imma Ditzah was one of the Forgotten Ones."

As the last two words bounce between the walls, I stand perfectly still, stunned and unsure of where I am, unsure of whose voice it is I hear.

I look around in wonder before realizing the voice belongs to Anush.

"Oh, you scared me Anush-jahn. I thought the women of the walls were speaking."

"I thought the same thing the first time I came here." She motions for me to come to her.

I walk in a daze to where she stands near the pool of water. "You said that my Grand Imma is a Forgotten One? What does it mean, Anush-jahn?"

"Yes, Katu, I spoke those words, but before I explain anything about Ditzah," she says with a sweeping gesture of her hands that takes in the entirety of this remarkable cave, "let's sit down because I can see that the excitement of this day and what you have discovered here has made you dizzy. There is much to tell and your future depends on it, so you will need to be very patient and listen quietly to what I have to say."

"Yes, Anush-jahn, I do feel a bit muzzy." I sigh and stretch my back before we sit beside the pool of water that flows so silently and slowly I scarce believe it actually moves. "And I will be patient. I promise." I look up at the top of the dome above us, where a large opening lets in streams of light, as though the sun itself has come to visit my face in this, my Imma's secret chamber.

My noorshma's shoulders heave as though she is letting go of a great weight. "Ditzah, as I said, was one of the Forgotten Ones. This simply means that she made choices that went against the wishes of her family, so they turned their backs on her."

"Turned their backs? What do you mean by that, Anush-jahn?"

"Tamar, what did I say about being patient?" she answers with a twizzle of impatience.

Oh-oh, she uses my real name. I look down at my knees.

She sighs and goes on. "It means they stopped speaking to her, vowed to never again mention her name, not even in their home. She was allowed to live under their roof, cook her own meals, eat and sleep there, but she was considered as dead, or as though she had never been born. If they entered a room where she was sitting, they turned and walked out of the room. If they passed her in a hallway, they walked by her like she wasn't there, like she was a ghost with no form.

"They never told anyone in the community about their decision, and Ditzah never said a word either. I suppose she felt too ashamed to talk to anyone about it. As far as others knew, the family had no troubles and everything was fine."

Anush looks into the water.

I say nothing.

She breathes in and out deeply and slowly several times before she continues.

"Imagine your name never spoken by your family again, your name forgotten, as though you had never felt their love, never laughed and cried with them, never played and fought with them, never worked with them, never eaten at their table. Imagine it, Tamoosh-jahn. Imagine it."

I try to imagine it, but cannot. Although Yergat treats me like I am trouble and a bad omen, at least he shows his feelings, even if they are cruel and hateful. Anush has always loved me and called me by her pet names. I can imagine Yergat acting like I don't exist (he practically does that now anyway), but Anush? No. Never. It would crush me to powder until all of me blew away on the wind.

"Eventually, all her family members moved away from the city where she lived, and she never heard from them again. They sold the house, and she married the man she loved. She raised a family of her own, but never told her children about her own family, never told anyone in the city what had happened."

My heart feels the weight of my Grand Imma's sadness, but I do not make a sound.

"You see, the reason they shunned her is this: she had fallen in love with someone they did not approve of. It was that simple. His family was a family that did not belong to their tribe, to their people. This was very important for them, and she knew it. They expected her to obey their wishes and stay away from him and his family. She dearly loved her family and tried with all her strength to honor their wishes. But he loved her desperately, and she felt the same way about him. I remember how they looked at one another. Like the moon and sun and stars all existed in their eyes only."

Anush pauses and loses herself in her memories.

I look at the paintings on the wall nearest me. The women and objects in them seem to stir as the sun moves over the dome above us. Shades of green, red and yellow in the kilim rugs they sit on shift, and merge in the changing light until it seems the rugs, and the women on them float in the air like clouds.

On another wall, water in a pool (like the real one near where we sit) undulates; the women who bathe in it twist in a slow dance. I blink my eyes. The light continues to slip and slide and ripple in ways that make the paintings seem alive.

Anush's voice pulls me back to my Grand Imma's story. "And still Ditzah told no one, not even her husband, or his family. Neither he, nor his family, nor her children, nor her children's children ever knew the truth of what she suffered in order to love them. No one knew until the day she told me."

I look away from the pictures, and study Anush's face. Lines crease across her cheeks, and her lips seem as pinched as raisins. A deep furrow in her brow looks like an ard has been at work there. At the outer edges of her eyes an eaglet must have wandered in search of prey and left its tracks. She has watched over me all her life with these deep brown eyes, but now their color is covered with watery-looking grey clouds. Her hair is streaked with silver, and the flesh on her chin has come loose. I wonder why I have not noticed these things as vividly as I do today. Perhaps it has something to do with this cave.

Anush seems to have come to the end of her story, or at least to the end of what she wants to tell me. I wait to speak until I am certain she is done.

"May I speak now, Anush-jahn, or is there more you want to say?"

"There is more, Katu, but I am finished for the moment, so you may speak."

"Thank you, Anush-jahn." My chest heaves as though taking in a breath of air for the first time ever.

She smiles and says, "Quite a shock, all this, isn't it?" She takes in the entire cave with a sweeping gesture of her hand.

"Yes," I chuckle softly, "to say the very least."

She nods her head, but says nothing, waits for me to continue.

"I'm not complaining, Anush-jahn, you know that's not my way."

I look at her to confirm that she understands me.

She nods her head again.

"It's just that I now have so many questions—about Ditzah and my family, about this place, about Moon Blood, and Illit, and Er, and the Dragon Blood Sovereignty—that it makes my head swim like these pictures that swim on the walls in the sunlight."

Anush looks at the pictures, and I imagine she recalls memories that continue to shape her life, her future, her hopes and disappointments.

"Tell me, my dearest noorshma, my Yakiri," I say with shyness that comes from an unfamiliar feeling, "you who have loved me, and taken care of me all these years, why didn't you ever tell me about this secret chamber, about Ditzah's life, about you? You've never told me much about you. We only talk about—"

Suddenly, I realize *why* she has not told me these things. It's because we only talk about me. Our conversations are always about me, and how Yergat, Bushra, Shulgi, Er, Illit, or anyone else affects me. They are never about Anush, and how she feels, or what she knows, or what she dreams about.

I feel like I have met her for the very first time and am suddenly embarrassed by my selfishness. I fall silent, and as tears form in my eyes, she pats my hand and says ever so softly, "Tamar," but not in an angry or vexed tone. No, she speaks my name like I am her daughter and she is my Imma.

All I can do is look into her eyes and try to show through my tears that I finally grasp all she has done for me, all she has suffered by having to hold her secrets inside as she listened to my childish thoughts and fears, as she soothed me through my hurts and slights from others.

In her eyes a twinkle breaks through the cloudy grey, as though she's always known this moment would arrive.

"Tamar, my dearest Yavrik, who is now a woman. It is time

for you to learn the ways of your Imma. It is time to wash in the waters of the hidden wellspring, wash in the waters that remove the chamas, the uncleanness, wash in the waters of the secret chamber and be renewed."

"What? Now? No, I can't go in there," I protest and look at her curiously. Is this what she has planned all long? Is this what she envisioned for me in the Moon Blood hut when I saw the sadness in her eyes because of my uncertainty about agreeing to marry Er, when my eyes pleaded for answers, and hers pledged to give them to me? I look at the water, afraid of what will happen if I go into it.

She smiles as though she knows exactly what I am thinking. "What stops you, Katu? Fear?"

"No... well, maybe. But couldn't I do this later? So much has happened today, and it's all too much for me. My eyes feel so heavy and..."

She gently touches my shoulder and softly says, "It is time, Tamar. It is time."

She is right, of course, and I know it. All she has revealed to me today makes me realize she has probably always been right.

"You'll be okay, Tamoosh-jahn. I promise."

When I look at her for reassurance, her eyes have that knowing look in them that I see when she and Numa talk about their secrets. What else does she know that she has not told me? Will she tell me if I go into the water?

As though my silent questions and doubts have jumped into her ears, she cups my chin and kisses my nose then simply tells me to remove all my clothing and walk down the steps of the pool then into the water. She says that I must allow the water to fully cover me, even to the top of my head and through all my hair. My heart flutters with an excitement and fear I do not understand, but I take a deep breath, stand up and remove my clothing then walk to the side of the pool.

I hesitate.

What will happen? Will the water be cold? Will it have a

strange smell? Will my eyes sting? I look back at Anush. She says nothing, only smiles, tilts her head and nudges with her chin toward the pool, as though this will give me courage.

It is time, Tamar. It is time.

Is it my inner voice I hear or the voice of Anush or the women on the walls… or my Imma?

It is time, Tamar. It is time.

I dip my right foot into the pool and to my surprise and relief the water is warm. I step into the water up to my ankles. Inside me, feelings rush into an empty cavern and flood me with the love my Imma would have given me had she lived.

I take another step down into the water, and then another and another until every trace of the fear that has haunted me since the shuk attack washes away.

Now I am up to my waist in the water, and a pleasure I have never known sweeps over me.

It is time, Tamar. It is time.

As I submerge the rest of myself and allow my feet to come off the smooth stone floor of the pool, every vestige of Yergat's cruelties vanishes into the cleansing flow.

I sense that the time for understanding the purpose of my life has begun; I float in contentment.

"Remember the Dukifat, Anush-jahn?" I ask as we sit on the rock by the terebinth outside the cave. I rest against her in the way I have always done.

"Dukifat?" She shifts her shoulder to get more comfortable. "No, I don't remember. What about it?"

"It was my friend that you chased away the day Angry Anat shook us in her fury." I laugh at the memory.

She says nothing and looks down at the fields below us.

I shift my weight now too. Her chest seems bonier to me, less cushy than when I was a little girl. She must have shrunk too because the last time I laid against her like this my head only came up to the crook of her arm. Today it tries to find a soft place on her shoulder, which also seems bonier.

I sing, "Boop-boop-boop... boop-boo."

"Ah yes, now I remember." Her voice sounds like it's returning from a long trip far away from where we sit. "It was that little bird you scared by moving the branches near its nest. You got mad at me and ran into the cave." She smiles at the memory too.

"Yes, my dearest and sweetest Anush-jahn. How foolish I was to storm off like that."

She strokes my hair. "No, Katu, not foolish, just young and fearless."

"I don't feel so fearless now."

"No? Why not? What do you have to be afraid of?" She holds me closer.

"I'm thinking about being married to Er and... well, you know. The things men and women do at night?"

She pats my hand. "Yes, Tamoosh-jahn, I know. I was married once too."

I turn to look into her eyes.

"There are still many things you do not know, little Katu. Many things, but you need not fear Er, or his family. And especially, you do not need to fear Yehuda as the head of that family. He is not at all like Yergat. Not at all." She shakes her head at the thought of Yergat.

"How do you know?"

"I know Yehuda in a way different from the way you know him. His family is not from here. They are not from the family of the Forgotten Ones either, but there *is* a blood link between the Forgotten Ones and Yehuda's bloodline. It's a delicate one, the threads of which have been stretched so far you can almost see through them, but they still hold. That is why I was able to tell Illit what I did... without lying. What I didn't tell her is that your line is not the same as her own.

"You will remember I never said that you were of the Royal Line of the Dragon Blood Sovereignty. I only said that you were of the *royal bloodline*, and that is why she took so long to decide whether I was telling her the truth or not. What you don't know is this: Illit later sent Yehuda to the temple to verify your bloodline with the priests, and they gave him no reason to doubt you are a worthy match for Er." Her eyes twinkle and her lips tremble slightly, as though she can barely contain a secret she wants to share.

In the hush of her pause that follows, I am tempted to ask her more about this, but I have promised to persevere in quiet patience, so instead I tell myself that if she wants to reveal the secret she will do so in her own good time. And if not, what does it matter? Forcing myself to remain mute like this is harder than experiencing the pains of a Moon Blood flow, but I dare not interrupt her if I am going to get to the bottom of anything she has to say. Just when I think I cannot quell my curiosity any further, she speaks again.

"You see, ever since you were born, ever since I knew that Yehuda lived in Adullam, ever since your Imma died, and ever since your father chose the road to bitterness and cruelty, I have prepared for that little talk I had with Illit in the Moon Blood hut. I waited and held my peace until the time arrived for me to set things in motion for you." She stops as though to consider what she has just said.

"What things?" I prod. "What have you set in motion for me other than a marriage to a family wealthier and more powerful than my own?"

Anush cups my chin in her hand and says, "The things I told you today will need to be enough for awhile. I am weary, my Yakiri, but we will talk again soon. Many changes are ahead for both of us. Let us go home now. I need to rest."

I take her hand and kiss it. "Yes, Anush-jahn, let's go home so that you can rest."

The Mohar

"Words contract a significance which clings to them long after the condition of things to which they owe it has passed away."
—Joseph Barber Lightfoot

DURING THOSE MOMENTS when I feel free to stand in the confidence of my own strength, when I think I am ready to proceed into the murkiness of the unknown life ahead of me, when I believe I am ready to fly beyond all doubts about myself, it is then that the plans of others bump into me with such force that my sure footing slips until I sink into the mire of everyone else's intentions and lose sight of my own.

Today is one of those moments.

Today is the day Yergat and Yehuda finish their mohar negotiations to put a price on my head, as though I am a goat, or a field of barley, or a sparkling stone chipped from deep inside a cave, or a sheep hide ripe for tanning.

Even though some part of me accepts the ways of Adullam, the ways of bloodline ties and the brokering of those bloodlines for the best bargains in what Shulgi and I call the "shuk-of-power-breeding," I balk at the idea of being reduced to the value of silver bits and clay shapes in a bulla.

I am not sure where the idea birthed itself into the minds of men and women that a person of the Moon Blood should live like a mute sheep barked back into the herd if she seeks to explore a new pasture on her own, like Ditzah did. I wish I had the courage to be more like my Grand Imma, to wait for love to set a marriage in motion instead of settling for this

Dragon Blood arrangement of being tied to a man who loves me not, nor I him. I wish I could say no to all of it, and then, if love didn't find me, maybe not even marry at all.

But this is not the way of things, not the way that works. At least that is what Anush has told me during our times in my Imma's secret chamber after each of my Moon Blood cycles.

Six of those cycles have come and gone since I first washed in the wellspring waters of the secret chamber. I remember when Anush and I returned to the city that first time, and I saw my first Moon Blood cloths flapping above our house like banners in the breeze. I had realized then that everyone working in the fields that day probably knew I had become a woman, and this made a deep impression on me.

On the one hand, I had felt proud to realize that I had become a woman who had agreed to a marriage that would move her into a respected position in the city as the future wife of the King of Adullam. I had reasoned that perhaps even Yergat would now respect me enough to stop treating me like I was the cause for all his misery. On the other hand, I had felt betrayed because I had had no say in the initial transaction between Illit and Anush that took place in the Moon Blood hut.

Nor will I have any say in today's final transactions as the men bargain away my future. Of course, Anush is doing her best to prepare me for what lies ahead, utilizing our trips to the cave to impart bits and pieces of information about the importance of the negotiations between Yergat and Yehuda and what happens after those negotiations end. Still...

Anush's arrival at the hut pulls me from my musings. She is early this morning, this last day of my sixth stay in the Mood Blood hut, with bag in hand, as usual. I no longer feel like twirling it with its soiled cloths and grasses inside like I did the first time, so we hurry home to wash the cloths and hang them to dry before we happily make our way to the cave where the women of the walls and the pool of many waters await us.

The secret chamber is like a sanctuary for me now, a private temple of renewal, a place where the colorful women with their various painted postures are my sisters. And Anush? My beloved noorshma? She is Imma to us all.

This is my real family now.

Neither Yergat's continued cruelty, nor the petty spitefulness of Bushra and her daughters hold power over me anymore. Each time I step into the pool and submerge myself in its warm waters, every nasty word they have spoken to me, every jealous look with which they have tried to pierce me melts into the living stream and washes away.

"Anush-jahn," I ask after I come up and out of the pool, "do you believe the men will actually finish their bargaining today? It's taken so long that my life cannot go forward, and certainly never backward. I feel like I am stuck like a terebinth tree whose roots prevent it from ever moving and whose branches can only thrash about when the wind chooses to blow. It's maddening. Isn't there anything we can do?"

My nipples, and the hairs on my arms, legs and Hill of Asherah, drip with water while I stand naked to allow the warm air inside the secret chamber slowly and pleasantly dry me. I look at the women on the walls and realize that with each passing Moon Blood cycle I have begun more and more like them, with their long limbs, luscious curves and radiant skin. Knowing this excites me.

"Hogoc, Katu, how many times must I tell you that these are complicated matters, and that the future of many people are involved, not just you."

"I know, I know."

Repeating the words she has spoken to me for the past several moon cycles, I change my voice to sound like hers, but with more of a mocking tone: "'The mohar is key to *everything*, and Yergat isn't sure he wants to give up on his idea of marrying you off to Shulgi because he doesn't want to pay the mohar he'll have to give to secure a different wife for Shulgi when the boy comes of age.'"

A surge of tightness in my chest and throat makes me feel like Angry Anat grips me from the inside out.

"Yeesh." I exhale the tension with a burst. "Yergat's stubbornness vexes me so! He certainly never hides the fact that he doesn't want to send me into Er's home with anything of value for my nedoonyat. Any fool can see that he will give as little silver and gold as possible to Yehuda for me to have if I later have need of it. And why not? He thinks that I'm worthless except for what he might get from the mohar he can extract from Yehuda. And you know as well as I do, Anush-jahn, that the mohar price Yehuda will have to pay for me is greater than any bride price Yergat will have to pay for a wife for Shulgi. Can he not count? Maybe I'm just a foolish young woman, but even I can figure this out. Has he no sense at all? Yeesh! He's so stupid!"

A chill races through me. Snatching a rubbing cloth from the pile of clean clothes that lies near Anush, I vigorously rub myself dry then thrust a clean halug over my head.

"Yeesh!"

She sighs. "Tamoosh-jahn, what else can I tell you that you don't already know? Although Yergat wants you out of the house and wants the status of his bloodline associated with a king's, you know better than anyone else how greedy and cruel he has become, and you also know that he wants to get the most out of any bargain no matter what it does to the people around him. You cannot make lechem from an auroch, so why do you let these things vex you when you have no control over them?"

"Hogoc, Anush-jahn, I know that." As I furiously rub my wet head of hair, my words come fast and loud. "Can I help it that he is so unreasonable?"

"Of course not, but you can also do nothing to change the way he is. That's the point. Why waste yourself because he wastes himself? There is no law in Hammurabi's Code that decrees you must do that..." She changes her voice to mimic me now. "Even Shulgi knows that."

Catching me off guard, she looks at me with such a purposeful twinkle in her eyes; my pursed lips cannot help but relax.

"You're right," I answer with less annoyance. "Sometimes the heat of my vexations makes me forget that I still have much to learn." My chest heaves with a frustrated sigh.

"Of course, Katu, of course, but a little heat now and then keeps us warm." Anush's eyes still shimmer, but with a little less light now. "Besides, we all have much to learn, and there's no incantation the priests can speak over us to show us all the secrets of the heavens, or the gods, or even our own world. We barely know the inside of our *own* thoughts, and yet we must each still seek out the path of our purpose." She closes her eyes for a moment before looking deep into my eyes. Then, without any hint of mimicry or mockery she says, "And I believe you are old enough to know that no one can do *that* for us."

I nod my head and sigh.

She turns away to look at one of the walls; an expression of longing on her face makes me imagine past images, past loves, past ideas, and past dreams, all of which must still tug at her mind.

"What is it, Anush-jahn?" I soften my voice, forget all about Yergat. "What are you saying that your mouth does not speak?"

Her breathing seems more labored. "Nothing, Katu, it's nothing, really."

Over the last few moon cycles, I have learned to curb my impatience and keep my peace until she is ready to reveal more of herself to me, and I am usually richly rewarded for my silence. Even though it is clear her memories are not all pleasant ones, the tiny fragments she has shown me thus far are such beautiful jewels of wisdom I don't want her to keep the rest of her private treasures hidden from me forever. So, I wait.

"There is much more I long to tell you, Katu. Never doubt

that. Everything will make sense to you in time. After the men finish their negotiations today—and I believe they will—you will begin the best part of the preparations for your marriage to Er."

This is the first time I have heard these words from her, but I contain the excitement of my curiosity about what those preparations might be so that she will continue.

"Oh?" I say as though I could care less.

Her eyes crinkle with amusement, for she knows perfectly well the game I play.

She looks away from the wall then back to me. "You are such a clever little Katu. You always have been. Now, let me familiarize you with all the many lovely things that will happen next."

Any remaining swell of Anat's anger in my chest settles down and disappears as I listen to her describe luxurious oil baths, massages, perfumes, new clothing made from soft rich fabrics, delectable foods from far-away places, prayers from the priests and priestesses, and finally, the matan, the expensive gift Er will present to me at the end of all the royal treatments.

Anush makes her voice sound mysterious. "Er will come to our house alone, and you will wait for him alone in Yergat's business room, where, at this very moment, Yergat sits with Yehuda to finalize your mohar negotiations."

"In Yergat's room?" All the delight she has so carefully woven to snare me vanishes, and I frown, for I cannot stand to be in any space where he has stood.

"Ah-ah, Katu, no furrows in that beautiful brow of yours now. Remember, the troubles caused by Yergat are all washed away, and now the trick to staying clean is to *keep* them washed away."

I sigh and look back at the pool of water.

"All right." I shrug in resignation.

"That's better. Now, as I was saying, you and Er will sit alone in Yergat's room. Er will give you a gift and say, 'I give you this matan, Tamar, as a token of your beauty and the beauty of our marriage to come.'"

"Er will never say that to me," I protest. "He hates that I always beat him at the Royal Game of Ur, and he has never stopped reminding me that I made him fall at the feet... I mean the *flipper* of Atagartis. Never once in his life has he told me I'm beautiful, and I don't believe he'll say it now. Besides, being told I'm beautiful is not all that important to me. Humph! Especially if it is Er who says it."

"It's understandable you think this way because you base your thoughts on your childhood experiences with Er." She eyes me like she is Asherah and I a mere mortal. "But how much time have you actually spent with him since he became king? Since he drank the cup of red mead?"

I have no clue what the red mead is, and she knows it.

"No time at all. You know that, Anush-jahn."

"Yes, it's true. And what is also true is that you do not know what the red mead is or what its powers are. Isn't that right?"

"You know it is, Anush-jahn. So, are you finally going to tell me about the red mead?"

Two can play this game.

"Yes, I am, Katu, so put on your sandals now, and let's go to our rock next to our terebinth tree. Some things are better spoken in the open light."

As Anush emerges from the cave, I am already sitting on the rock next to the terebinth tree. Noticing that her breathing is more labored, and that she walks more slowly and looks at her feet more often than she did on the day she first showed me the secret chamber six moon cycles ago, I spring from the rock, rush to her side, and put my arm in the crook of her arm.

So thin.

She looks at me sideways; her lips curl into that peculiar Egyptian cat smile I haven't seen since my first trip to the Moon Blood hut.

"Are you still hiding secrets behind that smile of yours, Anush-jahn?"

She chuckles and waves away my question. "What I have to say about the red mead must be said quickly, Yavrik, because I can see by the position of the sun that the men are most likely finished with their business, and that means Yergat will want to be fed soon."

"The cook will do it, Anush-jahn. You don't have to tire yourself with it."

"No, Yergat will feel like celebrating and want something to fill his belly tonight that the cook doesn't know how to make. I already began the preparations before I came to get you this morning at the hut."

"Do I know what it is?"

"Probably not. It's baba ghanoush cooked the way it used to be cooked in the city where his Imma, my sister, Kohar, once lived. But the secret is in the finish of the pomegranate and olive oil mixture, but the cook doesn't know the secret to that, only I do," she says with pride.

"Oh," I say, distractedly. She has never spoken about Kohar before, and this makes me think that she is only doing so now to let me know that she does indeed still hide many secrets from me.

"I don't know where that city is, Anush-jahn, and I don't know anything about Kohar. If she is Yergat's Imma, then that makes her my Grand Imma, is that right?"

She nods her assent.

"Why have you never told me her name until now?"

Sadness overspreads her eyes. "All in time, Katu. All in time," she says softly. Pausing to take a deep breath before continuing, she goes on. "Yes, she is your Grand Imma, and someday you will learn more about her, but right now it is more important for you to know about the red mead, and how to answer Er after he gives you the matan."

I shake my head. "I don't understand why you can't tell me now, Anush-jahn."

"All in time, Katu." She pats my hand.

I breathe out a heavy huff through my nostrils and roll my eyes.

When we arrive at the terebinth tree, I ask, "Do you want to sit on our rock to tell me about Er and the red mead?"

"No, child. Not today. I must tell you on our way home."

We turn away from the rock. She seems a bit unsteady on her feet.

"All right, Anush-jahn, but I'd like to keep holding your arm, if you don't mind."

"No, I don't mind. In fact, I would rather like that today, Yavrik."

As we begin our slow descent down the rocky path that leads back to our city, I give her arm a gentle squeeze.

"The red mead is drunk from a sacred cup in the temple, but only during the last two days of Gannitha." Anush's voice seems so distant as she says this that it is as though it comes from the clouds above us. "It is a mixture of red wine and the Moon Blood of a priestess."

I gasp. "No! That's awful, Anush-jahn." Letting go of her arm, I stop and face her.

She smiles that peculiar cat smile again. "As awful as it sounds, I assure you that it is true. On the tenth night of Gannitha, the king, whoever he may be, drinks one cup of wine mixed with the fresh Moon Blood of the first priestess. Then he and she are joined in the sacred marriage."

"What? Why have I never heard of this before? Sacred marriage? I don't understand. Does it mean that he is already married? How can he marry *me* then?"

Anush looks at me sternly. "Too many questions flying through the air at the same time."

I breathe in slowly then exhale my impatience. "Please go on," I say. "I am ready to listen." I take her arm again; we slowly make our way down the path.

"Good, Katu, good." She looks up at the position of the sun then pats my arm again. "You have not heard of this before because it is a sacred secret, and girls are not told of it until after their first Moon Blood. In your case, I didn't want to tell you until you had had enough time to adjust to the surprise of Trinjah's secret chamber... and the idea of marrying Er."

She waits for a reaction from me, but I keep my mouth closed as tight as a nursing baby on its Imma's nipple.

Satisfied, she continues. "On the eleventh night of Gannitha, the second priestess mixes her Moon Blood with red wine and also enters into the sacred marriage with the king."

I cannot imagine Er doing any of this. The thought of the red mead alone makes me want to lose my lentils. But two priestesses? I force myself not to flinch.

"The sacred marriage is not at all like the marriage you are to have with Er. It is simply a ritual performed once a year with the priestesses in order to please Ba'al, Asherah, El, Enki, Enlil, Nimna, and the other gods and goddesses. All of this is done because the power in the Moon Blood gets released when mixed with wine and drunk from the sacred cup. Or so the priests say. The sacred marriage takes place after the king drinks every drop of the red mead. This is the sacred union of the king with the priestesses."

I can scarcely breathe as I listen to her.

"For two nights the king imbibes the red mead, and couples with the two priestesses. Why two and not just one? It is believed that if after the coupling takes place the first priestess dies before the next morning, then drinking the red mead of the second priestess and coupling with her will insure that the gods and goddesses will give the king power to create life, will allow the rains to return for another year, will keep our city strong.

"This is the power of the Moon Blood and the red mead, the power of the sacred marriage, and the power of the continuation of the cycles of life." She looks up again at the position of the sun. "Do you have any more questions?"

"Is there anything *else* you need to tell me, Anush-jahn?"

She fidgets slightly then looks down at her feet.

"All in time, Katu. All in time."

More secrets. I feel like I am hearing the same voice I heard when I floated for the first time in the pool. *It is time, Tamar. It is time.* I peer at her sideways and can tell that she senses the depth of my discomfort. She does not look at me, though.

"All in time, Katu, but now we must hurry, for there is food to cook."

As the setting sun paints the sky with shifting red patterns, I know that I will never think of the color red the same way I did before I learned the truth about how red mead is made.

And Er? For the past six moon cycles I have worked hard to accept that I am to become his wife, to share his bed, to live under the authority of Yehuda and Illit. But after what Anush has just told me, how can I even think to let Er kiss my lips... ever?

Flecks of red still dot the sky as Anush and I open the door to Yergat and Bushra's house, the house where neither of us has been happy since we moved here after their marriage. I hear male voices in our courtyard and am surprised to see that Yehuda is still here. He stands like a massif as he speaks with Yergat, whose own stance suggests a pile of shifting sand. I lower my eyes when Yehuda sees us enter.

"Hello Anush... Tamar," he says with a broad smile that reveals his nearly perfect white teeth.

I feel a red heat rise to my cheeks, and my feet suddenly fascinate me. I look down and keep my eyes focused on them.

Yehuda continues. "I think you will both be pleased to know that Yergat and I have settled on the terms of the mohar and the nedoonyat, and have also set a date for the nissuin. It is my hope that Tamar will be ready to move to my home as Er's betrothed next year, one week after Gannitha, and there celebrate and consummate this great union between our families."

167

My head spins as I realize that everything is happening just as Anush said it would. I blink, draw in a deep breath then lift my head to meet Yehuda's eyes.

All at once, I am back in his arms again like I was on the day he spirited me away from the attack in the shuk; I am in the temple square on the fourth night of Gannitha when he gazed at me with all the light of the starry skies gathered in his eyes; and suddenly I am plunged under the living waters of the secret chamber and never want to come up for air.

The Nissuin

"Hope is the thing with feathers that perches in the soul and sings
the tunes without the words and never stops at all."
—Emily Dickenson

"Tamoosh-jahn, stop fidgeting with those fabrics!"

I stand on a long and sturdy cedar bench in the room Anush
and I share. Cascades of colorful fabrics strewn over it catch
the morning light, which streams through the window behind
my bed. Rich hues of purple, saffron, gold, blue and white
mingle with sparkles from the jewelry I will wear today for
my nissuin, the wedding procession which will take me to the
temple square and back to Yehuda's home for the celebration
that will end with me in Er's bed!

"I can't help it. You know I'm nervous about all this,
Anush-jahn. An eagle is flapping around inside my belly then
dipping and diving on a high wind. I'm not sure I can hold
my lentils."

"Never mind about your lentils, Katu, it's too late for that.
The mohar has been paid, and you accepted the matan from
Er weeks ago."

"I haven't accepted his bed yet!" I cry out as the thought of
lying naked with Er makes the eagle in my belly flap, dip and
dive all the more. "Besides, I'm not so sure I even like Er, so
how can I possibly marry him?"

"You might have thought of that before you agreed to the
marriage proposal." Anush retorts.

Two of Bushra's servants assist Anush with the fabrics.

Bushra sent them in place of herself and her daughters because she did not want to be troubled with helping me prepare for the nissuin. Besides, she has made it clear that she will be much happier when Anush and I live under Yehuda and Illit's roof rather than Yergat's and hers. So will I.

One of the servants, a twelve-year-old with rapidly blinking nearly lash-less eyes, bursts out in a high-pitched giggle. The other one, a forty-something-year-old with thin mealy hair the color of minced meat and onions flashes a warning glare at the silly girl.

Anush winks at the older servant then smiles reassuringly at me.

"What you feel is normal, Katu. My own belly felt like yours on the morning of my big day." Her voice softens as she immerses herself in a memory. "And later before my big night, too. Ha!" She winks again.

The older woman grins and grunts. The speed of the younger servant's blinking eyes increases as her giggles bounce higher and higher. Anush shakes her finger to hush the chortling girl then turns back to me.

"You'll be fine, just fine," she says with a smile.

I ignore her. "Surely I can give back the matan to Er," I plead, "and tell Yergat that he can take back the nedoonyat from Yehuda?"

"Foolish girl, of course you can't do that."

"But I've heard that it is written in Hammurabi's Code if someone slanders Er before I marry him—like Shulgi, for instance—then Yergat can demand double the nedoonyat from Yehuda." My words fly faster than the youngest servant blinks her eyes. "Don't you think Yergat would like that?"

"Hogoc, Tamoosh-jahn, you talk nonsense. Of course Hammurabi's Code will allow it." She bends to see if the fabric is hanging too far over my feet. "But you know as well as I do that Er has done nothing wrong." The cloth must be too long, for I feel her tug and pull near my waist to lift it. "So Shulgi has absolutely nothing bad to report about him that could

possibly be used as a reason to get out of this marriage."
She picks up a piece of golden gossamer silk, examines it.
"Besides, Yergat would never agree to it anyway. Yehuda gave
him such a generous price for you that not even getting back
triple your nedoonyat would make him change his mind."
With a bone needle, she stitches the silk to the garment that is
gradually being assembled on me.

Closing her eyes for a moment, Anush puts a hand over her
chest, then, concentrating heavily, she breathes slowly before
opening her eyes again. "My darling Yavrik, set your mind on
other thoughts." She keeps her hand over her chest. "Like
how pretty you are in your wedding garment, and how pretty
you will be when you put on all the delightful jewelry Er gave
you last week when he brought the matan, and…"

This time when she inhales, I hear a rumbling raspy sound
coming from her chest.

"Are you all right, Anush-jahn?"

She flicks her wrist and waves away my words.

Coughing now, she pounds her chest lightly with her fist
as she continues. "As I was saying, we will both soon be out
from under Yergat and Bushra's roof and have our own rooms
again." She stops coughing. "Now, for the sake of the memory
of Trinjah and the suffering of Ditzah, will you please stop
fidgeting and fussing with this fabric!"

I blow air through my teeth then release my fists, where,
without realizing it, I have been clutching the fabric of my
wedding garment.

Almost in unison, the two servants sigh heavily as they
readjust the cloth where I tousled and knotted it up.

"She's soiled it with her sweating hands," the older one
complains to Anush. The younger one giggles as though she
thinks my sweating hands are the funniest things since sheep
dung soup.

"Tamar!" Anush scolds. "How are we supposed to get that
spot out now? You must shoo that eagle of yours out of your
belly and away from your mind!"

"Yes, Anush-jahn, you are right," I answer distractedly as I look at the jewelry, and recall the night Er came to our house with the matan and presented it to me...

* * *

Fidgeting in Yergat's room, I wait for Er to arrive. A soothing scent of lebonah and lavender mixes with the faintly pungent and fruity smell of freshly pressed olive oil. The combination helps to settle my nerves. All the pampering I've received these many moon cycles, combined with the perfumed oils from this morning's massage, makes me practically glow by the time I hear Er's voice in the courtyard.

I have loved the daily baths and herbal treatments for my skin, hair and nails. Imagine, a whole year of mud baths, massages, special foods and exotic beauty treatments, and all without Yergat ever once having complained about them. It's been heaven!

Bushra has simply ignored all the fuss made over me, and since Hazibah and Mirah are older than me and still not betrothed to anyone, they've been jealous. Even though they have never once been kind to me, I feel somewhat sorry for them. It must be hard to watch me enjoy myself so much when they have little hope of ever experiencing this kind of pampering.

I have eaten too much and lounged too much and have been generally bored, but Anush has encouraged all of this. Laughing and talking about my upcoming nissuin and my "big night," as she calls it, we've spent many happy hours together

There has been sadness too, though. My dear noorshma has not always accompanied me to the secret chamber after I finish my seven days of Moon Blood. She claimed that it was just too hard for her "dried up bag of bones" to climb the hill then crouch down in the cave tunnel to get there. I've counted nine times now when she's not been with me. Going alone has not been at all as pleasant as when she is with me.

Shulgi has fluctuated between pouting and showing genuine happiness for me. Probably he hasn't liked it that we don't play or talk together much anymore. And although he's been supportive of me, and has told me that he understands why I have to marry Er, he hasn't fooled me one little bit. He has noticed all the lovely changes in me that the pampering brings out, and without having said anything with his mouth; his eyes have told me that he wishes he (and not Er) could be the one to marry me. I've tried to assure him we will still be good friends and do lots of things together, but he hasn't believed it. I don't blame him. I haven't believed it myself.

I hear Er's footsteps in the hallway now. I sit still and calm my racing heart, for I am not sure how I will feel when he enters the room. I know what I am *supposed* to do—Anush has made sure of that. I am just not sure that I can do it! I adjust the purple hattah on my head and smile.

When Er appears at the door and stares at me like I am someone he doesn't want to see, I lose all confidence, look down at my lap where my hands fidget with my clothes. He glowers as he strides into the room as though he wants to be anywhere else but here.

"They're right, you know."

His statement catches me off guard; I stop fidgeting.

"Who is right?"

"The people in the city… and Bushra and Hazibah and Mirah and Yergat. He's the most right of all, if you ask me."

Both the sound of my voice and the chamber below my belly tighten as I prepare for a fight. "I *didn't* ask you, though, did I?" I challenge.

"You see? They *are* right." He laughs at my nervousness, which is so thick you could slice it with an axe.

"I don't care what it is you think they are right about. I can *still* beat you at the Royal Game of Ur!"

He snorts. "Doesn't matter anymore. That's for babies. I'm a man now." He lifts his chin up and looks at me as though examining a piece of sheep flesh.

I feel my fists tighten again in my lap. I am grateful the table hides them.

He plops down a large silk bag on the table, pushes it until it is directly in front of me.

"Here. This is yours, and I'm supposed to say something to you."

Next, he rattles off words as though he is checking off a list of goods in a storage room. "I give you this matan, Tamar, as a token of your beauty and the beauty of our marriage to come." He looks away just as quickly as he spits out the words.

I don't move or touch the bag.

Now *he* fidgets.

"What is wrong with you? Don't you want the gift? I have to give it to you, so just take it and I'll go home." He clicks his tongue on his teeth and mumbles, "You are such trouble!"

I almost laugh as I repeat the words Anush taught me to say: "I receive your kind words as a token of my acceptance of your matan and our coming marriage vows." I don't look away, and I still don't touch the bag.

"Ehff," he fusses, "you really think you're something, don't you? You think because we will marry we will be equals. But I tell you we will never be equals. I have learned things from the priests, and the priestess... uh... *priestesses.* Yes, learned things you will never know."

His voice is as smug as smug can be for someone who has drunk the red mead and entered into sacred marriage with the "priestess... uh... *priestesses.*"

He looks at the still untouched bag.

"Don't you *want* it?" His voice sounds as though he would like to make amends for his rudeness. "My father bought these things in Megiddo when he and Hirah last traveled there on business. You cannot find them in our shuk." He nearly pleads with these last words.

When Anush and I have talked during my baths and massages, she has told me secrets about how men behave, and what women can do about it.

For instance, in this moment, Er, who has never been particularly courteous to me during all the years I have known him, has never behaved so rudely toward me as he does now. It seems that his position as king has made him cockier than ever. So what should I do? Easy. I remember Anush's instructions then smile serenely as I look at him with my kohl painted eyes and my pomegranate stained lips. I think about the naked women on the walls of the secret chamber and nearly laugh.

Er suddenly catches his breath as he notices (for the first time it seems) that I am beautiful.

Yes, I have finally realized that I *am* a beautiful woman. My breasts are high, pert and firm, my thighs soft to the touch, and my lips round and full. My purple-brown eyes draw him in while I smile as though curious to find out what kind of creature he is.

A slight red color creeps over his cheeks as I watch him as though observing Atagartis' flipper for the hundredth time then lift my right hand to look at my nails.

"I'm sorry, Tamar. I don't mean to treat you like this. You and I both know we are getting married because our parents want it, isn't that right?" His voice modulates slightly upward, as though he is not sure if he has put his foot into the fire or not.

I let him burn.

He sucks his breath through his teeth, looks down at the gift.

"Here, at least take this as a token of our friendship, won't you please?" Again he looks at me as if he has never seen me before. "You *are* beautiful, Tamar."

He is nearly breathless now.

Anush has taught me that a woman shouldn't play for too long when a man is in this state of mind: when he realizes he is wrong but doesn't know how to regain his position of supposed superiority. She tells me that when this happens, a woman must relent slightly in her silent power to train, control or punish, otherwise the man will burn too hot, and hate her for the dominant strength she can wield over him.

I place my hand delicately on the bag and say sweetly, "Thank you, Er, for this generous matan, whatever it may be. Since you say your father took the trouble to purchase it for me on your behalf, I trust that what's inside are items of beauty fit for a queen." I look past him to the door. "I will open the bag after you are gone." He is nothing to me now. He is not in the room. He is not even in the house.

His voice falls so low I can barely hear him. "I didn't mean what I said about you being trouble, Tamar. It's not true what they say. I think they are all just jealous of you."

"Hmm," I murmur as though all my thoughts have to be pulled back in order to hear his voice. "Why is that?"

He fumbles around for words. "You know."

Even though I know perfectly well what he means, I want to hear him say it.

"No, I can't say that I do." My words flick away at his diminishing confidence.

"Really? It's obvious to everyone else. You're going to marry the King of Adullam!" He smiles broadly, and I can see a resemblance to Yehuda on his lips.

I purr like an Egyptian cat. "You have a nice smile, Er."

"Thank you, Tamar." He stumbles over his words. "You... uh... you do too."

I smile as serenely as a queen. "Now, shall we walk out together so they will know all is well between us?"

"A great idea!" He jumps up like he's ready to kick a sheepskin ball around the olive groves and back.

Tranquilly, I come out from behind the table and wait for him to offer me his arm before I lightly place my well-oiled and perfumed hand on his skin.

He trembles.

I turn and smile at him.

Together we walk out the door and into the courtyard where all the listening ears peel themselves off the walls and jump back onto the heads of their owners.

* * *

Anush and the two servant women continue to fuss over my wedding garment as I gaze at the jewelry they will fasten to every visible part of my body. Among silver and gold chains of various lengths and thicknesses lie glass beads; carnelian, agate and jasper pendants fashioned into spirals, cones and grapevines; copper, silver and gold wrist and ankle bracelets; finely fluted gold and silver hair pins; and an amulet of pure amber.

The shape of the amulet is not like the ones I have seen in Adullum. Those are always carved or molded to look like a god or an animal, and are as common as barley in a field. However, this one must be rare, for it looks like a miniature cylinder. Tiny words are carved into it. The language is unfamiliar to me, but I don't mind that I cannot read it because this amulet has a beauty that is almost a power unto itself.

I love all the jewelry Er brought to me in the silken bag weeks ago. I like to adorn myself with different pieces each day and admire myself in the black and highly polished stone mirror that came as a surprise at the bottom of the bag. Anush told me that this strange and wonderful looking stone comes from a region close to where she used to live, and that it too is rare.

I get skin bumps every time I look into it and see my eyes looking back at me as though a spirit is inside the stone duplicating my every gesture. I wonder if what I see in the mirror is what others see when they look at me too, for other than seeing murky images of myself in the still waters of a clay bowl or a well bucket, I've never known how I look until Er gave me the mirror.

Among all these treasures however, one small item stands out from the rest. It sits now in the small cedar box it came in. The box is lined with thin sheets of pounded silver, and the lid is inlaid with shapes of highly crafted abalone pieces.

The lid is open and I can see the single and almost perfectly rounded pearl Yehuda bought for Er to give to me. It does not sparkle, but seems to compel light in the room to form soft waves that trick the eye and tell of the origins of the sea. Sitting atop wispy tufts of silken purple threads holding it inside the box, this exquisite queen of the jewels is pure luminance and makes everything around it seem imperfect and spoiled by human hands.

Suddenly, I imagine Er's hands touching and exploring all the secret treasures of my body!

"Anush-jahn, are you certain we cannot convince Yergat that he could strike a better bargain with Yehuda by marrying off Hazibah or Mirah or *both* of them to Er?"

The two servants snicker; Anush takes my hand.

"Step off the bench now, Katu. We need to do your hair next."

"But what about Hazibah and Mirah? What about my idea?"

"What about them? They will be fortunate to find anyone who will pay a mohar for them. You, on the other hand, are betrothed to a king who has a good father, and you will not go hungry or be ill treated the way many women are. So hush now, and let's get your hair into the headpiece."

In my failure to stop the forward march to the nissuin, I sigh and resign myself to the next part of the preparations.

Earlier today I had enjoyed the henna, oil and rainwater treatments for my "swirling cloud of blushing onyx," which is what Anush still calls my hair, but now I wish that she and the servants had not been able to untangle it with the ram's horn comb they used. Maybe that would have stopped them from braiding it as they do now, or from pinning it up and slipping the jeweled headdress over it. Maybe my unruly hair could stop the wedding even yet.

Anush hands me the mirror. "There. What do you think?" She smiles as though I should be pleased.

"I do not like this arrangement," I protest.

"What?" Anush seems almost hurt. "Is it the headpiece, or the hair under it?"

"No, I don't mean any of that. It all looks beautiful. What I mean is that it's not fair I have to marry Er, not fair that I had no real say in choosing a husband, and not fair that he might smell like a donkey!"

The two servants laugh out loud. Anush grins at the older woman, and I cannot believe what comes out of her mouth next.

"If he smells like a donkey, Katu, then you will have to wash him before you ride him!"

They all chortle.

"You are wretched, Anush-jahn!" I cry out as I try to hold back my own smile.

"Seriously now, Tamoosh-jahn, you need to think about the impression you'll make as you walk through the streets of Adullam to the temple then back to Yehuda and Illit's home. Think about the fact that soon you will have your own children, and will be able to give them many advantages because of this marriage."

"The last thing I want to think about right now is children... or at least how they're made, that is."

"You don't have to think about that until after the wedding feast, so stop worrying. You and I have talked at length about what will happen tonight, and you are completely prepared. It is a natural thing for a man to be in bed with a woman... a beautiful thing. It was for me, at least, and it is for most women. If you relax now you will enjoy the time with Er later.

"Here," she sweeps her hand toward the jewelry displayed near me. "Choose what you would like to wear. I know you like the pearl best, so tell us first where you want it to go."

Having to think about where to place the pearl takes my thoughts off Er's bed for only a split moment.

"Do you think Er is as nervous as I am?"

"Perhaps, but probably not. You remember what I have told you about all that."

I shiver at the memory of the red mead and the priestesses.

"I suppose you are right, Anush-jahn. Even so, will he be—"

My voice breaks.

Anush seems to understand that I might also break into tears at any moment, so she softens her voice. "Will he be what, my sweet Yakiri?"

To cover my embarrassment, I peer out the window in the direction of the cave before I answer so slowly and so low Anush and the other women strain to hear me.

"Gentle. Will he be gentle when he—"

I blush and cannot finish my question.

Anush, in probably the most delicate voice I have ever heard her use, finishes the question for me. "When he enters you, my sweet and brave Tamoosh-jahn?"

"Yes," I answer even more quietly. "Yes, that which you spoke."

"Ah, Katu, who can tell about these things? Each man is different and will do what he will do. There are never any guarantees in this world, least of all when it comes to men. All I can tell you is what I learned from my own marriage experiences, and what I have heard from other women.

"We all know that men are generally built the same way down there," she gestures by gently flicking her cupped wrist outward near her Hill of Asherah, "but they are not always built the same way up here." She taps her forehead.

I smile and nod.

"In my own case, I think I was fairly lucky. My man was gentle, or so it seemed, as far as I knew. If the stories I heard from other women in the Moon Blood hut I used to go to in my own city can act as a measuring stick, I think he was gentle enough. Of course, I can't tell for sure because he was the only man I ever knew... in that way." Anush smiles at me. "If Er is not gentle with you, there are things you can do to teach him *how* to be gentle."

"What things, Anush-jahn?" My voice quivers slightly, and

I feel a red heat rise to my cheeks.

"Ah, now, Yavrik, you mustn't jump ahead of yourself. You'll need to wait and see. All you can do now is hold your head up high and keep your eyes forward as you walk through the streets of Adullam. To be honest, much of what will happen is in your own heart and hands."

I look out the window again and yearn to be anywhere else but here. A tear takes a journey from my eye to my lips.

Unexpectedly, the twelve-year-old servant girl touches the tear away and looks at me. She no longer blinks or giggles.

"You'll be all right." She smiles sweetly at me then looks away and drops her hand to adjust a few unruly strands of my hair near my ear.

While each of us stands alone in our thoughts, all grows quiet in the room.

Suddenly, a dazzling dance of rainbow colors sparkle through the room as the sunlight catches the jewels in my headdress.

The utter beauty of it causes me to laugh so deeply the eagle inside my belly finally stops its lurching flight.

"All right, Anush-jahn." I let out a loud sigh. "Since I cannot stop this wedding, then tonight, and in the many nights ahead, I will simply have to discover what those things are that you said I can do to teach Er gentleness in bed."

I look in the black stone mirror one more time and see my eyes sparkle like the rainbow dance of the jewels on the walls.

"I am ready," I say in a regal voice. Gracefully walking to the front door of Yergat and Bushra's house, I hold my head high and look neither to the right nor the left as I step onto the stone pavement of the street that is festooned with flowers. I smile at the cheering people who will lead me to the temple then to the celebration that will lead me to the bed of my soon-to-be husband.

A Wedding To Die For

"It is silliness to live when to live is torment, and then have we a prescription to die when death is our physician."
—William Shakespeare

A<small>S MY EYES DART HERE AND THERE</small> to adjust to my new surroundings, my fingers graze Er's reluctant wrist. After all the feasting and drinking at the celebration festivities, Er is barely standing upright, so does not seem to notice my touch.

Oil lamps, placed cunningly throughout the bedroom, create a dim luster and cast playful shadows. The room is warm, and the blood in my head beats and booms with every movement of the flickering light dancing over everything. I take a deep breath to steady myself then lead the way to Er's bed.

Yeesh. So small for two people

Er staggers as we approach the bed, then flops down on it, face first. This does not seem like a good sign to me.

"Er, are you all right?"

He moans, but doesn't move.

"Er, I need you to help me with my wedding garments."

He groans again, but still does not move.

I sigh, sit down beside him and gently shake him. He moans a third time, but still doesn't move, so I look around the room.

Directly across from where I sit is a window, but no light comes through it at the moment because a heavy curtain covers it. For our privacy, I suppose. To the right of the window is a small alcove-like area to store clothes and other items. He has a lot of belongings in there, and I cannot imagine how I will fit my things in there too.

On the other side of the alcove is the door through which we just entered. I know where that leads: back to the dining area and the main part of the house. I can still hear the sounds of merriment as Yehuda, Illit, Hirah, Yergat, Bushra, and all the other guests continue with their celebrations. Shulgi is one of the guests too. The thought that he might be able to hear Er and I when we couple makes me cringe. I inwardly vow to stay quiet, very quiet during the ordeal ahead.

I shake Er again, but this time, just when I hope that he is asleep so that I can avoid the coupling ritual for at least one more night, he rolls over and opens his glazed eyes.

"Whad're you doin', Tamar, wife of mine? Tryin' to ge-rid of me a'ready?"

"Don't be silly, Er." I distract him. "I just need to take off my headdress, that's all."

He starts to sit up, sways a bit and leans on one elbow. "I know how to help you." He looks at me like a puppy that has just escaped from its mother and littermates.

"That is okay. Never mind. You don't have to."

Impatience begins to wear away at my confidence. I know Er's character, so why did I agree to this marriage in the first place? Why did I allow Anush to talk me into it? For one brief moment in the Moon Blood hut I had the chance to say no to her, to Illit, to all of Adullam... so why didn't I?

Er's words stumble out in slow spurts as he wobbles off the bed. "Oh yes I do. I'm gonna help you...b'cuz thadz my job." He stands... just barely, and teeters like a tree about to fall over in the wind.

I'm tempted to reach out and steady him, but not wanting to embarrass him, I say through my carefully placed smile, "All right, have it your way."

"Thad I will do too... have my way." Still teetering, his head nods up and down like an old man who can barely stay awake.

I want to think that maybe he isn't such a baby anymore. Maybe he's just confused. Maybe what everyone has believed about Illit thwarting Yehuda's training of his son is true and Yehuda was never able to teach him anything about how to be a man. Maybe that explains his shortcomings, his selfish ways, or even his anger when I beat him at the Game of Ur. Maybe there is something better inside of him that he has never been able to show the world. Maybe I can help him learn to do that.

He steps closer; I can smell him. He doesn't smell like a donkey, as I had feared he would.

"You ready for me, Tamar, my wife, my woman?"

"You are so silly, Er. Of course I am ready," I lie. "I've been preparing for this night for over twelve moon cycles. The real question is whether or not *you* are ready."

I use my kohl-painted eyes and eyebrows to play with him. Unexpectedly, the warmth of his body envelops me as his face changes like a ram near a ewe in heat. The heat that rises in my own body also surprises me. This is not a feeling I thought to feel with Er. In fact, in spite of the bravado I displayed this morning when I told Anush that I would figure out the things I could do to teach a man to be gentle in bed, I didn't really want to do that. I simply felt that I had to put on a bold face for her and the two servants... and maybe for myself too.

Er puffs out his chest, "So you wanna play, do ya?"

"Might as well. Nothing better to do." I'm surprised how good it feels to flirt with him. Maybe this *can* be fun.

His eyes gleam like the oil lamps. "Alridey-didey, you asked for it." The power he radiates both excites and frightens me at the same time.

"Off with your head first then." He lifts the jeweled covering away from the mound of my hair, and sets the hairpiece on a chair near the window.

Meanwhile, I take out the bejeweled hairpins and set my "swirling cloud" free, which makes me feel almost naked already and shocked that I enjoy the sensations rippling through my body.

He turns back and gasps.

"Ohhh. You're budiful."

He staggers to me and gently threads his fingers into my hair, touching my scalp.

I breathe a sigh of relief. It seems that this will not go badly after all.

"You like this?" He pulls me to his chest; I can hear his heart beat through his clothes.

"I do," I answer softly. "I... I really do." I almost hate myself for admitting this to him.

"Good. Therz much more ta come."

He touches my ears now; lightning streaks to my toes.

"Oooh." I feel like I am melting into an unknown world.

"Yes, thatz right, Tamar, thatz what you need."

"Oh yes, I think you are right," I say breathlessly. "Please don't stop."

"I don't plan ta stop. Off withtha clothes next."

As he lifts my garments, and as I raise my arms to help him maneuver them over my head and away from the burning sensations in my flesh, skin bumps pop up all over my body.

He tosses my garments aside then kisses my neck and lingers his lips across the skin that leads down to my nipples. They feel like they will burst as I stretch my chest forward and moan. He looks up and smiles at me before he gently kisses around them then closes his lips over them. Lightning strikes my Hill of Asherah, but instead of fire there is the sweet sensation of wetness between my legs.

He stops.

I pull him to me, but he resists.

"Off with *my* clothes next," he instructs me as though I am a child and he is a god. "*You* do that."

I remove all his clothing; his body seems like a god too.

He looks at me with a curious hint of sadness in his eyes, as though he doesn't want to hurt me, which, given the nature of his usual character, seems unusual to me.

"What is it, my husband?" It feels so strange to call him

that. "Your eyes look sad."

His voice seems to come from a distance, as though he were in a different room, a different world. He sounds sober now too, and his voice has lost all the playfulness that was in it before.

"Now I must drink the red mead. You must prepare it for me."

I close my eyes; my head shivers slightly as I try to shake away his words.

"The red mead?" I ask hesitantly.

His eyes still seem sad-looking, as though the images stored behind them contain too much awareness of the things in life over which he has no control.

"Yes Tamar," Er answers without uncertainty. "The red mead."

I remember Anush telling me that the moment would come when he would want the red mead. She tried to get me to think about it, to make a plan and decide how to respond when Er asked for it. I avoided those conversations like they were raiders in the shuk, and never did settle down into facing what I needed to face. Instead, I chose to believe that he would forget about it entirely. Now I realize that I was entirely wrong.

People do that, don't they? Believe what they want to believe, even when they know they are fooling themselves? Pretend that the moon shines when it is day, and that the sun illuminates the sky when it is night? Distract themselves by any number of this-and-that-these-and-those tasks until the truth is neatly tucked away out of view, out of mind, but never fully out of the subtle tensions in their bodies?

For my part, when it came to the subject of the red mead and what would be required of me on my marriage night, I always felt a tightness below my belly and in my shoulders and neck, but ignored what those three places seemed to be attempting to tell me: "We're trying to help you here, so don't just flick us away because you think you don't have enough time to deal with us right now. You'd better take the time to make the time, or we'll be forced to get louder and uglier until you face what you have to face and do something about it rather than running from it like you so often do."

Thinking that I could ignore these built-in warning signals, these muted tensions in my body, that I could spurn them until they disappeared altogether, and that by doing so the problem of the red mead would go away on its own, I fooled myself, and never did take the time to figure out what I would do when the moment came to face the inevitable.

Now the inevitable has arrived, and I have nowhere to hide.

* * *

Er's smile still looks sad to me as he asks, "You know how to make the red mead, don't you?"

"Yes," I answer so softly that it sounds like I do not speak at all. "Anush taught me."

"The vessel is there." He points to a bejeweled drinking cup that sits on a small table with an oil lamp beside it. "You are my priestess now."

"No, Er. I am not a priestess."

"Yes you are, and you must bring the vessel. My Imma filled it half full with wine earlier today. It is ready for you to mix with your Moon Blood."

I don't answer him.

"I *said* the wine is ready."

I do not move.

"What is *wrong* with you? Bring me your Moon Blood!"

I find my voice, and without malice or fear say, "I don't have any Moon Blood to give."

He stares at me with his mouth agape.

I gather my strength.

"And *even* if I had it, I wouldn't *want* to give it away."

The force of forcing myself to speak the truth makes me

nearly shout.

"I am *not* a priestess, and the ritual of the red mead *disgusts* me!" The power of my words feels like thunder in my chest.

"*Whaaat?*" He explodes as any remaining stupor from the feast flees from him. "*Not* have the Moon Blood? Not *give* it if you did? Are you *crazy?*"

He storms over to me, raises his fist within a hairs width of my face, the glaze in his eyes now a craze of anger.

I take a deep slow breath to keep the fear I feel in my belly, shoulders, and neck from rising to my eyes.

"No, Er," I speak more softly than the air that stirs around us. "I am not crazy."

He sucks in his breath, thrusts out his chest and snarls at me, "All right then, have it your way. I guess this means that everyone was right about you after all. You *are* nothing but trouble!"

I barely breathe.

He takes one step backward. "Doesn't matter. I don't love you anyway. I love Lilith. I love the priestess who gives me her Moon Blood and withholds nothing of her secret chamber from me. I don't need *you* to be king!"

His words swarm and sting at me, but I do not flinch.

Panting with fury, he glares at me one last time then stomps over to the vessel of wine, sucks it down in one furious swig.

I stand perfectly still and watch to see what he will do next.

Suddenly, he coughs as though he can't breathe, as though the wine goes not to his belly, but instead drowns his air. He grabs the empty space around him with his free hand. The vessel falls, shatters on the stone floor, all of its jewels scattering like mice in a pantry when a cat pounces.

"Er!" I rush to his side, but he crashes to the ground before I can reach him. His head strikes the stony floor.

"Er, no!"

Blood. Lots of blood.

I grab one of his wedding garments and wrap it around his head. It turns red as fast as I can move to see his face, to see if his eyes are open, to see if he is breathing.

His eyes flutter; he looks at me with the same curious sadness as before.

"Can you breathe?" I touch his cheek.

I look at his chest where my head had rested a few short minutes ago and realize that it no longer moves.

A thin smile creeps over his lips before all the food and drink from the celebration feast pour from his mouth then sink back in again.

His eyes roll upward, stare at the ceiling without seeing.

"No!" I scream over and over.

"No. No! NO!"

Shadowy figures encircle me.

Someone covers me with a blanket, moves me to the bed.

Shuffling sounds of a body being moved reach my ears.

A door closes.

Voices and flickers from the lamplights fade.

Darkness takes me.

Onan and Illit

"Who knows what true loneliness is—not the conventional word but the naked terror? To the lonely themselves it wears a mask. The most miserable outcast hugs some memory or some illusion."

—Joseph Conrad

WHEN I AWAKEN THE NEXT DAY, Anush sits beside me.

"What is this place, Anush-jahn? Where are we?"

She smoothes my hair tenderly, and looks at me with sorrowful eyes.

"We are in Er's room... on his bed."

I suck in my breath and can barely breathe. "It wasn't a nightmare then, was it? He's dead, isn't he?"

She touches my cheek so softly I barely feel her fingers on my skin.

"Yes, Katu. He is gone."

"But why, Anush-jahn, why?" Confusion squeezes my face until I think my skin will shatter into a thousand points of darkness. Only tears release the tightness.

Anush bends over and gathers me into her arms.

"Shoosh-shoosh, my darling Katu, shoosh-shoosh."

I remember these sounds from another time, another place, another nightmare that I thought I had pushed away forever.

I bury my head in her bosom and cling to her as though lost.

Over and over and for a time longer than I can count, all I hear is "shoosh-shoosh, my darling Katu, shoosh-shoosh."

Finally, after one last sob, I shudder and look up at her. "What happened? I only remember him drinking wine from a cup, then… then—"

She takes a wet cloth from a bowl of water on a table near Er's bed, wrings it out and dabs my tears that have started again, presses it to my brow to cool my skin, so hot now from crying.

"Please tell me what happened, Anush-jahn." I press her hand away.

"No one knows for sure," she says as she dips the cloth in the bowl again then wrings it out. "The priests came quickly and worked with the Apsu waters to expel the evil spirits from Er's body." She gently lays the cloth over my brow and leaves it there. I don't resist her this time. "But the bitterness and the evil in the waters of the wine were so strong that the Siptu incantations of the priests failed. Their water prayers could not bring back his breath nor rescue his blood from the chaos of Tiamat, or the dark fingers of Mot."

I fall silent at the speaking of these dread words, for only the priests know how to heal, only the priests know how to stop the powers of the evil spirits that cause our illnesses and deaths. Or so it is said.

Now, I am not so sure it is true, though. In fact, it cannot be true, or Er would still be alive. The priests would have been able to help him if they actually had the power to stop evil. Besides, how could wine have bitterness and evil in it? I've never heard of such a thing before.

"Do you believe that the wine held evil in it, Anush-jahn?"

"I'm not sure about all that, but the priests do what they do. And now, before you think anything more about it, you must do what you can do to rest, Tamoosh-jahn. You must regain your strength because your presence will be required for the procession of Er's body to the cave where the hogi of his Grand Abba Shua awaits him."

As she loosens her arms from around me, I breathe deeply and allow myself to rest against the pillows on the bed then shudder again before I close my eyes and fall back to sleep.

The nightmare continues the next day after I rise, bathe, eat and put on my widow's weeds, the dark rough clothing of a grieving woman; it continues as I walk behind the body of my husband—who was never truly my husband—while it is taken to the temple; it continues as the flowers and herbs tossed on Er's litter lose all color, and the songs of lamentation elude all melody; it continues after the required two days pass in which the priests remove Er's organs and prepare the rest of his remains for burial.

The sky is gray, the ground is gray, and my heart is gray as I walk into the tomb with the priests, Yehuda, Illit, Onan and Shelah. Black overcomes the gray as I watch what is left of Er descend into the box with his image on it that sits beside Shua's box. Black is the lid that is placed over him, and black his urn of organs positioned near Shua's urn.

I cannot tell if the Annunaki have judged Shua yet, but I wonder how they will judge Er, and whether they will blame me for his death because I had no Moon Blood to give nor would have given if I had.

An odd thought penetrates my gloom in the cave: I will never play the Royal Game of Ur again.

The next few days pass into oblivion. People come to the house, lower their voices and their eyes when they see me, pay their respects to Yehuda and Illit then go.

When Yergat, Bushra, Hazibah, Mirah and Shulgi arrive, I want to see none of them except Shulgi.

When he looks at me I try to smile, but my cheeks, which have sought the ground for shelter since Er's death, still feel stuck there. I nod my head in the direction of the courtyard, and we excuse ourselves to go sit near the pond in full view of everyone, and with an appropriate distance between us.

Shulgi's words spill out hesitantly, as though he thinks that an evil spirit attached to me might lurk in the waters where Atagartis, as always, silently watches everything from her unchanging position in the pond.

"I'm truly sorry for you, Tamar."

197

"Thank you, Shulgi," I respond quietly.

I have few words for him, and he for me. I can tell by the way he looks at me that our ideas about "god nonsense" are gone forever. The evil spirit that he believes is in the water divides us from the comforts of the friendship we shared before my marriage to Er.

Nearly a full moon cycle slogs by. Because I am now Yehuda and Illit's daughter by marriage, I am grateful to have been able to remain in their house. Even though sadness surrounds us all, the daily routines of the household begin to soften our loss into a dull pain.

Anush and I spend much time together, and Numa comes into the room often as well. Numa seems to have softened toward me because of Er's death, and I am still so grieved by the confusing suddenness and circumstances of the loss that I don't care about our differences all that much anymore either. Nonetheless, I have to force myself to laugh when she and Anush manage to find laughter themselves. I'm not sure why they are not as stricken as I am about Er's death, but even in my numb state of mind I am aware of the secretive talk and laughter they have always shared that has never included me. Today, however, their voices are louder and clearer than usual, so I catch more than broken bits of their chatter.

"And so, Numa, it comes to this." In my ears, Anush's voice sounds loud enough for even the birds outside to hear. "Yehuda, whom you know better than any of us because you have lived under his roof for so long, has decided to fulfill his obligation to Tamar. She will marry Onan before her next Moon Blood cycle."

Numa glances over at me to see if I am listening or not.

I stare at her in disbelief.

"She hears us, Anush."

Anush turns to me. "Katu," she whispers as though my face will break into pieces if she speaks any louder. "I know this is very hard for you to understand or accept."

She pauses to make sure I am listening to her, which I am, but not in a solemn way, not as though it matters one way or the other what she has to say next.

"You know the custom." She continues, her voice still hushed and concerned. "You know Yehuda and Illit have the right and the duty to marry you to their next son so that you can raise up his seed in the name and memory of Er."

In the next moment, and without me intending for it to, all the confusion, hurt and anger that has continued to crush me since Er died seems to roar out of me.

"What is this crazy custom?" I demand. "Do I *still* have no say about my future, even after what has happened? I cannot even think about another husband, let alone spending a single moment in Onan's bed with him. No! I tell you, no! Surely there is something we can do to put a stop to this absurd and cruel idea?"

My eyes flash as I defy them to challenge me.

They say nothing, but their eyes deliver their answer.

"Have they no pity for me, then?" I say with the waning strength of a sheep that's being barked and nipped back into the flock from which she has strayed.

I stare at Anush and Numa like they are statues in a courtyard, but I cannot long countenance the pity that has frozen onto their faces.

"I see."

I drop my head to my chest. Like a sheep that has been slaughtered, I say nothing more.

The preparations for my marriage to Onan are short, and the celebrations consist only of a quiet, simple meal with the family and Hirah and very little beer or wine. Even Yergat and Bushra are not invited. After Onan and I finish eating, we go to his room where he undresses himself as though I don't exist. I undress myself as though I am in the box in the cave that holds Er's remains.

Onan doesn't look at me, he says nothing, and I say nothing as we crawl under the blankets of his bed. Soon, he is on top of me, but I am not there. I am flickering in the lamplight on the walls; I am flying through the roof and into the night skies.

Before I know what is happening, he enters me with a thrust that makes me cry out. Never did I expect this overpowering pain that tears apart the door to my secret chamber, but the crushing pain is quickly over as he pulls out of me then rolls over and onto his belly to tremble there for a short time before he moves away from me to the other side of the bed.

I feel a warm substance on my thigh and touch it with my fingers then pull my hand out from under the covers to look at it in the lamplight.

Blood!

I want to get up and wash myself, want to run from the room, from the house, want to beat Onan's chest and scream away the memories of Er. But I'm too shocked and embarrassed to do anything except try to sleep and forget about the soreness between my legs.

There is just enough space between the two of us for me to roll to my left side and shift the position of my right arm to rest over my body and onto the bed.

"Yeesh, what is this?"

I jerk back my hand from a sticky substance that smells vaguely of wet barley.

Onan laughs. "That is my life force."

"What do mean? I thought—"

"You thought it belonged to *you*? It could and it should but it won't!"

"I don't understand."

"Of course not. You're not a man who has been made to marry you only so that his life force can be used to create children in his dead brother's name."

"You mean this stickiness is your *seed*?"

"Yes, my seed that will *never* be planted in you."

"How can this be, Onan? You know that we *must* make children. It is the way of things." I lower my voice before I say, "It is the way of your father that we should do this to honor your brother's memory."

Onan does not answer.

"Onan?"

Soon, his snores answer me.

Onan behaves the same way in bed for the next four nights: he mounts me, pulls out of me then releases his seed onto the bed before falling asleep. I have not yet asked Anush about this because it is too embarrassing. Still, I have hopes that Onan will see things differently soon. I've decided to give it another week and if nothing has changed by then, I will seek her out for counsel about what to do next.

When the morning light sneaks its fingers through the window on the fifth morning of my time in Onan's bed, I reach over to touch him.

His flesh is icy cold and as hard as a statue.

This time I cannot scream.

Many days pass before Anush tells me that I will be expected to marry Shelah next so that I can still try to raise up seed in Er's name. Shelah? Who makes these kinds of decisions? Illit? The priests? Yehuda? Does Anush have a say in it... or even Numa? Certainly I do not. They have all made that more than perfectly clear to me. Whoever it is, they are heartless. Shelah's barely thirteen, which is the same age as Shulgi. And what if he dies too? What then? And what about Onan's name? Doesn't anyone care about his name? Or will it be utterly erased from the seeds of time? And most of all, what about me? My name? My life? Do I not count at all... for anything other than to raise up seed for a man's name to be glorified? A man whose character showed that his name was never worthy of being raised up to begin with? Just because Er was Yehuda's son it doesn't mean that he was worthy to carry on Yehuda's name.

"Can't I just talk to him, Anush-jahn? Maybe he will listen to reason about Shelah if it comes from me."

My noorshma sits on Onan's bed next to me, concentrating deeply on my words. Since Onan's death, I have had to sleep in his bed instead of Er's. Frightful dreams cheat me of sleep at night and gloom haunts my days.

"You could, Yavrik, you could," Anush speaks haltingly, as though weighing how best to choose her words, "but I advise against it." She strokes my hair gently.

"Why? What harm can come from it?" My voice settles on my ears as though it comes from a distance. I try to sit up, but cannot. My head rings and my sight blurs.

"To begin with," Anush soothes, "Numa has heard Yehuda and Illit arguing about what to do with you." She pauses, continues to stroke my hair.

"Oh?" I close my eyes to wait for what she will say next.

"Convinced that you caused the deaths of both of her sons, Illit wants to take you before the priests and let them judge you. If they find you guilty, the punishment will be death by fire." She pauses to let her words sink in.

As a shiver runs down my spine, I breathe in deeply, but keep my eyes closed.

"Short of that, she wants you sent back to Yergat and Bushra's house," she says as though that alternative is a boon. "Thankfully, Yehuda is not sure about any of this, and defends you as best he can in her presence."

Without enthusiasm, I respond. "As he should, since I'm not to blame for the deaths of Er and Onan."

Anush says nothing.

A terrible thought enters my mind. "*You* don't think I'm to blame, do you, Anush-jahn," I say uncertainly.

Anush answers as softly as possible, "Of course not, my Yakiri, I know you are not to blame."

Breathing a sigh of relief, I now try to envision the debate between Yehuda and Illit, and how the outcome of it will change my life. I keep my eyes closed as I ask, "If Yehuda doesn't believe I am to blame either, don't you think that he would listen to me then?"

202

"Not necessarily," Anush responds. "It's one thing for him to defend you, and yet another for you to defend yourself."

"What do you mean?" I open my eyes.

"Think of it from Yehuda's point of view for a moment. He's a man, and as such takes a certain amount of pride in standing up to his wife," she says.

"Really? Why do you say that, Anush-jahn?" I try to sit up again, but do not succeed.

"Women observe these things, and talk about them when they work together over a hot oven, or in the fields... and most especially when they are in the Moon Blood hut." She says this as if the insight should be common knowledge to me by now.

"Oh." I act as though I understand so that she will continue.

"It's a man's way of claiming ground, if you will. Rather like a male dog that pees everywhere to stake out its territory. Since a man can't pee to win an argument with his wife, he will often take the opposite point of view from hers, even if he doesn't fully believe in it." She lifts my chin and says, "I think that is what Yehuda is doing, and if you get in the middle of this husband and wife dispute, you will be the one who gets peed on, I can guarantee it." Her eyes twinkle; I smile for the first time since Er died.

"It is good to see you smile again, "Katu." She kisses the tip of my nose.

Three days later, Numa helps us pack our things, and reluctantly, Anush and I return to Yergat and Bushra's house.

* * *

"You selfish goat," Bushra barks at me. "I always said you were trouble and bad luck and now all of Adullum can see I was right. I don't know why your father and I have to keep you here though, especially not after what it cost us to get rid of you in the first place."

I don't look at her or even shrug my shoulders. Why

should I? She only sees a selfish goat and will never even try to acknowledge my hidden sorrows, so there's no need for me to become vexed with her. Like Anush told me, "You cannot make lechem from an auroch."

And yet, I am weary of her crude insults and disheartened by the way they sap Anush's strength as well as mine, so I try a different tactic with Bushra.

"Perhaps there is something I can do in the house to help with the added burden I have caused you, Bushra. Perhaps some weaving of the wools, or dying of the threads?" I look at her like a guileless lamb.

She gasps as though someone has bumped into her from behind. "What? You? Help me?" she says all a fluster. "The last thing I need is *your* help. I just need you and Anush to stay out of my sight!" She turns and darts from the room.

"Hehh." As soon as I breathe out my relief, Anush walks in.

"What happened to Bushra, Katu? She brushed by me in the hallway shaking her head and letting out loud 'humphs' like someone had just cheated her at the shuk."

I smile at her. "Let's just say that wool and dyed threads didn't sit well with her today because you can't make lechem from an auroch."

Anush grins. "I always said you were clever, Tamoosh-jahn, so whatever you did to Bushra, you have proved me right once again."

"You are almost always right, Anush-jahn, you know that."

She shakes her head and imitates Bushra. "Humph!"

We both laugh.

"Oh, I almost forgot. Numa came by to tell me that Illit wants you to visit her in the courtyard tomorrow after the midday meal. She didn't say why, she just told me to tell you." Anush watches to see how I will react to this news.

"I will go, of course, but I can't imagine what she wants." I look away.

"Neither can I, but whatever it is, it will be for the best."

Anush fidgets with a loose thread on her halug.

"I suppose so," I stare at the floor.

The next day I sit on the same bench in the courtyard where Anush and Numa squeezed my legs so long ago.

Today I keep my eyes on Atagartis as I did when I first had to face Illit and apologize to Er for causing him to fall into the pond.

Today I have no apology to give. I have done nothing wrong.

Illit stands before me like a cold statue.

"The priests could not find anything to explain Onan's death." Illit's frosty intonations fall to the ground like heavy snow, and her pinched and icy eyes tell me she wants more than an expression of remorse from me today.

"Neither could they find anything to explain Er's." Morbid awe seems to freeze her face as she peers at me.

I remain seated and say nothing.

Now she pleads, "Tamar, please tell me what happened again." Her voice fluctuates between the sound of a subject pleading for mercy and that of a pitiless queen who is accustomed to making decrees and having them carried out without challenge. "There must be something the priests have missed. Something *I* have missed."

I meet her eyes with a royal gaze of my own.

"I've told you everything that happened at least three times now. What else do you think there is to tell?"

"I think, Tamar, that you are hiding something from us all and not telling the truth, not even to Anush or Numa. That's what I think."

"Have Anush and Numa said they think I am lying too?" I counter.

"It doesn't matter what they say or don't say. Numa is a mere servant, Anush a mere aunt. I see what I see, and I know what I know."

"And what is it you see and know, Illit? Tell me so that I can tell you whether you are right or wrong."

Her voice rises. "*Me?* Tell *you?* How *dare* you."

"No Illit, how dare *you* to suggest that I had anything at all to do with the deaths of your sons."

She looks at me with feigned shock. "I never said that."

"Not to my face, perhaps, but even in this time of grieving, I have not gone deaf. Don't you think that I know what you have said in hushed whispers behind my back? How you have planted the seeds of doubt about my innocence to everyone... especially to Yehuda, not to mention all of Adullam?"

She looks away, but the anger that has been building in me for days boils over I am not about to stop it.

"Besides, wasn't it enough that I should have been *forced* to marry those sons of yours, whether I wanted to or not?" My voice gets louder. "Wasn't it enough that Er died in my arms after I had begun to thrill to his touch?"

She twitches.

I'm surprised that I mention this intimate detail to her, but then again, I'm so weary of the accusations that follow her wherever she goes, I don't care what she thinks anymore, so I press on.

"Wasn't it enough that Onan would not give me his seed because of his jealousy?"

She begins to tremble. It feels good to finally speak the truth to her face, to watch the effect of my words on her oh-so-icily-controlled façade. But, I haven't finished yet.

"What do you want from me? Do you think I have some means of sorcery to bring them back to life: a secret incantation I can pray to make them rise from the cave where their bones now lie with your father's? Is that what you think?"

Illit looks as though she might slap me. Instead, she storms over to Atagartis then turns and screams at me.

"No, I don't think you can bring them back to life, but I *do* think you killed them for spite... to show your power." Her eyes blaze with a fire that seeks to burn me. "I think you poisoned Er, and suffocated Onan in his sleep!"

206

I laugh out loud. At last she is finally saying what everyone else seems to believe about me when they cower behind corners to point at me and speak in hushed whispers.

"You give me far too much credit, Illit, and far too little compassion for a twice-made widow who came to your house in good faith. For all I know, *you* poisoned Er. After all, you are the one who poured the wine he drank that choked and killed him. *You* are the one!"

She is so stunned by my words that she seems to melt before my eyes. She has lost her power over me, for it can never be that those who seek to hurt others instead of comforting them have any real power. Yes, she has *definitely* lost her power. In fact, I now realize that she never had any actual power over me to begin with, other than what came from the fear she fomented, the fear that I once bent my knee to, but have now challenged so that I can stand without shame before her—or anyone else.

She tries to regain her now diminished authority by seeking to expand every part of herself, as though she can conjure up an apparition to cover the truth of her smallness, her meanness, and her bitter pettiness.

"Tamar, of the house of Yergat, of the blood of Trinjah, and of the forgotten family of Ditzah," she shrieks, "I curse you in the name of Ba'al. I curse you in the name of Tiamat and the Annunaki. With the full authority of the lineage of the Dragon Blood Sovereignty, I curse you!"

I shudder but do not shake, for I am filled with pity for her.

"And I, Tamar of the waters which live," I answer calmly and evenly, "forgive you, Illit." My voice softens. "I forgive you."

"Oh you do, do you? How *dare* you!"

She raises her fists above her head and bolts toward me like Mot preparing to devour Ba'al. Her eyes now burn with the fires of Irkalla, but I do not budge.

In the moment when I am sure that she will strike me, her face suddenly turns the color of sun-bleached bones, as though all the blood of her Dragon Sovereignty has been drained from her in a split instant. She clutches at her heart as a look of icy terror replaces the fire in her eyes.

I gasp as she falls to the ground, dead.

Not believing what I am seeing, I stare at her as though I too am a corpse. Then I stand and cry for help.

What words can I use to describe my reactions to this third death?

I have no words.

I have no strength to eat. I have no strength to rise from my bed. I have no strength at all and feel like I am floating somewhere between the ceiling and the floor.

Anush watches over me day and night, and Numa comes to help when she can. Today is one of those times. Sitting on the other side of the room that Anush and I share once again, they keep their voices low so they will not disturb me as they talk, but it is not long before their mumblings find a way into my ears.

I shudder when I hear Numa whisper, "They think she is a servant of the Annunaki, that she is to blame."

"I have heard the same thing," Anush whispers back. "Yehuda is beside himself. Two sons taken… and now his wife too. Who has ever heard of such a thing happening so quickly? But then again, there was Sh'chem."

"Yes," echoes Numa sadly, "there was Sh'chem and Yehuda's family…"

Their words can't reach me. I won't let them. I float to the ceiling again where I am safe from their secrets, but their murmurs climb aboard my ears there too.

Anush's voice trembles. "All of Adullam listens to the priests who say that not even their most powerful incantations, or their most sacred waters can break the evil spells of Tamar. They spread rumors that she has entered into a pact with Mot that gives her powers they cannot match. The people are filled with terror and want to kill her. But the priests are too fearful of what Ba'al might do to them and to the city if anyone tries to get near her."

They do not realize that I can hear them as I try to float away forever.

I have no words.

I have no words.

I have no words.

It Is Time

"The woman who follows the crowd will usually go no further than
the crowd. The woman who walks alone is likely to find herself
in places no one has ever been before."

—Albert Einstein

HOW DOES ONE DESCRIBE the way blow upon blow upon blow
takes its toll on a life? How can one explain the price extracted
for so many losses, rejections, betrayals, cruel suspicions and
accusations from others? Can these costs be counted and
weighed like clay pieces in a bulla? Can they be measured in
syllables and symbols? Words are cheap imitations for telling
the truth of the stories that make a person who she is. She
herself is at a loss to recount her truths by using such paltry
expressions as words.

And so it is that after the deaths of Er, Onan and Illit, I
continue to try and make sense out of what happened, try to
go on with life as usual, try to convince myself I am not to
blame. Yet no matter how diligently I toil away at these goals,
I find little to say to others, and find what they have to say to
me of little interest.

It has been well over a year since Anush and I came back to live
under the roof of Yergat and Bushra again. Everyone continues
to shun me at every turn, except Anush and Numa (who still
comes to visit). Yergat will not even look at me, although that
is nothing new. Hazibah and Mirah rush off into places of the
house as far away as they can get from me. The servants stop
speaking when I enter a room and look at the ground.

I feel like I am getting a taste of what Ditzah suffered as a Forgotten One.

And Bushra? Don't get me started. Oh how her true character displays itself ever more clearly these days.

For instance, the first time my Moon Blood cycle came upon me after Anush and I were sent out of Yehuda's house in disgrace, Bushra told me that I could not use the hut closest to our home, the one I have always used. She told me that my Moon Blood was evil and that I would not be allowed to spill it where she and the other women regularly spilled theirs.

When I asked her where I should go then, she told me to use the hut in the part of the city that Shulgi and I ran through on that day so long ago, that place where filth and smells of despair fill every space. So I went there, but the women inside would not allow me in either. They held up amulets of Asherah and Ba'al and turned their eyes away from me, as though they might die if they even so much as looked at me.

I remember coming home that day and crying. Anush found me and wiped away my tears like she always does and said, "We will find a better place."

That better place turns out to be our room. During my Moon Blood cycles, I simply stay in it for the full seven days, and no one but Anush comes in or out, except Numa, who visits as often as she can. Any hard feelings she and I may have once harbored for one another have vanished, and we are both glad of it.

When my cycle begins, Anush and I pile the cloths and dried grasses in a corner, and spend the next seven days eating, drinking herbal infusions of sage, lavender and mint, burning lebonah to clear the air and rubbing each other's feet, hands, necks and shoulders with oils, all the while attempting to make plans for the future, even though we feel like there is no real future for us at all.

As each of my cycles comes and goes, Anush gets more tired and moves more slowly. She coughs a lot more now too.

212

Not the kind of morning cough she has always had that clears away the dusty air of sleep. No, this cough arrives with the daylight, stays past the time of the setting sun then chokes her dreams all through the night. It wakes me up most nights too, but there is nothing much I can do except to bring her water, or warm herbal infusions, and rub her head and back.

Numa stops by most every day during the days of my Moon Blood, and she is here today. However, I don't feel much like talking. Then again, I can't remember the last time I felt like talking at all.

"He's grown taller and broader in his chest," Numa tells Anush while stealing sideways glances at me to see if she can interest me in news of Shelah.

I smile the kind of wan little smile I am sometimes able to muster these days. The effect makes me feel like a mindless goat.

"So, he's old enough to marry now?" Anush looks at me with a small hint of hope in her eyes. "He's ready then?"

I gaze at her without interest in what the two of them are saying about Shelah.

With every passing moon cycle, the grey clouds in Anush's eyes continue to blot out the color that once was so strong in them. Sometimes, when I am near her and look directly into them, I think that they must have been cloudy grey all along instead of the terebinth trunk brown I remember from earlier days.

"Old enough? Yes," Numa answers. "Ready? Not at all. Well, that is to say, *Yehuda* is the one who is not ready... not ready to let him marry quite yet."

"Ah." Anush tries to hide the sound of disappointment in her voice.

I hide my relief by saying nothing and continuing to smile like a mindless goat.

Realizing that they will get no response from me, they turn to their favorite topic: Sh'chem. I now know that all their secrets for all these years have revolved around one thing and one thing only... the city of Sh'chem, the place they call "our home that used to be."

They nearly touch heads as they lean toward one another and lower their voices so I won't hear them as they launch into an animated discussion about this place called Sh'chem, which I know nothing about, other than the fact that they used to live there. Usually, I get nowhere when I pester them with questions about their "home that used to be," but today I am more bored than usual and am determined to learn something new. I wait for them to get comfortably unaware of my presence before I break into their conversation.

"Is it Sh'chem again today?"

They abruptly halt their conversation and look at me as though I just entered the room. They laugh like they have been caught stealing a loaf of lechem from a stall in the shuk but wish to deny it.

"I know, I know, it's your home that used to be, and so you can't help but talk about it, right?"

They glance at each other quickly then shrug their shoulders in unison, as though this is the custom in their old city. They say nothing more.

"Anush-jahn. Numa." I eye them both. "I think it's time for you to tell me more about this place that occupies so many of your thoughts and so much of your hearts."

They look like they've been caught stealing purple silk this time.

"Ah, clever Tamar." Numa always uses this phrase when I get too close to the truth. "Perhaps another time, but not today. I've stayed longer than I should and have to get back to help with the evening meal."

She stands to go.

"Ah, how clever of *you*, Numa, to have timed your visit so well."

She laughs, and I smile a little more than a mindless goat might.

Anush begins to chuckle, but a fierce wet cough fights to

steal her breath away.

I pat her back gently. "Are you okay?"

She tries to speak, but cannot. She waves me away with her wrist as if to say, "It's nothing at all."

Numa goes to a table in the corner of the room and pours a cup of water from a clay pitcher then hurries back to Anush with it. Anush waves it away too.

"Does this happen often?" Numa looks at me.

"More and more with each moon cycle, but this is worse than usual."

"Has she gone to the priests? Have they sprinkled the Apsu water over her and said the Siptu prayers?"

"No, she won't go… says she doesn't believe in it anymore."

"I don't blame her."

Suddenly, the cough stops. Anush breathes as though she's been underwater for days and has just come up for air.

"Oh thank Ba'al, you are still with us!" Numa crouches down and gives Anush the cup of water, which she eagerly accepts this time.

"Yes, thank Ba'al I am still here." She shrugs. "But I need to rest now, Numa, so I hope you won't mind if I don't get up and walk you to your house."

"Of course I don't mind, Anush. Rest, dear friend."

Numa looks at me with a worried expression.

"I'll stay with her. This is my last day for the Moon Blood, so tomorrow I'll be sure to get her outside for some fresh air."

"Good, good. I'll go now then. Be well, and may Ba'al protect you both through the night."

"And you," Anush responds.

Then Numa is gone.

I turn to Anush. "The cough is much worse, Anush-jahn. Last night in your sleep it sounded like you were choking."

"It's nothing, Katu, nothing."

"Stop trying to fool me. Of course it is something, something terrible, and you know it."

Her face softens with a far-away look, as though some

215

secret still occupies her eyes.

"I know, Katu, I know. I am not fooling you or myself. I know how serious this is. So serious, in fact, I need you to do something for me."

"Anything, Anush-jahn, anything. Just tell me what you need me to do."

A rasping sound in her chest is almost as loud as her sigh. "I need you to take me to your Imma's cave tomorrow."

I stiffen.

"I know you don't want to go there, don't want the waters anymore, not after what people have said about your powers being evil and greater than that of the Apsu waters and the Siptu prayers of the priests... about your waters causing death."

I say nothing.

"Katu, you *know* what the people say is nonsense."

I refuse to speak.

"You know you did not cause the deaths."

"Do I? Do I know it is nonsense? No, I think they might be right. I think it might be the waters in the cave that give me this death power. What else could it be? Why else did Er, Onan and Illit die? Only you and I go to the cave, no one else. But I am the *only* one who was present at the deaths. You didn't see the terror in Illit's eyes, you didn't feel the coldness of Onan's flesh, you didn't watch the blood turn Er's wedding garments red, didn't witness his food and drink rise and fall back into him, so it cannot be *you* who caused the deaths. No, I do not know if it is nonsense or not."

I turn away from her as the full wave of guilt for the three deaths pours over me.

She doesn't speak for quite some time, and I wonder if she is asleep. I turn back to her. She looks straight at me as though I never moved.

I wait.

She waits.

Then she speaks. "Tamoosh-jahn, there are things I must

tell you, and there is no time left to do so. You must take me to the cave tomorrow. We must go to the secret chamber. You must help me to get there. You *must*."

"No! I don't want to go, Anush-jahn. Tell me these things anywhere else. Tell me here or out in the fields, but *not* in the cave, not even *near* the cave!"

She pauses as though considering my suggestion.

"You don't understand yet, Katu," she says at last. "No, I must tell you in the secret chamber. Otherwise you will never know."

"Never know what? Why can't you tell me now? Here, where you will not have to walk up the rocky path, where you will not have to crouch into tunnels and hurt your back. Tell me here, Anush-jahn. I beg you, tell me here."

She breathes slowly and deliberately, as though trying to hold back the rasp in her chest as it marches toward war.

"If you take me there tomorrow, as I ask, if you honor your promise to do anything at all to help me then I will tell you more about Sh'chem. It is time, Tamar. You must take me before the sun reaches the highest point in the sky. You *must*, Yakiri."

She uses the one word that can bring me back to her then implores me with her cloudy eyes.

I let out the tension of my tightened breath.

"All right. You win. Even if you don't tell me about Sh'chem, I will take you there, Anush-jahn."

Tears spill from my eyes.

"Shoosh-shoosh, Katu, shoosh-shoosh."

* * *

At times along the steep path leading to the cave, I think Anush will not make it through the dust and heat; but she stops often, gathers her strength then leans on me so that we can go on. By the time we make it to the terebinth tree and the rock near the cave, she barely stands upright. We rest against the rock until she is ready to walk the last few steps to the cave entrance.

"Your Dukifat's nest was here, was it not?" She tilts her head toward the branches of the tree and smiles mischievously. "You see, I do remember."

I squeeze her hand. "You remember everything, Anush-jahn. I realize that now."

She squeezes my hand. "Shall we go on then, Katu? I am ready."

"Yes."

She breathes hard as she makes it to the cave entrance, breathes harder as she makes it to the tunnels where we turn and turn but do not scrape or bump our heads. She makes it to the secret cavern and the women on the walls, makes it to the pool of waters, makes it to all of these places, but only just barely.

I help her sit down near the pool. She is weak and cannot help me with her own strength, so her weight seems heavier to me than when we started.

She labors to keep breathing as her chest heaves and rasps, heaves and rasps.

I look around while I wait for her to gather enough strength to tell me what she must tell me.

Even though I have refused to come here since Illit died over a year ago, the women on the walls do not seem to have missed me at all. They still smile and dance naked in their places, they still pour oil over one another and rub each other's shoulders and feet. They are still content to be where they are, content to do what they do best, content to defy time and all the trouble it brings.

The unchanging pictures of the stories they might tell could they but speak mingle with the impermeability of their abiding and joyful strength. All of this floods me with a sense of relief, a sense of sacred awe, as though they include me in their secrets, as though they allow me to breathe in vigor of my own from what they know.

Anush coughs; I turn my eyes away from the women on the walls.

"I am ready now, Tamoosh-jahn." Anush's voice is weak but determined.

"I am ready too, Anush-jahn."

A look of contentment washes over her face as she smiles at the women on the walls, smiles at the pool of waters, smiles at what must be memories formed here long ago. She sits in the stillness of the moment as though she will never experience it again, then takes a deep breath and gathers her eyes back to me.

"What I am going to tell you I have told no one else, not Numa, not even your Imma. I have locked these secrets inside me since the day I left Sh'chem. All these years I have wanted to speak, wanted to tell the story, wanted you to know what happened."

She pauses and breathes heavily before continuing.

"Yes, I lived in Sh'chem. My life there was neither hard nor easy. It was a happy life filled with the love of a husband and children who made me laugh, made me cry, made me live every moment as though another might never come.

"Then, one fatal night arrived on the heels of a day that should never have dawned, and everything came to an end, not only for me, but for all the men, women and children of Sh'chem. One horrible measure of time that changed hundreds of lives forever."

I barely breathe.

"On the night that robbed us of all we held dearest, two men... wait, I get ahead of myself."

She coughs and pauses.

"Are you sure you want to go on, Anush-jahn? Perhaps these memories will swallow your breath too fast."

"No. It doesn't matter now. All that matters is that I go back in the story a bit, for I must first tell you more about one person, someone you already know."

"Numa? Besides you, she's the only person I know from Sh'chem."

"No, not Numa."

"Who then?"

She breathes heavily then catches her breath before answering.

"Yehuda."

I gasp. "Yehuda? He was in Sh'chem too?"

"Yes, for a short time," she rasps, "and if he had not been, I would not be alive today, you would not know about this place, nor would I be telling you this story."

She peers at me, and seems to hear the questions forming behind my eyes.

"Yes, Yehuda lived in Sh'chem. Not inside the city's walls though. He and his family—a rather large one—lived outside the city in ohelim."

"In ohelim?" I ask, intrigued by this idea. "Do you mean they lived like the Elamites who roam the region? I've always wondered about the ohel that Yehuda keeps outside Adullam's walls, but thought that he had kept it as part of his sheep business, as a place for his overseer to live in. But are you saying that his family actually lived in these ohelim like the Elamites?"

"Somewhat like that," she answers, "but different. Yehuda's family bought a piece of land from Hamor, who was the king of the city, and on that land they pitched their ohelim. And yes, they did live in them. It was as if they were a part of us— those who lived inside the city gates—but were not, if that makes any sense."

It doesn't, but I don't ask her to explain as I wait for her to continue.

"Hamor had a son named Sh'chem, the same as the city name. Yehuda had a sister named Dinah. She was very beautiful and the only girl in the large family of Yehuda's father, Ya'akov, who had four wives and twelve sons. Yehuda is Ya'akov's fourth son."

I have never thought about Yehuda having any family other than the one I know, the one I grew up with here in Adullam;

but I keep my thoughts to myself because I want to hear the rest of what Anush needs to tell me.

"None of that is important now." She coughs again and stops.

I pat her hand and take a deep breath, wondering how long she can continue to tell this tale. She squeezes my hand and waits a bit more before she continues.

"The important thing is what happened to Dinah, for that is what set everything in motion. Sh'chem fell in love with her, and some say she loved him as well. He took her into his bed. Some say against her will, some say with her blessing. We will never know the truth of it, for Sh'chem is dead and so are all the men and boys from my city."

She braces to keep breathing, and we both wait for a coughing fit to pass.

I brace myself for what might come next.

"The problem with the two of them sleeping together was a simple one. No one had asked for Ya'akov's permission, no one had negotiated a mohar or nedoonyat, and no matan had been given."

"That's terrible, Anush."

"Terrible that they broke the rules, yes, but such outrageous behavior is not uncommon. What came next was far more terrible than a man taking liberties with a woman, or a woman allowing those liberties without the proper negotiations between the families taking place."

These words set off another coughing fit, and I try to help her, but she waves me away then presses her hand hard against her chest, as though keeping it there will force her short and diminishing puffs of air to continue long enough for her to finish the story.

"When Hamor realized what had happened, he hastily assembled a group of elders and negotiated a mohar bargain with Ya'akov and his sons. Hamor and the men of the city agreed that as part of their bride price for Dinah, all of them—from the oldest of the elders to the youngest of the boys—would submit to the ritual of what Yehuda's family calls the milah, the cutting off of the foreskin from the male sex member."

I don't say anything, or even flinch. After what I have learned about the red mead and the strange rituals of our *own* priests, and after the shocking deaths I have witnessed, nothing surprises me, not even hearing about this peculiar practice of cutting off the flesh from a man's organ.

She pauses and looks at me as though asking if I want to hear more.

"Go on Anush-jahn. Finish your story," I say softly.

"Sh'chem was the first to go under the knife. His father and all the males in the household were next. Then the rest of the men in the city carried out their part of the bargain too, the bargain they believed would later allow them to marry and have children from the bloodline of Ya'akov, which in turn would then allow them to partake of his wealth.

"I and the other women of Sh'chem felt strongly that their thinking about this last part was the wrong way to look at things. Oh, we understood why they would want to enjoy the somewhat legendary wealth of Ya'akov, not to mention the legendary wealth of his Grand Abba, Avraham, who had come through Sh'chem before him, but we could see that they were letting their greed get in the way of their common sense. We voiced our concerns about it to our husbands, fathers, and the other male members of our families, but what man ever listens to a woman?"

I have no answer for that question, so she shrugs then pushes on.

"Three days after the milah, while they were all still in pain on their beds, two of Yehuda's older brothers stole into the city in the dark of night. They slaughtered every man and boy, old and young. Not one male was spared."

Anush closes her eyes as though the memory of that horrible night seeks to blind her. She breathes heavily again, and the rasp in her chest sounds like it is winning the war.

"Rest a bit, Anush-jahn. This is too hard for you."

She flicks the air with her wrist and shakes her head.

"No, I must go on. There is still more you need to know."

"Why must I know, Anush-jahn? What does this awful story have to do with me?"

"All in time, Katu. All in time."

She shifts her weight to lessen the pressure on her back.

"Help me to lie down, Tamoosh-jahn." She struggles to get these words out.

As I gently lower her into a reclining position, I worry over the hoarseness in her voice, but say nothing.

"A few of the women tried to save their men and boys. Those women were killed too. I was one of the women who tried to save my husband and my sons."

"You had sons? I never knew that, Anush-jahn."

She looks at me sadly, pats my hand. Another coughing fit hits her.

"Isn't it enough now?" I urge. "Surely you can stop so that you can breathe better?"

She closes her eyes and shakes her head then waits for the cough to stop before continuing her story.

"I did not succeed in saving my husband or my sons, though."

She looks at the women on the wall.

"It was Yehuda's brother, you see," she says, her voice barely above a whisper. "Levi. His name was Levi." She pauses as though the memory is too hard for her to continue, then shakes her head as if to push away the pain.

"Yehuda's brother?" My voice trembles. "Oh, Anush-jahn, I can't believe it."

She doesn't seem to hear me as she drones on like she is walking among the dead.

"When I saw the lifeless bodies of my husband and sons, I screamed and screamed, but this only enraged Levi. He shouted at me to stop. I tried to stop. I honestly tried to stop... but I could not."

Her chest heaves with a rasping sigh. My own breath comes in shorter and shallower spurts as the full horror of the story envelops me.

"I was wearing a pair of earrings at the time, and Levi wanted them. I would have given them to him to save my life, but by this time he was so filled with the feeling of power in his veins that he didn't want to wait. He wanted more blood. He lifted his knife to slit my throat so that he could rip the earrings off my ears.

"At the very moment that I thought I would never see the sun again, Yehuda crept into the room, and before Levi could strike me with the knife, Yehuda grabbed his brother's wrist. They fought. Levi slashed Yehuda's hand, but Yehuda overpowered him. Levi released his grip, growled in defeat and ran back into the streets."

I feel like I am back in the shuk, reliving that horrible moment before Yehuda rescued me, that moment when I too thought I would never see the sun again. My heart thumps now with the panic I felt back then.

Anush coughs again, and the sound of it pulls me away from the memory of the shuk.

"I ripped a piece of cloth from my dead husband's sleeping garment, and without saying a word, wrapped Yehuda's hand in it. Silently, I handed him the earrings then faded into the darkness of the inner rooms of my house. Since my family members were all dead, I later stole out into the night to find a safer shelter, a safer place to hide.

"The morning after the slaughter, Ya'akov, Yehuda's father, gave orders for all the dead bodies to be piled in a pyre and burned. He also told his sons to gather up all the women, girls, livestock, jewelry, food, and anything else of value.

"I wanted to rush at Ya'akov and his sons and tear out their eyes, but I kept myself hidden and watched as all that was left of my friends and our city's possessions became the spoils of war."

Anush's shoulders droop as though a great weight has

fallen on them. She coughs now and again, but does not speak for a long time.

I do not move or say a word.

When she stirs again, her voice is barely a whisper.

"Of all the people in the city, I was the only one who escaped."

Haltingly, she continues as though the sound of her voice might carry her back into the memory so far she will not be able to return.

"Near one of the sacred altars under the great Terebinths of Moreh, Ya'akov ordered the women to throw all their jewels and idols into a deep hole his sons had dug. Hidden behind one of the terebinths, where no one could see me, I watched as the women and girls dropped their treasures into the dark dirt. I watched as they left behind their previous lives, and were herded like sheep to the road that would take them to the Ridge Route. As everyone disappeared into the hills, I listened to their cries join with the howls of the jackals, and out of my life forever.

"Until I found Numa here in Adullam—

"No, I cannot speak of that now. There is still too much to tell you before I do that."

She has little strength left, but I know she will not stop until everything inside her is set free.

"Yehuda stayed behind to cover the hole holding the jewelry and idols. I saw him take my earrings out of his bag and place them on top of the pile. The moon cast a light on them, but it seemed as though the light came from *within* the earrings rather than from the moon. Yehuda saw this strange wonder too, gasped then reached out to retrieve the earrings. He hesitated before he touched them, though, then pulled his hand away, covered the hole and was gone.

"I waited until I could no longer hear the jackals howling in the hills. Then I dug away the dirt from the top of the hole. I quickly took my earrings back and rescued every piece of the most valuable jewelry I could find. I placed it all in a large sheepskin bag then covered up the hole and returned to my hiding place."

Anush's effort has been too great. When she coughs this time I see red specks on her hands. She sees them too and looks at me as if asking me to wave them away from her because she can no longer do so herself.

I gently wipe off the red specks with the skirt of my halug then stroke her hand and give her kisses on her cheeks.

"You do not have to tell me more, Anush-jahn. This is enough."

"No, there is more. I will finish. Just let me lean on you."

I hold her as she leans on my chest. She seems so small now, as though the release of her memories has robbed most of the flesh from her body.

Her voice is even more breathless than when she started, and her coughs frequently interrupt her words.

"The bracelets I gave you on your twelfth birthday... they came from what I rescued that night... other things for you were purchased... with jewelry from the bag... but most of it is still there... enough wealth... to live comfortably... no matter what Yergat does... no matter what the city says... no matter what Yehuda decides... about Shelah."

Anush's eyes blaze with an inner light that pierces through the cloudy gray pools that have made me wonder if she has seen the world as a gray place for this past year, this year that has taken away so much of the color from both of our lives. That blaze of light now seems to rush into her arm. She takes my hand as though her remaining strength marshals itself into each of her fingers. Her grip is so strong I almost cry out in pain.

"Remember this Tamar. As a widow... you are still under Yehuda's... legal authority, and you... must make sure he fulfills his obligation to... marry you to Shelah. You must raise up... seed from the bloodline of his family."

I suck in my breath and stiffen.

"You *must*, Katu."

She releases her hold on my hand, and we sit in the ancient silence that speaks from the women of the walls.

"Now help me sit up. I must tell you how to find the jewels... how to keep them hidden, how you must never... never take them into Yergat's house. You will need to know... who you can trust in the city... to sell them if the need arises."

I say nothing as I help her to sit upright.

"Go to the other side of the pool, Katu."

"But Anush-jahn, I need to stay by your side and—"

"No! Do not take my strength away by hesitating. I have little time left. Go!"

Trying hard not to feel like I am abandoning her, I stand, walk around the pool and leave her by herself.

"Behind the women... directly past the pool... one woman wears a pendant... gold chain... around her neck. Do you see her?"

I peer at all the women.

"I think so. Is the color of the pendant amber?"

"Yes. Touch the pendant... an indentation... pull the stone toward you. Gently."

Her voice fades, and I look back. She flicks her wrist at me, but does not speak.

I turn back to the stone and feel for the indentation.

"I found it, Anush-jahn." I look at her. Again she flicks her wrist.

I pull on the stone, and to my great surprise, the outlined edges of a large square I could not see before form a frame around the woman.

"Keep pulling... slowly."

The stone moves effortlessly, as though hinged, but I see no hinges, and cannot understand how it moves.

"Put your hand... inside."

Anush's voice is so weak I want to forget the bag and the jewels and rush to her side.

She notices my hesitation and shakes her head as if to say, "forget about me."

JOY SIKORSKI ~ MICHAEL SILVERSHER

I feel behind the stone with my fingers. There is a space there, a hidden alcove. I cannot see anything, but I search with my hand for what I am sure will be Anush's bag from Sh'chem.

"Did you find anything?"

She sounds frightened, as though she has held back her secrets for so long that the bag may have been stolen.

Suddenly, I feel the bag. "I found it," I call out.

"Good." I hear her breathe deeply. "Bring it."

I pull out the bag and take it to Anush. Her eyes are pinched in pain, but her lips curl into a grin that looks like it has waited all the years since the massacre to find a way out of its dark hiding place.

"Yes, that's it. I have long envisioned this moment, Katu." She closes her eyes and breathes more easily than she has for weeks. "Now open it."

I set it down beside her and pull on the sheepskin straps that bind it. I am astonished by what I see inside. Treasures from an entire city are there: necklaces of gold and silver, amulets and bracelets, hairpins and rings, golden cups and small idols.

I do not touch anything. These are sacred objects purchased with the lives of those who lost their freedom and all they held dear, purchased by their loved ones whose ashes *surely* must still cry out as they continue to seek rest on the winds of the desert.

I look at Anush. "What should I do, Anush-jahn? What should I do?"

"Find the amber earrings. They are the most valuable pieces. They are the ones that Levi sought to take from me, the ones that Yehuda buried, the ones that I rescued."

Her voice is less labored than before, and her next words come at me rapid-fire, as though all her remaining strength musters to snatch away the looming victory of the rasp in her chest.

"They belonged to your Grand Imma, Ditzah. She treated

me like a daughter, and gave them to me. I was married to Ishkhan, the son of the brother of her husband. There is a story to these earrings. It goes back beyond Ditzah... beyond her Imma, and her Imma's Imma. So far back that I cannot take the time to explain it now.

"Find the earrings... let me see them... near your face... then we will go."

She is losing the battle. Quickly, I dig through the jewels until I see something glowing as though the full moon shines from within it. One of the earrings! I carefully lift it out of the bag and take the matching one beneath it too. I turn so that Anush can see me better. She smiles. I place them near my ears. She sighs deeply. A quiet sense of contentment fills me.

Now, as though the moon has also taken up residence inside of Anush's eyes, I watch as she too succumbs to contentment, even as the rattling breath of Mot hovers around her next words.

"It is time, Tamar... It is... time."

* * *

In the darkest moments of the night, when only owls and jackals dare to move about, our house is quiet as Mot curls his deathly fingers around the one I love, the one who struggles for air so near the threshold of his dark and dusty kingdom.

In short, barely audible sounds Anush's breath seeks its resting place.

I sit beside her on her bed and wipe her brow with wet cloths and sing the melodies from my childhood she once sang to me.

I do not weep. I will not waste these last precious moments of her life with my tears. Later, I will water my garments of grieving with my sorrows. Now I only want to look upon her and wonder at all the strength she conveyed to me through the silences of her secrets. I want to hear her voiceless words echoing from her heart to mine before they speak no more. I want her to know that I am here.

I look out the small window in our room and search for the light in the black spaces between the brightest stars, the ones Anush told me I would learn to see. Tonight, however, as though a think veil covers all light, even the brightest stars seem as though they've been snuffed out.

All of a sudden, my noorshma groans and cries out with a great noise.

I gather her in my arms.

"Shoosh-shoosh, Anush-jahn. Shoosh-shoosh."

Widows Weeds

"None of the daughters of Yisrael shall be a kedeshah."
—Devarim 23:18

EACH MORNING before the moon hands its scepter of light back to the sun, and before anyone in our house stirs, I rise, dress quietly and slip out like a cat in the dark to make my way to the rock beside the terebinth tree near my cave.

I have done so every morning since the day Mot swept Anush up and out of her body in the same way that the sun, moon and stars devour one another in a never-ending cycle of time.

Today, I sit and listen to the sounds of birds and other animals rejoice over another day to live, another day to busy themselves finding food and fussing with their nests and sleeping places, another day to dispel yesterday's digested grains and bugs and catch up with one another on what goes on in their lives.

I ponder everything Anush told me before she died and try to piece together the most important parts that will lead me in the direction I must take to form my future.

After I returned the jewels to their hiding place, Anush and I painstakingly made our way out of the cave, down the path and back to our room where she tried to tell me about the source of the amber that gives the earrings their strange and wondrous inner moonlight glow. By then however, the rattle of Mot was too strong, and she fell silent.

Clearly, she meant for me to understand the power of the

earrings, to perceive when to wear them and when not to wear them. But without knowing the last part of the story Anush meant to tell, I am not sure what to do with them now that they are mine.

Nonetheless, of this I *am* sure: she made it clear that I must find a way to hold Yehuda to his legal obligation to marry me to Shelah, so that I can raise up seed from his bloodline.

As of yet, he has not honored his word to entrust me with his third and last son. In fact, I am now certain that he fully intends to leave me at Yergat's house indefinitely and keep me from his own home so that he can find Shelah another wife. I know this because I overheard Yergat complain to Bushra about it one night when they were in Yergat's business room and didn't know that I was in the storage room peeking through the crack in the wall. Not only that, their conversation alerted me to an even greater danger.

Fortunately, or perhaps not—only the ongoing cycles of the sun and moon will show me for sure—Anush foresaw the likelihood that what I heard that night might come to pass. Before she died she told me what to do if either or both of these dread possibilities began to materialize. Her words still make me cringe: "Before you do what I suggest, be very sure that you understand the consequences; for as I have clearly explained, if you should have to carry out this plan, and you succeed with it, Yehuda will have the legal right to have you killed."

I shudder.

Oh, if only I could hear my beloved noorshma's voice again, if only I could lean on her this morning, if only I could listen to her assurances that what I plan to do with the earrings will work.

But I cannot. Her voice is only a murmur on the wind now.

Suddenly, a dukifat sings out, "Boop-boop-boop… boop-boo."

I sing back to her, "Boop-boop-boop… boop-boo."

She laughs and changes her tune. "Boop-boop-boop… boo."

I echo her then carefully part the branches where she hides. She still looks like she doesn't know her front side from her backside.

As I watch her build a new nest, I realize that whether or not she looks like she's coming or going she knows exactly what she is doing.

I smile and say, "That is okay, my little Dukifat friend. Never mind. You and I both know what to do, don't we?"

I look over the city of Adullam and almost laugh at its position on the hill, at the walls of stone that pretend to have the power to keep out all intruders.

I am Adullam.

Anush was the wall that protected me during these seventeen years of my life.

She is gone, but the secret of her inner strength is not, and because of it I am no longer in doubt about what I must do to open the gate of my own strength.

As the sun continues to awaken the vibrant colors in the Valley of Elah and to search out the hidden darkness in the secret spaces which surround the rocks and trees, flowers and leaves, soil and water, I stand and walk to the cave.

* * *

Gannitha has come and gone.

Sheep shearing has begun.

Yehuda, Hirah, Yergat and other men from the city make their plans to go to the annual sheep-shearing festival where they will eat, drink, carouse, buy and sell animals, wool, leather items and anything else that finds its way into the shuks of Timnah.

I prepare too.

The time of grieving for Er, Onan, Illit and Anush is over, and the time for my future has arrived at long last.

Early in the morning, I make my way up the hill to the cave. Once again I go to the pool of waters and wash away all that troubles me. Once again I walk naked to the woman on the wall and touch her amber pendant. Once again I take out the bag of Anush's treasures, open it and see the light of the moon radiating from inside Anush's amber earrings.

I take out her earrings along with other jewelry too. Bracelets, gold hairpins, silver and gold necklaces, glass beads, rings, and anything else that will make me shine like the moon tonight.

Near the pool, my widow's weeds lie in a heap. Dark in color and coarse in texture, these garments will not serve my purposes today.

The women on the walls laugh as I slather myself with perfumed oils and tenderly pat myself with soft linen cloths to soak up the excess.

Beside my widow's weeds, soft tufts of silken fabrics that I have purchased in the shuk catch light coming down from the opening high in the dome of the cave. Vibrant colors dance through their threads as I slip them onto my body, wrap them around my head, cover all my flesh with them, even my face.

Especially my face, for no one must know who I am today.

I place bejeweled slippers on my feet—they are the kind that a new bride might wear. Next, I layer myself with the jewelry I have chosen to wear.

The last things I put on are the amber earrings.

They belong to me now and give me the final strength I need to complete my task.

As I sit beneath a terebinth tree beside the road that leads to Timnah and wait for Yehuda to pass by on his way to the sheep-shearing festival, I know that I am not alone. Anush's voice whispers through the warm air, Ditzah calls out to me from her memories in Sh'chem, and I hear a faint melody from a far-away voice I cannot identify.

Under my veils Yehuda will think I am a zonah, but I am not. I will take no payment for what I am about to give him.

Nor am I a kedeshah, for I will give no Moon Blood, nor

enter into any sacred marriage.

With anyone.

Ever.

I see him now. He makes his way along the road with Hirah at his side.

The last slanting rays of the sun reach through the purple and gold luminance of my veils to gently touch my face, and then they combine with the inner moonlight power of the amber earrings.

My time has come.

Yehuda sees me, points then says something to Hirah. Hirah looks at me, nods to Yehuda then continues on the road to Timnah alone.

Beside me terebinth leaves rustle.

Through my veils I whisper to the wind.

"It is time, Yehuda. It is time."

Glossary

NOTE: Places and terms are understood to be transliterations of actual Hebrew, Canaanite, Sumerian, Babylonian, Armenian, Persian, Phoenician, Akkadian or Arabic words unless otherwise noted with two asterisks (**). Asterisks indicate terms or names we have created.

Adama: Adam

Adon or adon: Hebrew term of respect similar to sir, master, father

Adullam: one of the royal cities of Canaan located northwest of Kirjath-arba (Hebron) where Hirah lives and where Yehuda settles. Also see the Valley of Elah

Alashiya: ancient name for Cyprus

amnoon or amnun: freshwater fish native to Israel, commonly known as talapia

Annunaki: Sumerian fertility deities of the oldest primordial line; and judges of the dead

** Anush: an older woman who raises Tamar. Also see "noorshma"

Apsu: a Babylonian or Akkadian term for the waters of the deep that have medicinal powers of healing in the Babylonian religion (also see Enki)

Aqhat: a purple merchant (also see tamkarum) of Adullam and husband to Bushra

Araratyan: the plains and hills near Mount Ararat

ard or bow ard: a primitive hand plow used as early as 3,000-2,000 BCE

Asherah: a fertility mother goddess sometime identified as the wife of the Sumerian god Anu or the Ugaritic god El, the oldest deities of the Kn'n pantheon

Atagartis: chief fertility goddess of ancient northern Syria, popularly known as the "mermaid goddess"

Auroch: a now extinct species of wild cattle, probably the forerunner of the zebu in India and the domesticated cows of today

Azeka: an ancient town outside the Valley of Elah

Ba'al: Biblically, this name is used to mean any number of local spirits or deities in the ancient Near East that are worshipped in a cult

baba ghanoush: Arabic for an eggplant recipe made from eggplant, tahini, olive oil, lemon and spices and sometimes dressed with a mixture of olive oil and pomegranate syrup

Be'eirot: Beirut, Lebanon

Beersheva: Beersheba

Beleti: Sumerian for "lady," which the authors turned into a name for Illit that means "woman of high and royal birth"

bulla: In Sumerian and Babylonian times, a round ball of hollowed out clay with a lid and identifying marks on it. Inside, small tokens were used as a form of monetary exchange for goods, services, loans and receipts. The bulla and tokens were marked with the symbol of its owner as evidence of who bought or sold items

Bushra: wife of Aqhat and mother of Shulgi, Hazibah and Mirah

Calanit: Hebrew name for a flowering plant (Anemone Coronaria) that is native to the Mediterranean region. Its name comes from the root word for bride (Cala) because the beauty and majesty of the flower evokes the idea of a bride on her wedding day. It became the national flower of Israel in 2013

Canaan: a land in the ancient Near East, the borders of which would roughly approximate (according to various archeological sources) the land masses of present-day Israel, Syria, Jordan, Lebanon and parts of Turkey. In our *Judah and Tamar Trilogy*, it is the place where Ya'akov and his family lived before they moved to Egypt. The inhabitants included the sons and daughters of Noah, Shem, Ham and Japheth (see also the definitions for the word "Kn'n")

chamas: Hebrew for unclean in the ritual sense

da-na: Sumerian measurement of distance roughly equal to a league or 10,800 meters

Ditanua legendary figure who may have been the primary ancestor of all Ugaritic and Caananite kings

dukifat: a hoopoe bird, the national bird of Israel

Ebla: an ancient city southwest of Aleppo, Syria (Aleppo is one of the oldest cities in the world that has been consistently and continuously inhabited)

el-ee: Hebrew word for pestle used for grinding grains and legumes. Used with medokah (mortar)

emmer: ancient form of wheat that grew wild in the ancient Near East

Enki: (or Ea) a Sumerian god of the water of life (or Apsu waters) who is married to Nimhursag, goddess of earth. As mentioned in the epic *Enki and Nimhursag,* these two and their doings represent one of the oldest creation myths and are part of the Annunaki pantheon

Er: first son of Yehuda and Illit; also Tamar's first husband

erusin: first part of the ancient Hebrew wedding ceremony that is known as the betrothal of a bride and groom. At the betrothal the woman and man were legally married, although the woman still remained in her father's house and the marriage was not yet consummated. She could not belong to another man unless she was divorced from her betrothed (also see nissuin)

Galil: Galilee

** Gannitha: a sacred festival the authors created by combining Sumerian, Babylonia and Canaanite religious and agricultural festival practices (Akitu, Gannu, Ba'al Cycle

Great Sea: the Mediterranean Ocean

Habiru: name given to various roaming bands of bandits and marauders who struck at villages and city-states from Mesopotamia to Egypt from 1800-1100 BCE. They were not necessarily organized by cultural or language ties, but they were also known to join with mercenary groups from the region to create a more powerful force for battles and looting

halug: an outer tunic made of fine linen or wool worn by both men and women in ancient Kn'n. Consisting of a large rectangular piece of cloth with holes for the head and the arms, it was gathered up at shoulders and held with a clip or a tip-loop so that it would drape gracefully. It was worn with a belt of leather, metal or cloth, it, which was either simple or elaborate, depending on the wearer and the amount of his or her wealth

Hammurabi's Code: more often known as the *Code of Hammurabi,* which is a Babylonian code of law written in circa 1,772 BCE by the sixth king of Babylon

hattah: Arabic for a scarf worn as either a headscarf or a loose head covering by women

Hattusa: Hittite city burned and cursed by Anitta, King of Kussara, a Bronze Age kingdom in Anatolia (modern-day Turkey)

Hava: Eve

Hayk: modern-day Armenia before it was called Urartu. The word comes from the name of the ruler Hayk who is considered to be the great-great-grandson of Noah.

Hazibah: Bushra's oldest daughter and one of Tamar's stepsisters

Hazor: ancient Canaanite city located north of the Sea of Galilee (Sea of Kinneret). From the Middle Bronze era (circa 1750 BCE) to the Israelite period (circa night-century BCE), it was the largest fortified city in the region and one of the most influential ones in the Fertile Crescent

Hevron: Hebron (see Kirjath-Arba) in Israel

Hirah: purple merchant in Adullam and friend/business partner of Yehuda (also see tamkarum)

Hittite: an ancient Anatolian (Turkish) people

hogh: Armenian hill or mound

hogi: Armenian for soul

hogoc: expression (possibly Armenian) for a sigh of frustration or exasperation or weariness

Hurrian: a people of the Bronze Age Near East in northwest Mesopotamia that heavily influenced the Hittite culture

Hyksos: A Canaanite people that took over the Nile Delta and ended the Thirteen dynasty of Egypt and began the Second Intermediate Period of Egypt

Illit: daughter of Shua, wife of Yehuda and mother of Er, Onan and Shelah

Imma: Hebrew word for mother

Irkalla: a city in the dusts of the underworld of the Babylonians (see Kur), similar in meaning to Sheol, Hades, Hell, Gehenna

ka'mun: Semitic word for cumin

Kassites: an ancient Near East people (most likely originating in the modern-day Iran region) who eventually ruled the Babylonian culture for approximately five hundred years

Katu: Armenian transliteration for kitten

kedeshah: Hebrew for a sacred prostitute in ancient pagan religions who did not take payment for her services

Khnum: one of the earliest Egyptian deities, he was considered the god of the Nile

kilim or killim: from the Persian for a colorful rug, usually of wool or linen that is made by tightly weaving together the warp and weft strands to create a flat surface with no pile

Kingdom of Mot: a dark dusty place where all who die live as "ghosts or shades." Mot is the Ugaritic god of death who is defeated by Ba'al during the spring festival

Kinneret, Sea of: Sea of Galilee

kinnor: Hebrew for ancient harp

Kirjath-arba: ancient name for Hevron (Hebron), a city approximately 19 miles south of Yerushalayim (Jerusalem). This is the place where the Cave of Mamre, or the Cave of the Patriarchs and Matriarchs is located. It is also where Ya'akov lived before the famine that took his family into Egypt

kisum: in Sumerian and Babylonian times, a merchant pouch for money and/or weighing stones, as well as marked clumps or small balls of clay with the merchant's identifying mark on them to indicate values for items purchased, or as a form of receipt

Kn'n: Ancient Canaan (see also the definition for "Canaan")

Kohar: Anush's sister; Yergat's mother and Tamar's grandmother. Derived from an Armenian name that means jewel.

Kur: the dark place of the underworld in Babylonian mythology. Also known as Kurnugi

Lebonah: Hebrew for frankincense

lechem: Hebrew for bread

limnu: the Semitic root (Babylonian) for the word evil

Magan: Sumerian for an ancient region in Mesopotamia, perhaps Oman, Yemen or possibly Nubia, Iran or Pakistan

marru: the Semitic root (Babylonian) for the word bitter

masgouf: Iraqi Arabic for an ancient and traditional Middle East dish made from roasted carp

matan: gifts given to the bride by the groom. This is not part of the mohar, or bride price that has been previously agreed upon

mazzevah: Hebrew for a simple altar of unhewn stones, sometimes called a pillar of stones

mecholah: ancient form of circle dance usually used danced in celebrations of joy

medokah: Hebrew for stone mortar used for grinding grains and legumes. Used with an eli or el-ee, which is a pestle

Midyat: an ancient Hurrian town in what is now southeast Turkey

milah: Hebrew for circumcision

Mirah: Bushra's youngest daughter and one of Tamar's stepsisters

Mitanni: a Hurrian speaking state in north Syria and south-east Anatolia

mohar: the bride price that is paid by the groom's father to the father of the bride. It is paid because the bride's family loses a valuable home and reproductive asset—the woman—and the groom's family gains it

Moloch: an ancient Ammorite god usually associated with the ritual of passing children through a fire to make the immortal

Mot: the Ugaritic god of death

nedoonyat: a dowry payable by the father of a bride to the groom's family

Ninma: Nimhursag, one of the original fertility goddesses; the wife Enki (see Enki) and also one of the Annunaki (see Annunaki)

nissuin: the second part of the wedding ceremony in ancient Israel and still utilized today in some circles. The nissuin meant only that the betrothed (see erusin) woman, accompanied by a colorful procession, was brought from her father's house to the house of her betrothed husband, where the legal tie with him was consummated

**** noorshma**: a caregiver/nursemaid/nanny/wise woman (usually a member of the father's family and never a young woman) who raises a baby who has lost its mother in childbirth or infancy. We created it from an Arabic word that means light and a Hebrew word that means listen to or pay attention to, so you might say that it means to listen to the light, with light meaning wisdom

ohel: Hebrew word for tent (plural ohelim)

Onan: second son of Yehuda and Illit and second husband of Tamar

Paltibaal: Kn'n male name meaning Baal is my refuge

Paras: Persia (modern-day Iran)

Rapi'uma: the Ugaritic concept of the shades or spirits of the dead

Ridge Route: ancient north-south trade route in Kn'n that follows the watershed ridge line of the Samarian and Judean Mountains. It runs from Megiddo and Hazor south to Beersheba by way of Sh'chem, Bethel, Jerusalem, Ephrath and Hebron. Unlike the Via Maris and the King's Highway which were international roads crossing the territories of many peoples, the Ridge Route was wholly within the territory of ancient Israel

Salt Sea: the Dead Sea

Set: or Seth, the son of Adam and Eve that replaced Cain after he was slain

sharmuta: Arabic for whore

Shephelah: Location of Adullum. Present-day Elah Valley in south-central Israel stretching from Mount Hebron to the coastal plain, where Adullam was located

Sh'chem: Hebrew for Shechem, an important trading center in Kn'n and where Avraham landed after leaving Haran. He built an altar there near the Great Terebinths of Moreh. Sh'chem is also the place where the incident with Dinah occurred that resulted in the slaughter of all the males of the city. Ya'akov fled to Kirjath-arba (Hebron) after that incident. Today it is called Nablus

shekel: Hebrew word based on the root word for "weighing." First use of the word occurred circa 2150 BCE during the Akkadian Empire; and later in the Code of Hammurabi, circa 1700 BCE. It was equivalent to .35 troy ounces. Payment was often made with silver rings from which various sized pieces were cut off and then weighed. However, the measurement could also be used to weigh gold, bronze, copper and other forms of monetary exchange or bartering

Shelah: third son of Yehuda and Illit

Shua: father of Illit and in some literature known as King of Adullam. Most likely he was a merchant in the sense of the word tamkarum, which, in those times meant that he was the "king" or the leader of a city-state

** Shulgi: son of Aqhat and Bushra

shuk: an open air marketplace

Siptu: prayers associated with the Babylonian ritual [Apsu] of using sacred water to drive out the evil spirits that were believed to cause all illness and death

Sokho: ancient town outside the Valley of Elah

sudra: a headdress made of a square of cloth, used by Jewish men in the ancient Lavan (Middle East) to provide protection from direct sunlight and to protect the mouth and eyes from blowing dust and sand. Similar to a keffiyeh (Arabic)

tabun: outdoor baking oven made from clay and stones. Usually used for baking risen and flat breads

taharah: traditional cleansing performed on a body before burial

ta'lab: Arabic for fox

Tamar: (pronounced Tah-mar) daughter of Yergat and Trinjah and daughter-in-law of Yehuda (Judah)

tamkarum: loosely, a merchant. As early as the Old Babylonian Era, the Akkadian word tamkarum could mean anything from a travelling merchant, to a broker whose goods were sold by agents, a financier for trade enterprises and/or a money lender, as well as a messenger or perhaps a diplomat

Tanith: Illit's mother (from Phoenician for "estate")

tannur: Persian (Dari) or Arabic for a slight conical and horse shoe shaped clay cooking hearth, often dug into the floor of one of the several food preparation rooms in the home. It had a hole in the front to feed in fuel and was often covered with pebbles or stones to increase its durability and heat efficiency. It is also known as a tandoor or tandur, especially in Indian cooking

Tehellim: Hebrew for Psalms

terebinth: a tree common in Israel and Syria. Often called an oak in the Bible, it is a much smaller tree and not actually an oak

Timna Valley: this area is not mentioned in the Bible but is the site of the oldest copper fields in the world. It is also where the famous Eliat green stone is found

Timnah: a city mentioned in Genesis 38 that was located north of Adullam and known for its sheep-shearing festival The other is not mentioned in the Bible and is actually known a instead of Timnah. It is located near Eliat and is famous for the copper and green stones that mined there since

* Trinjah: Tamar's mother

Valley of Elah: known as the valley of the oak or terebinth, this still fertile region in Israel is located between Bethlehem and the Mediterranean Sea and is where David is said to have slain Goliath. It is also where the city of Adullam was located—the ruins are called Tel Adullam—and where there is to this day a large terebinth tree that provides a breadth of shade encompassing seventy-five feet in the Adullam Grove Nature Reserve

Yakiri: Hebrew for Darling

Yarikh: a moon god in the Canaanite religion

Yavan: Hebrew for Greece

Yavrik: Armenian (adapted from Turkish "yavru") term of endearment meaning "little one"

Yehuda: (pronounced ye-HOO-dah). Hebrew for Judah, fourth son of Ya'akov (Jacob) and Leah and father of Tamar's children

Yergat: Armenian male name for Tamar's father and Anush's nephew

za'atar: Arabic for a common and plentiful Middle East spice blend

zeret: Hebrew for a measurement that equals the span of three palms

zonah: Hebrew for a common prostitute who takes payment for her services

Acknowledgements

The authors wish to thank the following people for their indispensable aid in helping us to realize our vision for this first book in the *Judah and Tamar Trilogy, Song of the Terebinths*.

Dawn Powers, Esq. for your invaluable comments that helped us to dispense with excessive exposition and encouraged us to find the real story, the one driven by an authentic voice. Your kindness and patience in helping us fulfill our vision is appreciated beyond mere words.

Adryan Russ for your observations and editing skills. Your honesty about the work we did on our previous story, *Betrayal*, helped us to find our way to the one we needed to write, which was this one.

Rona Liu for introducing us to a unique style for our cover art that so brilliantly conveys the important elements in our story, and for delivering on a tight deadline so very late in the process. The world needs more people like you.

Phil Baron for your help in introducing us to Rabbi Ed Feinstein and for your thoughts on Yehuda, Yosef and Levi.

Rabbi Ed Feinstein for your insights into the meaning of Hebrew words, phrases and context; and for your sense of humor while sharing your perspectives.

Our Readers. Without you, where would our words go?

About the Authors

JOY SIKORSKI

Although Joy grew up in Los Angeles, for many years she also lived in a log cabin in Alaska that she helped to build, where she birthed and raised her three children. In addition to being an award-winning composer, she has also written *Singing Through Life With Your Mouth Closed* and has been published in the *Los Angeles Family Magazine* and the *Inlandia Journal*. In addition to the Judah and Tamar Trilogy, her current book projects include *CHEMO?*: the true story of how she overcame a disastrous cancer diagnosis without chemo, radiation or other drugs; two illustrated children's books in collaboration with Pixar artist, Rona Liu; a true-life memoir about her life in Alaska; and too many other how-to books, novels, short stories, poems and articles to count. Her music projects take up her spare time. Joy lives in Idyllwild, California.

MICHAEL SILVERSHER

A Grammy Award winning songwriter and a three time Emmy-nominated composer, has worked with The Walt Disney Company® and The Jim Henson Company on movies, records, theme park parades and many TV series. He has also written numerous musicals for theatre with The Kennedy Center, Los Angeles Opera, Mark Taper Forum and South Coast Repertory. He was resident composer and musical director for Robert Redford's Sundance Institute from 1991-96. Michael lives in the Los Angeles area with his companion, Clicquot the Wonder Dog.

Explore more about the authors at
judahandtamar.com
joysikorskiworld.com